DRAGON

EARTH DRAGONS BOOK 4

CHARLENE HARTNADY

DEDICATION

To Mike,

You know you're getting old when your wife says to you "Let's go upstairs to make love," and you answer, "Choose one… I can't do both."

The quickest way to a man's heart is through his chest

Why don't they spell it 'ordervs'?

For being such a fantastic guy. For always making us laugh. For taking such good care of my mom. You will be sorely missed.

CHAPTER 1

Her stomach growled noisily. "We should go." Macy got up and started towards the back door. Scout bounced around her legs, making her feel guilty about leaving him.

"Are you sure you want to wear that, hun?" her mom asked, genuine concern laced in her voice.

Not this conversation again. "We already talked about this when you first arrived."

"Macy, my girl, I am your mother and it is my job to be honest with you."

Here we go! Macy turned around to face her mom, thankful when her pup pushed his nose into her hand. She stroked his sleek fur.

Her mom's expression grew pinched, which meant that she probably shouldn't say what she was about to say but she was going to say it anyway. "You don't have the nicest thighs, dear. You should wear skirts and dresses with the hem on the knee or lower. I can see too much of your thighs in that, hun." Her voice was soft and soothing. "Please don't take this the wrong way. You're extremely pretty. You have the most beautiful face."

"It's just the rest of me that's up to shit." She struggled to keep the hurt out of her voice.

"Language, Macy! That's not what I said at all."

It was implied though. "Mom, I'm thirty years old. I can say a little swear word. Is there anything else you don't like about this dress?" She looked down at herself, starting to feel pissy.

"Now that you mention it…"

Macy rolled her eyes. "Really?"

"Well… that neckline is all wrong for a bigger-busted woman. You should…"

"I'm not changing. I happen to like my breasts and my thighs. I happen to love this dress. I'm going to put Scout outside and then we're going."

Her mom opened and closed her mouth a few times. *Good! That shut her up!* Thing was, her mom wasn't actually a bad person. She meant well. It came from a good place, but hell, it could be irritating. "I haven't finished my coffee." The older woman held up her mug.

"I made that for you half an hour ago. It must be cold. Leave it, you can get more coffee at the restaurant."

"You need to get your dog settled out back. I'll finish my coffee while you do that." Her mom smiled sweetly, looking the picture of innocence. "We have time."

What the hell was going on? Her mom wasn't normally quite this bad. Come to think of it, she looked nervous. They'd discussed her outfit twice, her weight once and the fact that her clock was ticking once. Her mom was bad, but not this bad. Also, it felt like she was stalling.

Macy watched as the other woman tried to sneak a peek at her watch.

"What's going on?" Macy folded her arms.

She watched her mom's face turn a touch pink. "What do you mean?"

"Why are—?"

The doorbell rang. *Holy shit! No. Nooooo!* "Mom, who is that? Why is there someone ringing my doorbell on a Saturday afternoon?"

Her mother licked her lips. "All I ask is that you keep an open mind."

"Moooom." She moaned the word, feeling like she was ten again.

"I love you and I want to see you happy. That's all."

"I *am* happy. I told you to stop this shit."

"Language." Her mom widened her eyes. "You need to be on your best behavior."

The doorbell rang again.

"He's a lawyer and even made partner at his firm last year." She smiled broadly, looking like the cat who had gotten herself, not just the cream, but the whole damned cow.

"But this is my house, mom. You gave him my address? You *do* know that's a no-no. He could stalk me or kill me," she whispered. "I don't care if he's a lawyer."

Her mom snorted. "Nonsense. That's Shirley's oldest son, Markus." She pointed at the door. "I know him."

She frowned as the doorbell rang again. "Coming," Macy yelled. "You've mentioned him before a couple of times." Her mom loved to talk about how well other people's children were doing. "Isn't he married with kids?"

She shook her head, smiling. "He recently got a divorce."

"What? Mom! A divorce?" Her eyes widened and her mouth fell open for a second or two.

"You're not getting any younger, my girl. You've reached an age where you need to start compromising. The men who are interested in you might have some baggage." She got this sympathetic look.

The doorbell rang yet again.

"You'd better get that, hun."

This wasn't happening! *Arghhh!* Macy headed for the door, Scout jumped around all excited about who the visitor could be. She opened the door while holding onto his collar so that he didn't run out or jump all over the guy.

"Hi." He was smiling. It was a nice smile, she noted. At least he had that going for him. Nice straight teeth. That's where it ended, however. He was bald, which, in itself, wasn't the end of the world. Except, he had hair around the sides of his head. Why didn't he shave it off? It made him look like Friar Tuck.

"Hello," she quickly said, realizing that they been standing there staring at each other for a good couple of seconds. "I'm Macy," she managed to push out.

"Markus." He held out his hand and she took it. He gave her this silly, soft 'lady' handshake. She hated it when guys did that. It felt demeaning in an odd way. Like a woman couldn't handle a proper handshake.

"Come in." He wore a really nice shirt. It looked fancy. She recognized the label as designer. Unfortunately, he left the top three or four buttons open and the guy had chest hair. Mounds of the stuff. It was greying too.

Yuk!

Hopefully he was nice. They could at least have a good lunch together. Outward appearances weren't everything. She knew this only too well.

Macy stepped to the side but as he walked in, Scout got so excited, he broke free, immediately jumping on Markus's chest.

Scout was only eight months and technically just a puppy, but he was pretty big all the same. Markus looked horrified. He scrunched up his nose in distaste and held up his hands like he didn't even want to touch her beloved pet. Yeah, it looked like a nice lunch was not on the cards after all.

"Control your mutt, Macy," her mother piped up.

Scout, seeming to sense that he was not wanted, dropped back down to the floor and went back to her to seek reassurance. She petted his fur. "Please don't call him that."

"It's better than mongrel." Her mother raised her brows. "I thought mutt was quite a sweet thing to say." It was official, her mother was clueless.

"He might not be a pure-bred dog, but I love him all the same. Since he is a mix of two breeds, I like to call him a hybrid."

Markus snorted, like the concept was hilarious. Her mother seemed to agree and the two of them had a good old chuckle. It looked like she was in for a long afternoon. How the hell was she going to get out of this? "I'll take him out back and then we can go."

"I'll bring the car around," Markus said.

"Thanks, but I'll go in my own car. I have an errand I need to run straight after lunch." She just needed to think of what that errand was so she could use it as an excuse to leave early.

"What errand—?"

"Come on, Pup." She spoke in a singsong voice. "I won't be too long, my little Scout," she continued. "I know how you cry when I'm away for too long." She continued to speak to her dog as she walked.

When she got back, it was just her mother in the living room. Her expression was stony. "You need to be nicer," she whispered.

"I *was* nice."

"In hindsight, maybe meeting here wasn't the best idea."

This whole thing was a terrible idea. She bit down on her tongue to keep from saying it.

"We'd better get going. I can't believe we're taking three cars. You should have gone with him."

"I would prefer to drive myself. I don't even know this guy. What happened with his last marriage? Why did they get a divorce?"

"He cheated on his wife." She said it like it was no biggie.

"What?" Macy almost fell over her own feet. "He cheated? How the hell could you set me up with someone like that?"

"Don't be such a drama queen." Her mother began walking again. "He made partner and it got to his head. It was one of the secretaries at the firm. Not a big deal. He learned his lesson."

"I highly doubt it," she mumbled as she locked the front door.

"What was that, dear?" Her mom raised her brows. *Was*

she really that oblivious?

"Mom, let's get this lunch over and done with and then you and I need to have a serious talk. I'll come to you after work on Tuesday. We need to set a couple of boundaries."

"I'm not sure what you mean." She looked completely flummoxed.

Lord help her!

CHAPTER 2

*H**oly fuck!*
 Her scent.

It was sweet like candied apples. Tangy… green apples. Crisp. Fresh. Fucking delicious. It filled his nose. He could taste her on his tongue. Make that, he could *almost* taste her. He wanted to taste her. Sand knew that she would—

Druze's chest vibrated with an almost inaudible growl. "My mouth is watering," the male announced, eyes on the human.

Oh yes! Sand's mouth was watering too. He swallowed his lust down. Or he tried to, at any rate. They watched as the female bent over to open a drawer. Her ass was lush in those jeans. Holy shit. The fabric strained to contain the well-rounded globes. His hands itched to squeeze.

"Shit!" Druze cursed. "She's trying to give me a hard-on." He shifted uncomfortably, putting a hand over his dick. "She *is* giving me one."

"Quit it!" Sand warned. Like he wasn't affected at all. He spoke under his breath. "We don't want to scare Georgia's friend. We're supposed to be helping her, not perving over her. I mean…" Sand licked his lips, his eyes glued to her ass, which bobbed up and down as she continued to rummage through the bottom dresser drawer. "I'll admit, she's hot as fuck, and most likely about to come into heat." He suddenly felt the urge to shift his weight and to palm his dick as well. Heck, a quick jerk-off would come in handy right about then, but they were on duty. Here to protect the human while packing up some of his brother's mate's things, but hell, it was proving to be a difficult task. Far more challenging than he had thought it would be.

He forced his gaze off the lush female. "Go and grab a packing box," he ordered Druze, pointing to the other side of the room where some unmade boxes were stacked against the wall.

Sand turned back to the human. "Um…" He cleared his throat. His voice was thick and husky. It had been months since he had last been with a female. He was a non-human. A dragon. Testosterone levels were high in his kind. They were apparently driven to mate. To procreate.

Not him.

He *was* driven alright but not for any of the tie-down nonsense. He wasn't going to fall for it as his brothers had. Sand was driven to fuck. That was it. The beginning. The middle. The end. Simple. To fuck.

Right then, the urge was almost overwhelming. Another time, another place… maybe. Sand tamped the urge down. It didn't matter how amazing her scent was.

How lush her figure looked in a pair of jeans and the shirt…

That shirt.

The shirt was designed for a male. It was one of those plaid, button-down types. It did nothing to hide her full breasts. It seemed to enhance everything that was lush and feminine about her and in a big, bad way. "Um," he said again, sounding like an asshole whelp.

The female turned. She smiled. Her eyes were a beautiful bright blue. Her mouth was really full. Almost too lush, like the rest of her. He could picture those lips wrapped around his—

He needed to stop this shit.

He wasn't a kid anymore. He *could* control himself, dammit. "Can I help with anything? You're busy while we're just standing around."

Those lush-as-fuck lips curled into a smile. It was shy and sweet. "I don't think Georgia would like a bunch of guys rifling through her stuff. I'm almost done." She put her hands on her hips for a second, before pointing at an almost full box. "You can seal that with the tape over there." She gestured to a table. A roll of masking tape and a couple of other supplies were lying on it.

"Okay." He nodded once, heading for the box. "Let me know what else I can do. We really shouldn't be standing around watching you work." As amazing as looking at her was, it needed to stop. If they were busy, they wouldn't be ogling Macy like they were.

She looked back down at the dresser. "I'm nearly—"

Both he and Druze looked up, senses on high alert.

"Did you hear that?" Druze asked, from the other side of the room, his eyes flashing to Sand's.

Sand nodded. "It sounded like someone landing or… I'm not sure. There was no one from our party instructed to return to assist, was there?" They wouldn't approach in their dragon form. Not in the middle of town during the day.

"No. The other two left to escort Georgia's mother back to our lair with the Water dragons." Druze was frowning heavily. "Storm may have instructed some of his team to come back to assist us but… can't be, though. Should I go and check it out?" He seemed to relax as he spoke.

"I didn't hear anything," Macy said.

"It was very soft," Sand explained. "Probably nothing." He hadn't heard anything more since. No footfalls. No breathing or heartbeats detected in the vicinity. He breathed a little easier too as he nodded. "Yeah, go check it out just to be sure. I'll stay with the female."

Druze nodded and headed out the front door.

"Should I be worried?" Macy made a face.

"Not at all!"

"Because Georgia mentioned something about dragon slayers in her email to me. You see," the female went on, "we've been chatting back and forth. She's my best friend. I hope she won't get into trouble or anything. She swore me to secrecy." She touched her chest. "I wouldn't tell a soul." She widened her eyes.

"It's fine. I know how close you two are." Sand chuckled. "Shale told me the whole story about the birth of his whelps and how you guys didn't believe him." He laughed some more, noticing how Macy was laughing too. "Georgia thought he was batshit crazy. Did she actually ask Shale if he had taken his meds?"

Macy nodded. "Yes, she did. You should have seen her face when she realized she was having another baby. When she realized he was telling the truth."

"I wish I could have been there." Then again. That would have meant watching his sister-in-law give birth. He sobered up. "To answer your question. We're safe. It would take a whole team of slayers to take two dragons out," he said simply, not wanting to scare the female.

"What about silver?" She raised her brows. "It kills you if you come into contact with it."

Sand could hear Druze walking the perimeter. He couldn't hear anything else within his range of hearing. "It doesn't kill us that easily. It would take more than just contact with the substance. For that, they would have to get close enough and that's not going to happen. Forget about it." He shook his head, again playing it down. Why scare her unnecessarily over something that most likely wouldn't happen?

Macy sucked in a breath, about to say something when she looked behind him. Something glinted in her eyes.

Fear.

Cold. Hard. Raw. Her eyes widened. Her face turned white in an instant. Her mouth opened in a silent scream. *Fear.* He began to move, trying to turn. Before he could get around, Sand felt a sharp pain. His skull cracked. He both heard it and felt it happen. His spine seemed to compress from the severity of the impact, just before his knees buckled. It seemed like Macy actually screamed then. Sand couldn't be completely sure though, since everything went black.

CHAPTER 3

S and groaned. The sound hurt his head. He put a hand
to his skull, which made the throbbing worse. He grit
his teeth which… *arghhh*… hurt like fuck. Making him
want to grit them harder. He tried to shift his weight
and… it hurt like a bitch on steroids.

Worse than that even!

Throb. Throb. Throb. He couldn't think coherently. Not
beyond the pain. *He couldn't.* It didn't matter how hard he
tried. It only made his head throb harder. He needed to
though. There was something important he needed to
remember. Something he needed to do. Something—

Sand cracked open his eyes and groaned. *Fuck!* Light.
Blinding. *Throb! Throb! Throb!* He closed them again,
pressing his fingers to his temples. It didn't help. He
realized he was lying on his belly. On something soft.
Throb. Throb. Throb.

Pain.

Screaming pain. Blinding fucking pain. All-consuming! He'd never felt anything like it. Not when he'd crash-landed and had broken three… could have been four bones… somewhere in his body. Not when he'd sliced his hand open preparing dinner… or was it breakfast? Not even when Stone – or it could have been Rock – had accidentally nearly taken his leg clean off in a sparring match.

Never this bad!

He was still struggling to think. Trying to form half intelligible thoughts. How had he been injured? His brain felt bruised. It felt like it might be bleeding. He couldn't remember how he had been hurt, but he could remember the sound his skull had made when… it had cracked. *Who… what… how…?*

He frowned. Then groaned when the pain redoubled. Thankfully he felt himself passing out. A warmth was wrapping itself around him. *No!* He couldn't allow himself to be taken back under. He needed to stay awake. He needed to… Sand couldn't remember why, however. Instead of fighting it, he let himself sink deeper and deeper into oblivion.

Some time later – he had no idea how much time had passed – Sand tried to sit up but slumped back down instead. His head pounded. This time when he groaned, the pounding didn't worsen. He opened his eyes, feeling dizzy and nauseous.

His mouth filled with saliva, which he swallowed down. He realized he'd closed his eyes and tried to open them again. With difficulty, he cracked the one open and then the other. The light was blinding, making him feel dizzy all over again. Thankfully the bout of nausea that had rolled through him before, didn't make another appearance.

It took a good half a minute for his eyes to focus. A wooden coffee table was directly in front of him. There was a rug under that. He didn't recognize either. Sand's feet were on the ground but the rest of him was... on a sofa. He turned onto his side, feeling another bout of nausea hit. He grit his teeth for a moment until it passed. The pounding in his head was almost bearable. Still hurt like hell. Still throbbed, but not nearly as badly as before. Thank fuck for superhuman strength and advanced healing or he would most certainly be dead. Whoever had hit him, had hit him damn hard. Harder than he'd ever been hit before.

Wait a minute.

Hit him.

Hit.

The human. *Fuck!* The female. *Where was she? Was she okay?* He sat up, groaning hard as he did. Sand had to squeeze his eyes shut for a few seconds as bile rose in his throat. The pounding worsened but he ignored the pain, opening his eyes instead. It only took a few seconds for his eyes to focus this time. A few long-ass seconds, since worry flooded every part of him.

His eyes finally focused, landing on a bed. *Thank fuck!* She was sprawled out on top of the covers. Her blond hair fanned the pillow. She wasn't moving though, and his head pounded too hard to be able determine if she was breathing. If her heart was still beating.

Shit! He lurched to his feet, groaning against the pain. Sand took a few staggering steps before bending over and dry-heaving. Thankfully nothing actually came up, but the retching made his head pound harder. He needed to get to the female. He pulled himself upright, taking deep breaths. Sand forced himself to walk the last few strides to the bed. "Macy," he croaked. His throat was dry. His tongue felt thick. "Macy." He sat down heavily next to her. Sand swiped some hair off her face, pushing out a sigh of relief when he felt how warm her skin was. Her chest was rising and falling. Slow and steady. His head still pounded too much to be able to hear anything. Even his sense of smell had been affected by the blow. His mouth had this terrible metallic taste.

"Macy," he tried again, cupping her cheek.

She made a small noise that told him she was waking up.

"Are you okay? Macy! What happened?" He forced himself to shut the hell up. She was still mostly out of it, so throwing questions at her wasn't going to help anything.

He watched as her eyelids fluttered. "That's it," he urged. "Wake up, Macy." He gave her a small shake when it seemed like she might go back to sleep. "Wake up, Mace, come on!" he urged her some more.

She moaned.

"That's it!" he growled.

Her eyes fluttered again and then opened. The moment they did, she sucked in a deep breath and sat up, pulling backward, her face a mask of terror. "Noooooo!" she yelled, her eyes darting across the room. "Keep it away from me. Keep it—" She was panting, clutching her hands to her chest. Looking wildly about the room. The female was having a full-blown panic attack.

"Hey," he used a soothing voice. "It's me, Sand. You

remember me, don't you? We're alone. You're okay. I won't hurt you."

She swallowed thickly, her blue gaze moving to his. He watched as most of the fear bled from her. Her breathing eased and her shoulders relaxed. "It's n-not h-here." She looked around them again. "Where are we?" Her eyes moving to the ceiling before meeting his once more.

"I was hoping you could answer..." he grimaced as the pounding in his head flared back up, "that particular question. What happened?" he half growled the words, gritting his teeth and putting a finger to his right temple to try to ease the pain.

"Are you okay? That thing hit you so hard." Her eyes welled with tears. "I thought you were dead for sure." Her lip quivered. Her eyes were even more blue against the unnatural pallor of her skin. They looked huge.

"I have a headache from hell." He underplayed his agony.

She frowned. "I was sure I heard a cracking sound." Macy went on, "You went down like two tons of bricks. Out before you hit the ground and..." she made a face, focusing on his right eye, "the white of this," she touched a thumb to his right cheek, peering at him more closely, "eye is completely blood red. The pupil looks dilated as well. You need a CT scan and a hospital, and it doesn't take a medical degree to know that much."

"I'm a shifter. I heal quickly. Give me another hour and I'll be as good as new. What happened? Are you okay?" Her top was half untucked from her jeans. She seemed alright otherwise. Her hair was a bit tousled. She was pale but he couldn't see any actual damage. "Are you hurt?" he added.

She shook her head. "I'm fine. I... at least," she smoothed her hands over her shirt and jean-clad thighs, "I think so." She nodded.

"What happened? Someone... came up behind me and hit me over the head. Hard enough to crack my skull like a ripe coconut. That takes some strength. Also, some stealth... I didn't hear a thing. Didn't scent anything either." It was puzzling.

He watched as her eyes darted across the room all over again. Macy swallowed hard. "It wasn't a someone. It was a some*thing*."

That might explain it. "What kind of something? What did it look like? Did it say anything?" About a half a dozen more questions entered his head but he grit his teeth to stop himself from bombarding her more than he already had.

"I've never seen anything like it before. It was a demon." She shook her head. "It was big, at least as tall as you. It had the scariest eyes I've ever seen. Terrifying." She lifted her eyes in thought. Macy hugged her arms around herself. Her hands shook. "There was death in its eyes. They reminded me of a lion or a... definitely a predator. It was muscular too. Big arms. Massive pecks. A six-pack..." She frowned. "The weirdest part... the reason I think it's a demon... I mean," she licked her lips, locking eyes with him, "demons are fallen angels, aren't they?"

"I have no idea." He shook his head.

"It had wings, like an angel, only not." She frowned.

"Whatever this thing is, it's not human. Wings? What did they look like?" He frowned. This didn't sound like anything he had ever seen before. The human had been terrified, so maybe her recollection was bad.

She shrugged. "They looked like wings. Wide with

feathers. They were dark, though. I always imagined angels' wings would be white. Then again, this thing was no angel." She hugged herself tighter.

"What did it do after knocking me out? Did it say something to you?"

"No, he didn't. The demon advanced and…" Her eyes welled. She chewed on her bottom lip for a few seconds before taking a deep breath. "It hugged me."

"Hugged you?" That didn't sound right.

"Tightly. Tighter and tighter and tighter until I couldn't breathe." She lifted the side of her shirt and true enough, there was the start of a bruise blossoming on her side. She winced as she ran her hand up the other side. "Not hard enough to break anything but so hard that…" her lip trembled. Her whole body seemed to give a shudder as her eyes lifted in thought. "Hard enough to leave bruises. Hard enough…" She swallowed.

"That you couldn't breathe."

She nodded her head. Her mind still far away. "I couldn't. I've never been so afraid. My last thought before I blacked out, was that I was going to die. I was never going to see my mom and dad again. Or my brother. He can be an ass sometimes, but I love him. I'm sure you know how it is with siblings?"

Sand nodded while she seemed to ramble unconsciously.

"My biggest regret was not meeting the man of my dreams or having the family I've always wanted. That there would be no kids. No picket fence… you know?"

He nodded again, even though he didn't know. Not at all. "You're not hurt, though? Aside from the bruising?" His eyes ran up and down the length of her body.

CHAPTER 4

"No, I'm fine. Well, as fine as can be expected after being kidnapped. What's going on?" Her voice hitched as she recalled the creature's freaky eyes. "What does it want with us? The demon." She whispered the last, almost afraid that if she said it too loud, the thing would come back.

"I don't know, and I don't plan on sticking around to find out." He winced as he stood up. He had blood all down the back of his shirt. It was caked in his hair as well.

She must have made some kind of a noise because he turned back to her. "What is it?"

"Your head." She pointed. "You bled quite profusely. Are you sure you're okay?"

He nodded once. Sand pulled the shirt over his head, examining the blood on the garment. "It's a head wound." He shrugged. "They bleed." His muscles rippled under his skin. Her eyes were drawn to the golden marking on his chest for a moment before moving back up to his face. She was shocked at how calm he was being about the whole thing. It helped keep her calm as well.

"No doors," he muttered, almost to himself. Sand walked around the room, taking it all in.

The area they found themselves in was big and round. The walls were made from chunks of rock. There was a section that was walled off. It had a door. She assumed that was the bathroom. Otherwise, the space was mostly a large bedroom and lounge area with a small kitchen. There were no electronics other than a fridge. It was very rustic and sparsely furnished. There were candleholders attached to the walls. And two freestanding candelabras as well. They were made from – couldn't be… gold? They glinted like they were gold, but they had to be copper or brass. There was another freestanding candelabra next to the bed and one on the table.

Sand was right, there were no doors. "That is weird," she replied. There were drapes over sections of the wall. Maybe there was a door behind one of those, she thought.

She slipped off the bed.

Sand dropped the bloody shirt on the floor at his feet. The blood had long since congealed. It was a rusty color, which was a silly thing to notice at a time like that.

Focus, Macy!

He walked over to the first curtained section. All the drapes were closed. He pulled the fabric open. Sun streamed in. It was a wide, windowless space. There were bars though. Plenty of silver bars. They glinted in the sun.

"What the fuck!" Sand muttered, walking to the next drape. He pulled it open as well. Sand did the same thing to the other drapes. They were high up and seemingly in the middle of nowhere. Open land and hills stretched for miles and miles all around them. There wasn't a single soul in sight. Not a single building, or road, or man-made structure, for that matter, either.

"What is this place?" she asked.

"Fucked if I know," Sand growled.

All in all, there were four large exits. All of them had bars across the openings. He walked over to the last exit. It was the size of four or five doors and maybe one and a half times the height. Sand gripped two of the bars in his hands and attempted to pry them apart. He groaned, his face turning red. His muscles bulged. Biceps, triceps… muscles she didn't know the names of, all roped and swelled. He was a huge guy. Super strong, certainly not human, but still, there was no give. Not even half an inch. He stepped away, wiping the sweat from his brow. "Must be silver-infused," he muttered, walking to the next exit.

Macy trailed behind Sand. There was a ten- or twelve-foot ledge on the outside of all the exits. Enough space for something big to land on and enter.

Something not human.

The *thing*.

A shiver ran through her. She suddenly recalled that its mouth had also been weird. Those eyes though. The way it had looked at her was cold and calculating. "This doesn't make sense," she whispered. "Why are we here?"

Something flashed in his eyes as he looked at her. "I… I'm not sure." She could see he had been about to say something. That he had changed his mind at the last second. Sand had an idea why they were there, he just didn't want to share it with her.

"What?" she asked. "You know something. I can tell."

Sand continued to walk around the room. "I would rather not say anything until I know more. No use scaring you unnecessarily."

She folded her arms across her chest. "I would rather know what you are thinking. I'm a big girl, I can take it." It had to be bad. Had to be if he thought it would scare her.

"I have an idea as to why you're here, but I'm puzzled about why I was brought here as well. Which leads me to think that I might be on the wrong track, but..." he rubbed his jaw, "I can't think of any other reason." He spoke more to himself.

"Spit it out already," she urged. "It's a theory. I get that. I would like to know, please."

His jaw tightened. She could see he was thinking it through.

"You just said that you're probably wrong. I won't freak out. I'm over the initial shock."

"Whatever took us isn't human. I've never encountered a creature such as you describe, although I have an idea of what it could be." He narrowed his eyes in thought. "There is only one other non-human species I know of that can fly. They call themselves the Feral."

"I don't think I like the sound of that. Feral as in uncontrolled and savage?"

"Yep. The Feral, and from what I understand, they mostly live up to their name. They're griffin shifters. We didn't even know of their existence until recently. They're the strongest of the non-humans but," he shook his head, "we can't be sure it was one of them."

"What is a griffin? I have heard the term before, but I can't remember." She shook her head, trying hard to recall and failing.

"They're half bird and half lion. They're strong, powerful and completely uncivilized."

"I don't like the sound of that. That thing did have a weird mouth. I don't know… he was…" She shook her head. "I don't recall seeing paws, or claws or… then again, I couldn't look away from its eyes. I was too afraid. I thought he was going to kill me."

"It might not have been a Feral. We didn't know the griffins existed until recently. What if there are more non-humans out there? It's distinctly possible."

She nodded. "Yeah, well, I certainly didn't imagine that thing." Macy looked around them. "We're trapped in here. We're not imagining that. Something has us." Then she had a thought. Macy sucked in a breath. "You still haven't told me your theory as to why we're here."

He pushed out a breath. "It's just a theory." He shrugged. "The only thing I can think of is… because you're a female, and females across all the species are in short supply. I think he wants… you."

She narrowed her eyes. "It wants me to… to…" Panic *did* well up in her, despite her statement earlier of being able to handle whatever it was he threw at her.

Sand took a step towards her. "Hold up! That doesn't explain why *I'm* here, though. If it wanted to take you as a mate, why bring me along? This creature rendered us *both* unconscious and took us *both*. He had the opportunity to leave with you and you alone, but it didn't happen." He ran a hand through his hair. "It doesn't make any sense."

Macy forced herself to take in a couple of deep breaths and to calm down. "It can't be for that reason then. I hope it's not for that." She shook her head. It could be, though.

It could very well have taken her for just that.

Calm down!

"Listen," he walked right up to her, standing in front of her, "I'll protect you." He touched the side of her arm for a second. "I'll do whatever it takes. I was assigned to your wellbeing and I take my duties very seriously."

"O-okay." She nodded once. "Thank you."

"Right now, I need to try to get us the hell out of here before it returns. Quite frankly, I don't want to find out why he took us. I'd like to be long gone by the time he comes back."

"I'd rather not find out why we are here either." She shook her head. "Leaving sounds fantastic. I didn't mention my puppy earlier… he's all alone at home. I'm trying not to worry too much. He'll start barking when I don't come home. My neighbor, Colin, will go and check on him. I know he will." Concern ate at her. "He's a sweet guy. Not really a dog person but a sweet guy, he'll take care of my pup for me. His name is Scout but I call him Pup. He'll be so lonely."

"I'm sure your puppy will be okay," Sand reassured her, his eyes on her. "In fact, what do you say I get us out of here so that you can get there before he even has a chance to bark?" Sand asked, smiling. "I'm going to partially shift… might even go the whole hog, if I have to. I need to break us out of this place." He looked around them as he spoke.

She nodded. "Okay. I'm sure you can do it." She glanced back down at his chest and biceps. He wasn't as bulky as Rock had been, but Sand was taller and just as powerful looking. "I'm pretty sure you can do it."

"Go stand on that side of the room." He pointed to the

far side. "Get yourself behind the bed. Rock and debris might go flying. I don't want you injured. Also," he unclasped the first button on his jeans, "you might want to close your eyes if you're squeamish about nudity."

She watched in fascination as he turned the other way. Sand took two steps, his hand moving down as he unzipped as he walked. He stepped out of the jeans in mid-stride and her mouth dropped open.

She'd seen a naked shifter before. Macy had spent the night with one, for goodness sake, but still. Seeing his meaty ass and muscular back. *Wow!* She was reminded of how well built they were how—He turned around and her eyes moved down his muscular chest and abs to his… She swallowed thickly. He was sporting a semi. *Why was he sporting a semi?* Maybe it was normal just before a shift. Something to do with blood flow in the body or something. It was possible. *Wasn't it?*

"Normally, I wouldn't mind a beautiful female starring at my dick," Sand said. "But unfortunately, we don't have much time here."

Oh shit! Caught staring. "I wasn't… it…" she stammered. "Ummm… you didn't give me time to look away."

"Riiiiight." She could hear he wasn't buying it. Sand grinned for a second or two before becoming serious. "I need you to hunker down behind the bed and to stay put until I give you the all-clear."

"O-okay," she stammered, working hard to keep her eyes on his. What the hell was wrong with her? Macy quickly turned and rushed to where he wanted her. She did as he said and crouched down behind the bed.

"Keep your head down. Don't get up until I tell you."

"Sure." She ducked down, listening. Within seconds she heard pounding and the sound of rocks and dirt showering on the floor below.

Sand grunted with each hard blow. There was a cracking noise, followed by more debris landing on the floor.

Macy risked a glance, since it didn't sound like any of the rubble had made it anywhere near where she was hiding.

She gasped as she caught sight of Sand. He was much taller than he had been. His muscles were bigger too. Scales glinted where they mingled with his skin. There were patches of them. His hands were curled into large fists. Beautiful wings had sprouted from his back. Dragon wings. She couldn't take her eyes off of him as she watched his muscles shift beneath the scaled patches of skin. "Fuck!" he snarled. The sound guttural. So far from being human it sent shivers down her spine.

He stopped, letting his hands fall to his sides. She noticed that his knuckles were dripping blood. The wings receded, the scales pulled back disappearing on his skin as well. As he breathed out, his muscles seemed to normalize. Going from huge, to just plain big. "We're in a cage," he announced, in the same harsh, guttural voice. "A fucking silver-infused cage. Not huge amounts of the metal in the steel but enough to hold us in here." He grabbed his jeans and yanked them on, looking irritated.

She moved her gaze to where he had been focused, namely, the hole in the wall. It too contained the same silver bars between where the rock had been broken. It looked like if Sand were to break this whole place to pieces, they would still be trapped.

He looked up at the ceiling. "I have a feeling we're enclosed by these cage bars everywhere." Without warning, he punched up in one hard move that brought a large clump of rock down. It smashed on the floor below.

Sand cursed as more bars became apparent in the ceiling.

"We're trapped," Macy whispered. "Sitting ducks," she added, feeling adrenaline hit her veins. "What are we going to do?" she asked. She forced herself to take deep breaths as she pictured the creature. Its eyes. Its sheer size.

Not bigger than Sand had been. It wasn't. It was freakier looking but—

"Hey." Sand's voice had a soft edge. He took ahold of her upper arms and gave them a light squeeze. "I said I would protect you. I will."

She nodded once, feeling slightly better. "What if there are more of them? What if…?"

"We will end up driving ourselves mad if we start going down that path." He let her go. "Look over there." He pointed at the side table next to the bed. "If this creature meant us harm, it would not have left that jug of water and those apples."

"Oh," she pushed out. "I hadn't even noticed." She shook her head, eyes on the filled jug. There were two glasses next to it and the reddest apples she had ever seen.

"There are blankets on the bed and those are folded towels." He pointed to the foot of the bed where, indeed, a couple of folded towels had been left. "This place might be a cage but it's a fairly comfortable cage."

"So, you're just going to settle in and—"

"No one said anything about settling in." His jaw tightened. "I am, however, going to regroup. I'm going to try to save my energy. My head is pounding again." He touched his right temple. The white of that eye was no longer the deep scarlet it had been before, but more of a pinkish color.

She nodded.

"First a shower and then I should try to catch some z's." He looked around them, his gaze settling on what was most likely the bathroom.

"You're going to sleep at a time like this?"

Sand nodded. "Yes, back to needing to regroup. I have a feeling I'm going to need my strength if we hope to escape. He'll come inside here, and I'll attack."

"Maybe he won't come in." There was a panicked edge to her voice.

"Then we'll have to come up with a plan to get him in here, so that I can take him out."

She clutched her hands together. "I'm not sure I like that idea. The part about him coming in that is."

"We need this cage open if we have a hope in hell of getting out of here. Once it's open, I'll strike and that will be the end of that."

"You sound really sure of yourself?"

"I will do my best, and yes, I am that sure of myself. I'm a dragon shifter and a prince. I'm one of the strongest males in my tribe." He flexed his pecs. They *bounced!* His chest was solid muscle. "This male caught me unawares before. It won't happen again. I have to be at full strength, however. We'll have to take turns sleeping."

Macy pushed out a heavy breath. "No worries in that department. I might never sleep again." She watched as he did the whole 'bounce the pecs' thing a second time. If they had been in any other situation, she would probably have laughed. Flexing muscles was such a male thing to do. It was right up there with comparing the size of a just reeled in fish, or bragging about the size of their package.

Then again, in that regard, Sand would have most guys beat. She tried not to think about that last comparison as she watched Sand walk to the foot of the bed. He grabbed a towel. "I'll be right back."

"Wait!" Her voice was high-pitched. "You can't leave me out here alone."

"I'll be two minutes. You can shout if he comes back. I'm sure I'll be able to hear if—"

She shook her head. "No… no way I'm staying here!"

Shale smiled. "You are welcome to join me."

She frowned. "What… no… I…"

He pushed out a breath. "If you don't want to be left alone, you're going to have to come with me." He began walking towards the bathroom. "You've already seen me naked, so what's the big deal?"

Her legs moved even though she told them not to. She didn't want to watch Sand shower. The thought of being out there, though – *shiver* – all alone. No… nope… forget about it.

Sand turned back towards her in the bathroom, which was very basic but looked functional. His jeans were hanging open. His abs were… spectacular. She forced her eyes up. "You're welcome to hang out. You can even wash my back… if you want, but I'm afraid we can't have sex." He shook his head, looking serious.

She frowned. "What?" *Had he just said that? Was this guy for real?*

"It would divert my attention too much." He shook his head again. "I need to keep my ears open for… the obvious." He shrugged, looking completely serious.

No way! He couldn't be. Macy waited for him to laugh, or to point his finger and yell, *'gotcha.'* It didn't happen! Good lord, but he *was* serious. "That's fine. I think I'll be okay."

Sand nodded once, not picking up on her sarcasm. He pushed his pants down without warning and she realized how close she was standing to him. She turned away but not before noticing…

What?

Surely not?

Sand may have been sporting a semi before but… she glanced at him over her shoulder and gasped. His cock was full-on hard. It jutted from his body, bouncing a little as he stepped into the shower. "What the hell?" she squeaked, unable to take her eyes off the thing. "What is that? Why do you…? What the…? Why are you…?" She pointed at his erection.

Sand shrugged. "It's your scent. Ignore it."

Okay. She needed to look away, and right then. It seemed to actually get bigger under her scrutiny. Macy looked at the floor. "I'm not sure what that even means. We're trapped and about to be… who knows what the hell is about to happen to us and you're… you're… You have an erection?" Her voice was filled with shock.

"It's not a big deal."

"Why the heck do you have an erection? My scent… what does that even mean?" She sniffed her armpit.

Sand chuckled. She made the mistake of looking at him. His cock bounced as he laughed. "Ignore it. I am! Non-humans are very sensitive. You're not on any birth control." He made a face. Like it was a terrible thing.

"How would you even know that?"

"I can smell that you're about to come onto your heat… it's…" He paused, his eyes lifting in thought. "Oh shit!" He shut the shower door. The whole cubicle vibrated. "This is bad!" He scrubbed a hand over his face, the stubble catching.

She frowned. "What's bad? Why is it bad?"

Sand pointed at his erection. "Your scent is amazing. I can't help my body's reaction. It's about to get a whole lot better… or worse, depending on how you look at it." He spoke more to himself.

"What do you mean 'better'? Or worse? What does this have to do with anything? With that?" She pointed at his dick, which was pointing right back at her.

Eyes up!

"You're becoming fertile." He shrugged his massive shoulders. "Non-humans are base creatures in the end. We're driven more by our instincts than humans are. You're a good-looking female…" He licked his lips as his eyes skimmed over her body.

Her nipples tightened. The stupid little nubs actually reacted to this guy. Right then, and at that moment. In a cage. In extreme danger… and yet they reacted.

"Sexy as fuck, in the prime of your life and about to go into heat. Your scent is amazing. Your pussy is…" He cleared his throat. "That was vulgar of me."

"It was!" She smoothed a hand over her shirt. Trying hard to ignore the tightening she had felt in her belly as he said 'pussy.' This whole thing was ridiculous. She was afraid. Her hands felt sweaty and her mouth dry. That's how nervous she was and yet… her stupid body was still reacting to him. It was ludicrous!

He nodded once. "Whatever took you isn't human.

He's going to be just as affected as I am. Maybe even more so. He will want to breed you as soon as he gets a whiff of you. Every instinct in him will be telling him to do so. You need to shower. Right now." For the first time, he sounded a touch afraid. It unnerved her. Then she thought about what he was saying.

"What?" *Maybe she had heard wrong.* "Did you say shower? I'm not taking my—"

"Get in the stall. Wash! Do it now!" His eyes narrowed in on hers. "Wash your underwear as well. They'll be…" His nostrils flared, and he groaned. "They'll be soaked in your juices. You smell fucking amazing. If it's a Feral, or some other base creature, he'll go off his head with need for you."

Her mouth fell open for a moment. "You can't be serious."

"Oh, I'm very serious, human. You need to do as I say, and right now. Wash yourself well down there. Use soap. I saw some in the stall. Wash your underwear as well, hopefully it will be enough, at least for now."

"Why for now?"

"You're only at the start of your heat. It's going to get much worse." She watched his Adam's apple work. "Much worse. Don't worry about me though. Dragons have control." He swallowed again.

"I can see that." She muttered, looking pointedly at his erection.

"You have nothing to worry about… not from me. I've never spent time with a female in her heat but… I am strong. Some other base creature would have you on your knees in seconds."

She gasped, clutching her chest at the horror of his

words. Her eyes were wide. Her mouth even wider. Her heart suddenly raced. *Surely not.*

"A male will have increased strength after catching a snoutful of you, so I might not be able to stop him. He'll be out of his mind with need. It'll be base, instinctual… raw…"

"Okay!" she yelled. "That's enough. You've convinced me. Turn around!" She was still yelling but couldn't stop herself. "I'm going to shower. I'll do as you say."

Sand walked to the door of the bathroom. "I'll stand just outside. Be quick and be thorough," he barked.

Shit!

Crap!

Her hands fumbled as she undid the buttons on her blouse. They were shaking so much. Her breathing was ragged. *Was this really happening?* She quickly stripped out of the rest of her clothing, placing them on a small table. Then she turned on the shower, waiting for hot water. It didn't take long before steam filled the shower.

She got under the stream of water, trying hard not to panic. This was going to be okay. Sand was there. He would protect her. He'd said so and she trusted him to do that. She quickly washed, lathering plenty of soap in *that* particular place. Then she washed her underwear. Lastly, she rinsed off, again concentrating between her legs.

Her skin was flushed red when she got out. Macy toweled her hair and body, quickly dressing. She only wished she had more layers of clothing to protect her from that demon monster.

On her knees.

Macy squeezed her eyes shut and chewed on her bottom lip. It was going to be okay. It was! That scenario was not going to happen.

"How are you doing in there?"

"Almost done." Her voice was shrill.

"It'll be okay, Macy," Sand said, using a reassuring voice. "I swear I'll protect you, even if it means getting gravely injured or even death. I'll do whatever it takes. When that creature returns, I'll tear it apart."

"Thank you." He was quite sweet, even if he was a little arrogant. "I appreciate it. You can come in now," she added.

The door opened and a still naked Sand walked in. She noticed – even though she tried not to – that his penis wasn't as erect as it had been before. He pulled in a big breath through his nostrils. "Much better," he announced. "I'm going to take a shower and then I really think we need to try to get some sleep. Like I said, we'll have to take turns. Unfortunately, I'm not completely healed, and sleep is one of the… ways to help that along. I have to be at my best when the time comes."

He had taken a knock she didn't think he'd ever recover from. His head had cracked. She was pretty sure it was his skull breaking on impact.

Macy nodded once. "I'm too wired to sleep. I'll keep watch."

"I'll be quick." Sand stepped into the shower stall and turned on the water. He made a groaning noise as he put his head under the stream. Half a minute later, Macy realized she was staring at him while he showered. While he lathered his body in soap. While he tilted his head under the stream of water, eyes closed. Macy forced her eyes off of the dragon. *Shit!* She was stuck in a cage with someone she was attracted to. This wasn't good at all.

CHAPTER 5

She felt Sand sit up in the bed behind her. He grunted as he stretched. Macy glanced back, watching as he yawned. He scrubbed a hand over his face. His eyes still hazy with sleep. "How long was I out?" His voice was croaky.

She glanced at her watch. "Two and a half hours."

He lifted his brows. "That long?"

She nodded. "By the way, you talk in your sleep."

He nodded once. "I know." He smiled, still looking sleepy. His eyelids were hooded. His eyes were hazy. "Did I say anything interesting?"

"I couldn't hear much, just a whole lot of garbled nonsense."

He shrugged. "My head did get knocked in. I've been known to have full-blown conversations. To give away trade secrets… okay, not as bad as that, but bad enough that I don't let myself sleep with humans… ever.

Especially since they, generally, don't know about the existence of dragons."

"They'd think you were dreaming."

"We don't like to take any chances." He shook his head. "Your turn." He pointed back at the bed.

"I'm fine. I don't need to sleep… but I could do with a double cheeseburger and half a ton of fries."

Sand rubbed his abs. *Eyes up, Macy!* "That sounds so good."

They'd eaten the apples earlier. The sustenance long gone. "I'm sure whoever put us in here will have to come back soon to feed us."

Sand shrugged. "We can survive just fine for days on water."

She widened her eyes. "I hope they don't starve us. I must warn you, I get hangry when I'm denied food. I'm an eater. Breakfast, snack, lunch, snack, dinner, dessert… snack on occasion. I won't lie. I should probably be too nervous to eat right now." She shook her head. "But I'm not. In fact, I eat when I'm stressed."

Sand chuckled and she waited for him to tease her about her eating habits. "You sound just like a shifter. We love our food as well. There's nothing better than a female who enjoys her food." He turned serious. "I'm sure we won't be left to starve. Here," he poured a glass of water, handing it to her. "It'll keep you 'pretend' full for a while."

Not really, but he was sweet for trying. She nodded, taking the glass and sipping it. "How are you feeling?"

"Much better." His eyes were completely clear. They were a gorgeous light brown. Almost golden in color. Very warm. "I'm so glad my splitting headache is gone." He widened his eyes for a second. "I'm back to full strength, which is great."

"So, what's the plan… when it comes back, that is?"

"Simple… you need to get down and out of the way. I don't want you getting injured in the crossfire. I'm hoping this non-human comes inside, in which case I will attack immediately. I'll go at him full force…" He narrowed his eyes on hers and his jaw tightened. "There won't be any second chances. It doesn't matter if its species is unknown or if it's a Feral. You need to be clear of the action. It could get crazy in here."

"I hope it's not one of those griffin shifters."

"Me too." He nodded once. "They're hardcore. Stay out of the way." He looked worried.

"Do you think you can take it? If it's one of those Ferals, that is?"

"I'll give it all I have. I'll have to catch it unawares. Thing is, your scent is going to get stronger by the hour. I need to take action ASAP. There will be no waiting. No asking questions. It came hard at me. I plan on returning the favor." He turned his neck to the one side and then the other, eliciting a click.

"What if he doesn't come inside?"

"We'll cross that bridge if we have to. We'll gather info, regroup, plan and take action. Our goal will be to get this cage open, so that we can escape."

"You make it sound so easy." She sighed. "What if there's more than one?"

"I won't be able to take more than one Feral. I'm betting it's alone, though. Then all you have to do is get down and out of the way. The rest will be up to me."

"Again, you make it sound so simple." She choked out a nervous sounding laugh.

He shrugged. "It is." Sand pushed the blankets aside and got out of bed. He was wearing his jeans. He stretched, putting his hands above his head. His muscles roped and tightened along his back. "I think you should rest. It's been an ordeal." He pointed at the bed.

"I'm really not tired." She shook her head.

"Humor me," Sand said. "It's dark out. At least lie down and rest. I'll let you know if anything changes." He sat on the edge of the bed, facing towards the four entrances to their… cage. It might look fairly decent, but it was ultimately a cage. A jail. A cell. They were locked in.

Don't think about it!

Macy slipped into the still-warm bed. She lay down, noting that the sheets and the pillow smelled of him. It was a masculine, woodsy scent. Not unappealing. Not unappealing at all. *Moving on swiftly.* Sand was fairly sweet, but he was also arrogant and she was sure he was a bit of a player. She'd had a one-night stand before. With a shifter. A dragon shifter if she was going to get technical, and they weren't for her. Not shifters, one-night stands. Not that she hadn't had a good time – because she had. She really, really had. A *very* good time. Rock had been amazing. Sweet, kind, attentive and amazing. So much so that she'd found herself thinking of him often over the last six months. She'd been disappointed not to see him at the bar when Shale had turned up. Truth be told, she had been looking for Stone. Not Shale. Shale had been a complete coincidence. One she was glad about, since her best friend's twins had him as their father. Since it seemed like the two of them were actually seeing one another as well. Making a go of it. Who would ever have thought?

Macy was happy for Georgia. It only made her want the

same thing for herself even more. A one-night stand? Nope, she was an emotional person. Macy associated sex with feelings. She struggled to separate the one from the other. It's just how she was wired. Besides, she was made to be a mom. It *had* to happen for her. She loved kids – absolutely loved them. She would never have studied to become a preschool teacher otherwise. She had been warned that she might learn to dislike kids, working with them so much. That at the very least she wouldn't quite love them as much as she had before, and yet, here she was, ten years later and nothing had changed. She looked forward to the first day of school each year and cried on the last day when it was time to say goodbye to her kids. After all those hours a day, for a whole year, she would have come to think of each and every one as being a little bit hers. Then she'd watch them leave. On to the next year. On to bigger things. Not her kids at all.

She wanted her own. She burned with the desire. Maybe—

The bed shook as Sand stood up. He inhaled sharply, causing the hairs on her arms to rise. "Someone is coming," he whispered. "It's flying. Coming in fast." He sounded a touch panicked. Sand kept his eyes on the entrances. "There is only one," he growled. More confident. "You ready?"

"What?" *Shit!* She needed to hide. To get out of the way. "O-okay. Yes!"

Macy threw the covers off herself just as claws scraped against the stone of one of the ledges. Those terrible eyes looked in on them as its beak receded.

Beak? Did that mean it *was* one of those griffin creatures? It let out a loud screech as its body folded in on itself. Using a key on a lanyard around its neck, it opened the cage. The sound of the key turning in the lock made her spring to action. She dropped over the side of the bed, huddling against the edge, her head under her hands. There weren't very many places to hide. Any second and Sand was going to attack. Fists against flesh. It would be harsh and violent. She squeezed her eyes shut. Then again, maybe she should leave them open. She needed to see in case she had to move out of the way. Macy opened them again.

She was breathing heavily. Macy had never been this afraid in her whole life. This was worst-case scenario. A Feral. It was stronger than Sand. *Shit!*

"What do you want?" Sand asked. His voice laced with confusion.

What? Why was he talking to it? He had said that catching it unawares would be most important. He'd said he would go at it hard. No questions. No small talk. He'd said he had one shot to bring it down. This was that one shot, and yet he wasn't doing any of those things. No hitting. No attacking. No blindsiding.

"You are a decent specimen." The creature had a strange high-pitched voice. It was melodic. Quite beautiful actually. The voice didn't match what she had seen moments earlier.

Sand cursed under his breath. "Did I get this the wrong way around?" he asked. It sounded like he was talking to himself. "I'll ask again, why are *we* here?" More forceful, definitely directed at the creature. "You can let the female go. You have no use for her."

What?

No use. Why was that? Macy slowly lifted her head,

wanting to get a look at what was going on.

"I most definitely have use for the human." That same pretty, melodic voice, only it sounded… She frowned, sneaking a peek over the bed. *What?* Macy felt her eyes widen. *Pecs.* Those weren't pecs, they were breasts. The demon wasn't a *he* at all. It was a *she*. Macy's gaze dropped lower and lower to the juncture between her thighs. A *her*. Oh, yes… this was very much a woman. Her vagina was hairless. There was no question as to the sex of this creature.

Not a demon… The female creature had been partially shifted before. So big and toned, Macy had accidentally mistaken her for a man. A big, scary, demon-like man with broad shoulders and pecs. The nonhuman woman was still tall in her humanoid form. Not as tall as before, but almost as tall as Sand. Her eyes were still that freaky yellow color but that's where the strangeness ended. Her muscles were toned but they were also lithe in a feminine way. She had abs that would put many men to shame but above them were breasts, for sure. Small, high… but definitely boobs. Her hair was medium length, it was tousled about her face. Her jaw was distinctly feminine, as was her neck. Long, giving her a graceful appearance. If Amazons existed, this is how one would look in the flesh. Tall, toned, seriously athletic and yet distinctly feminine. She noted that Sand wasn't checking the woman out like she was. In fact, he seemed more agitated than before. His eyes were locked with the woman's.

"Why are we here?" Sand asked, his hands were clenched into tight fists and his muscles were bunched. "My people are looking for us. I'm a prince amongst my people. You have made a grave mistake by taking us. Bring us back right now and I will be willing to forgive and forget."

"Calm down, dragon. I can see that you are a royal. Superior blood runs through your veins. You are strong." She cocked her head, in a quick movement that reminded her of… of a bird. That was it exactly. A bird of prey. Her eyes too… they were predatory but at the same time, they were distinctly birdlike. "It is one of the reasons I picked you over the others of your kind," her head cocked to the other side, her eyes still on Sand, "for your blood and your strength." Sand may have seemed unmoved by her nudity, but she did check him out big time. "You will pass these traits to your young. It is your seed that I want."

What the heck!?

Seed? As in sperm?

Macy watched as Sand's jaw clenched. His muscles rippled beneath his skin. His jaw ticked. "I'm not interested!" he all but snarled. "If you have a condom handy," he opened his arms, "I'm all yours, but otherwise," he shook his head, "forget about it! I have no interest in becoming a father."

"Good." The Amazon nodded and smiled. It lasted all but one second. "Because I don't intend on making you one."

"I thought you said you wanted my seed." Then he chuckled. "Wait just a minute. Let me guess." He glanced back at Macy, winking at her. She wasn't sure if it was suggestive or conspiratorial in nature. He looked back at the Amazon. "You have interesting tastes, female. Very interesting indeed."

What did that mean?

Her blood ran just a little bit cold. Was he

suggesting…? Was the Amazon wanting…? The three of them? *No!* This was too kinky for her. No freaking way. Macy stood up, intent on putting her position forward on the matter, namely, *'No way. No how! Not happening.'*

"I can tell you right now," Sand said before she could say anything, "the human won't be game. She is timid and prone to crying. Her eyes leak for no reason. I just looked at her the wrong way earlier and the waterworks opened. She's a noisy crier too. She'd completely ruin the mood. Take the human back. I'll wait here. You can have at me once we're alone. I realize that," he glanced back at her again, "that she's hot. Those mammary glands… fuck!" he growled, sounding like he meant it. "Believe me, I get it. Those hips and thighs…" He made a low whistle, eyes back on the Amazon woman. "She wouldn't be into it though. Not even a little bit." He sounded disappointed. At this point, she was sure he was talking shit. Sand was laying it on too thick. "You and I can have far more fun without her. That's all I'm saying." He was trying to get the woman to let her go.

"I'm glad you like the human so much. That you are attracted to her." The Amazon turned those yellow eyes on her, and Macy wanted to shrink away. She was that intimidating. The Amazon cocked her head, those beady eyes scrutinizing her. Moving from her face to her breasts and lower, before slowly moving back up. "She is a good specimen indeed. Wide, childbearing hips."

Macy gasped.

"Her mammary glands are indeed… made for nursing babies."

"What?" both she and Sand said in unison.

"The human…" The Amazon woman sniffed the air.

"My sense of smell isn't nearly as good as yours and yet," she sniffed again, "even I can tell that she is about to come into her heat. Impregnate the female and you can leave, dragon."

"What?" they both said again, in unison. Sand turned back to look at her. His eyes were stormy. He was frowning deeply.

"I just told you I was in no way interested in becoming a father and I have a funny feeling the human won't want me anywhere near her either."

"And I told you, dragon, that I don't need you to be a father to the young. You see..." She pulled in a deep breath, her eyes shone with... pain for a moment or two before she schooled her emotions. "I cannot have children of my own. I'm barren. A terrible, cruel fate for a non-human. I crave a child. I must have one." She smiled. "Your kind have two in one go... is that right? A dual birth every time." Her eyes shone with excitement. "Get the human with child and you can go." She spoke to Sand, using harsh tones, even though her voice was methodical. "Human," she turned those eyes back onto her, "you will stay here until the eggs," she shook her head once, corrected herself, "whelps are born. I will release you once I have my young. You will want for nothing. I will take excellent care of you. You will also be rewarded financially."

"Not happening!" Sand growled.

"Firstly," Macy stepped forward, knocking her leg against the side of the bed. "Firstly," she repeated. "Like Sand pointed out earlier. I won't let him anywhere near me and then, let's just say I did get pregnant. Not happening!" she added. "But let's just say, for argument's sake, that it happened — I would never in a million years hand my babies over to you." She shook her head. "Not for any sum of money. I hope that's clear." This woman was mad. She might seem lucid, but she was out of her damn mind.

"Why not?" the Amazon woman cocked her head. "You could do with financial reward. Your nest is small."

Macy's mouth fell open for a few seconds. "Are you for real? Are you seriously for real here?"

"I am not sure what you are asking." The woman touched herself, running a hand over her arm and then her belly. "Of course I am real. You can see that I am here. We are talking."

Sand chuckled. He held up a hand. "I'm sorry. That was funny. It shouldn't be… I guess. But it was."

She gave him a dirty look and Sand wiped the smile off his face. "That's not what I meant," Macy went on, her voice laced with frustration. "I can't believe you would ask such a thing. I would never hand over my children."

The woman frowned, her eyes filling with confusion. "You can have more. Many more. As many as you wish. Besides, I wasn't—"

"That's not the point. People don't just give away their kids. Well, I guess they do sometimes, under certain circumstances."

"This is such a circumstance." The woman stared at her, unblinking.

"No, it's not."

"It is!"

"I'm not rutting this human. I refuse to get her with child," Sand growled. "End of discussion."

"I have a feeling your body might betray you, dragon. You will be stuck with her for an entire cycle. It will be hell for you. Why not just give me what I want? The young will be well taken care of. Follow your instincts and rut the female."

"You can stop!" Macy put up her hand. "Sand won't... hurt me in that way."

"He wouldn't hurt you." The Amazon snorted. "On the contrary, he would give you great pleasure." She looked him over. "I think you would enjoy the rutting very much. Even humans must be governed, somewhat, by their instincts. Your body wants to be filled with seed."

"Humans are not governed by their instincts at all. I can tell that you don't know the species very well." Sand pushed out a breath. "The female is right. I would not lay so much as a finger on her, despite what my body wanted. You might as well let us go now because there will be no rutting, no impregnating, no whelps." He shook his head, folding his arms.

"You have one heat cycle, dragon. I will find another male if you do not get this female with child. I am certain I could convince one of my own kind to do the deed. The males of our kind are starved of females. Desperate. I am sure that one would not be able to deny his instincts when presented with a female in her heat. My concern is that he might injure or even kill the female. Such would be his need, his drive." She shook her head. "I have thought this through. You would be the better candidate. My young would still be strong. They would be winged. I would raise them as my own. And even though a child of my own kind would be preferable, it might take two or three human females before one survived the mating but—"

Sand snarled.

The Amazon ignored him and shrugged. "I will have to do what I must do to achieve my goal of becoming a mother."

The horror of what this woman was saying sunk in, turning her blood to ice. "You can't do this," Macy begged.

"I have no choice, human. I must be a mother. I must obey my calling."

"But at any cost? Sand and I… we… we're people. We have feelings. We're not animals, to be used for breeding. Emotionless, uncaring. I should just go ahead and let him use my body and then give away my babies?"

She cocked her head. "I told you it would be pleasurable. One of my own males however…" She shook her head. "I suggest that you kneel down for the dragon."

"I'm not a baby-making machine. I'm not—"

"Of course you are not a machine. You are a delicate human. I will take care of you. You will be safe here. You can write a list of everything you need. I will do my best to acquire them for you. Your time here could be pleasant. You would be greatly rewarded for your efforts. You would not need to toil a day in your life."

"I don't give a shit about financial gain. It isn't a motivator for me," she added when the Feral cocked her head in question.

"Oh! I thought all humans were motivated by financial reward. I plan on giving you three pounds of gold for every month you spend here in my nest."

Macy ignored the bizarre offer. As if something like that would sway her. "And then, what? When the time comes, I have the babies and leave them with you?" With this crazy bitch! *No way!*

"I would raise them as my own and you would go back to your life. You could have as many whelps as you want." She smiled. Nothing they were saying was getting through to her. They may as well talk to the wall.

"I'm not agreeing to anything," Sand said, his voice gruff. "I can see that this conversation is going in circles, so we'll think things through and discuss them further with you tomorrow. Until then, we will need food."

"Of course." The Amazon inclined her head for a second. "That is where I was just now, sourcing some of the items you will need. I have done my research on the matter. And yes, I have food as well." She nodded, looking pleased with herself. "Just a word of caution, dragon. I am much stronger than you. It doesn't matter that I am a female. I will hurt you if you attempt to escape. Any attempts would be futile. I built this nest especially to house the two of you, and then to house the human. Let's save ourselves the trouble, shall we?" She didn't wait for him to answer. Instead, she turned and headed to the exit. She opened the door, Macy watched as her muscles began to bulge and rope. As fur and feathers sprouted up on her body. She didn't bother to close the cage door when she left.

Sand began pacing. He stopped, looking at the open door. His muscles were tense. His jaw was tight. He must be clenching his teeth.

"You should have attacked," Macy whispered.

"It's a female. A damned female. I'm sorry but that blindsided me. I'm not sure I can even harm a female unless it was in direct self-defense and even then…" He shook his head, running a hand through his hair. "Even if this particular one is completely fucked in the head." His eyes had this wild look.

"Is she really that strong?" Macy whispered.

Sand nodded. "Oh yes."

Macy heard the familiar scraping noise. Followed by a clunking sound. The Amazon carried a wooden chest, which she set against the wall. She headed out a second time, returning with a large canvas bag, which she placed on the table. "I will be back with more food tomorrow. This can be easy, or it can end up being difficult. The choice is yours." Her voice transformed into something more high-pitched as she half shifted, looking very much to Macy like a demon all over again. It was the eyes and the black wings that did it. The Feral woman closed and locked the cage before she took to the sky. Macy clasped the bars of the cage, watching as she flew away. Her lower half was lion and her upper half an eagle. Her wings were wide and feathered. She screeched once as she picked up the pace.

"We're fucked!" Sand announced from behind her. "Completely fucked."

Sand turned as he sat down heavily on the edge of the bed. He scrubbed a hand over his face.

"We can't just give up."

"You may as well get naked and in this bed." He gestured behind him.

"Bullshit!" she yelled. "I am not accepting this, and neither should you."

"We don't have any choice here." He shook his head, looking defeated.

"We absolutely do have a choice."

"Your only choice is whether you want me to father the

whelps, or whether you want one of those Ferals to do it. I would pick me if I was you. The last thing I want is to father children – you can trust me on that one – but if you think the females of that species are scary, you'll be horrified by the males. They're big fuckers. They're strong and base in their way of thinking. Feral is a good description. One of them might just tear you in two. Being pregnant and handing over your offspring would be the least of your worries. Trust me! You'd be lucky to survive the ruttings. Plural. You would be on your knees for days. That female wasn't lying when she said it was risky."

"I'm not giving up or giving in." She shook her head. "I refuse to be used in that way. It's sick." Her voice shook. Her hands too. Macy tried not to think too much about the scenario that was being painted. "We'll figure this thing out. There has to be another way. If it came to one of… them… being thrown in here with me, I would deal with that. Maybe I can talk to—"

"There would be no talking." He ran a hand through his hair, messing it up. "Look, we do have some time. Two or three days. Maybe we can figure something out."

"Yes! Exactly! We can't just give up. We definitely can't give in to her demands."

"You're right, but if there are no other options—"

"Don't say it."

"I don't want to see you get hurt." His eyes shone with sincerity. That and concern.

"We'll start by checking this cage again. Maybe I missed something."

She nodded, watching as he stood back up. Macy prayed to god he had indeed missed something. By the severity of his stance, she doubted it.

CHAPTER 6

Sand groaned in frustration. The emotion was due to more than one reason. Firstly, there was no way out of this cage. It was final. He flexed his hands. Thankful that they were already healing. The blood on his knuckles drying more slowly than his skin was knitting back together. He'd knocked several holes in the floors and walls. There was no doubt that they were completely surrounded by a silver-infused cage. He couldn't break the bars. Or bend them. He flexed his fingers again, feeling his healing skin pull tight. Although he had known this would be the case, he had needed to try one last time.

"Do you need me to take a look at your hands?" the female asked, walking towards him.

Her scent hit him square in the snout. Frustration number two. Her heat was on its way, big fucking time. It was like that shower she had taken had never happened. His dick throbbed against his zipper. That particular problem was something he needed to take care of and soon.

"They look pretty bad." Her eyes were still on his hands. Macy reached out and clasped one.

Sand pulled away. He didn't need the human touching him. "They're not as bad as they look." His voice was thick with need. Hopefully, she'd mistake his arousal for pain.

She raised her brows. "You're bleeding."

"I'm also healing." Sand tried hard to breathe through his mouth, instead of his nose. He took shallow breaths. It didn't help. The scent of her pussy filled his nose and his mouth. Sweet and wet. She'd be hot, tight. Her body would be oh so fucking soft. He had a feeling—

"Are you okay?" She frowned.

"I'm fine." His voice had a gruff edge. "I need to take a shower. That's all." He took a step or two away from her, heading towards the bathroom. Needing to put some space between them.

"A shower?" She made a face. "You just showered."

"I'm going to need to shower often over the next couple of days. I might end up looking like a wrinkled old man. Ignore me. That's the best advice I have to give."

She frowned, her eyes narrowing in thought. "Why do you need to shower that oft—?" And then the penny dropped. Her mouth made an O-shape and her eyes widened. "I see. Okie dokie then. I'll make us something to eat while you're… busy. I wouldn't mind taking a look at what's in there." She pointed at the plain, wooden chest the Feral had left.

"Food would be great. I won't be long in there." He pointed to the bathroom. "A couple of minutes. I'll help you with the cooking once I'm done."

"A few minutes… that quick?" She giggled. The sound of her laughter quickly turned into a sob. Macy covered her mouth with her hand. Her eyes welled with tears. "I can't believe this is happening." A tear rolled down her cheek.

Shit!

Fuck!

What the hell did he do to make this better? Sand felt powerless. "Hey…" He closed the distance between them and put his arms around her. Sand kept his body away from her. He didn't want to scare her with his erection. He tried to breathe through his mouth, feeling like an asshole for the thoughts he was having while she was crying. "I wish I knew what to say. What to do. Fuck!" he growled, looking up at the ceiling. Trying not to breathe. "I'll do whatever you say. Just say the word. We can try to come up with some sort of a plan. We can—"

"It's okay." She pulled away, wiping her face. "I'm okay now. Sorry." She shook her head. "I can't do what she says. I can't give in to that particular demand. There has to be another way." Her face crumpled and she burst into tears. Sand watched as she quickly pulled herself together, taking deep breaths and blinking.

Sand wasn't sure she had thought that one through. She might still end up changing her mind.

She shook her head once, as if to dispel the emotion. "Sorry. There I go again. Crying at the drop of a hat. Being all noisy and stuff." She snort-laughed.

"I just said all that to try to…"

"I know." She sniffed. "Thank you."

"I have to say… I'm mighty thankful she didn't take me up on that offer." He widened his eyes. "That female would have hurt me."

She laughed. This time it sounded real. "You're full of shit. I'm sure it would have been terrible. Just the worst fate imaginable," she rolled her eyes. "I mean what guy doesn't want sex with a gorgeous woman like that?"

Sand put up his hand. "Me. I don't want anything to do with her. Aside from not being my type at all, she's a total mental case, which also has a tendency to spoil the mood."

"That is very true. I can't believe she's doing this. I can't believe a woman would do this to another woman. Is she that cold and heartless? She said it isn't a big deal because I can have more children." Macy clicked her fingers, looking shocked. "Just like that. Like giving my kids away is no big deal because I can have more. She is crazy."

"I think she's desperate and, yes, mentally unstable. I told you that the Feral are base creatures. They're clearly even worse than I imagined."

"She's not all there. That's for sure!" The human pushed out a breath. "My worry is that we're not going to be able to get through to her. It seems like she's made up her mind."

"We'll find a way. Don't worry." Sand shifted uncomfortably. His cock was throbbing. His balls felt achy. "Are you going to be okay on your own for a few minutes?" he asked.

"Yeah, I'll be fine."

He nodded once, heading for the bathroom. "I'll leave the door open a little. You can shout if you need me." His hearing was going to be less than stellar with his dick in his hand. "Oh and," he turned back, "I wouldn't mind the steak." His mouth watered. He was about to burn a ton of calories. Sand needed to keep up his strength. There had to be a way out of this. An opportunity might present itself and they needed to be ready. That meant food and rest… okay, make that food for the time being. Rest might be difficult with a monster erection.

"Steak?" Macy frowned. "What steak?"

"There's plenty of food in there." He pointed at the bag. "I can scent a couple of juicy steaks as well." He touched his nose.

She rolled her eyes. "Of course. I keep forgetting how good your sense of smell is."

Sand headed into the bathroom, leaving the door slightly ajar. He quickly removed his jeans and started the shower. It took seconds for the water to heat. Sand stepped in under the stream, the water felt good. Steam had already filled the cubicle. His muscles were tight. Everything ached. Especially his balls. Sand looked down, shaking his head when he saw how tight they were. Pulled right up. His dick was huge and as hard as nails.

Sand grabbed the bodywash and squirted a decent amount into his hand. He palmed his cock, his mind going instantly to the human. He pictured her in that plaid shirt. Just the shirt. Nothing else. The buttons were undone. The shirt slightly parted. Not all the way open but just enough to see the sides of her soft mounds. Full. So fucking full. He pictured turning the female around. Her legs were splayed. Her hands on the table. Her ass in the air. Her pussy glistened with her need. He groaned, trying to keep it down. He didn't want the human to hear him jerking off. Sand fisted his cock, moving backwards and forwards, from tip to base. He pictured sliding into her tight little pussy. He could almost hear her moans. He placed one hand on the wall and pumped a little harder, his eyes closed. The water cascaded down his back.

His mind settled firmly on what her tight, hot pussy would feel like. He pictured the human moaning. By the sound she was making, she was close. Very close to… A few more hard tugs and he was coming and coming and coming. He crunched over, gritting his teeth, working hard to keep it down.

The whole ordeal was over in less than half a minute. *Fuck!* This was going to be a tough couple of days. That was for sure. Her scent was nowhere near as compelling as it was going to get. He sighed, looking down at his dick. It was flaccid for the first time in hours. He enjoyed the relief while it lasted.

Sand washed up. Then he turned off the water and exited the shower stall. He quickly toweled off. *Wait just a minute.* He frowned. It was too quiet out there. He should be able to hear movement. Macy's heartrate was elevated. He heard a moaning noise that had him running out of the bathroom, his jeans clutched to his dick. "What is it?"

Her eyes widened as he jogged into the room. "Oh," she said, her eyes drifting down. "You could have dressed first."

"I panicked. I couldn't hear you moving around anymore and your heartrate went a little nuts. I thought you might be in trouble." He took the jeans away from his already hardening cock. *Damn.* That hadn't lasted long at all. He watched as her eyes landed on his cock. She licked her lips. Blinking once or twice before quickly lifting her gaze. Too quickly. Like she had been caught eyeing the cookie jar. Now that, right there, was going to make the next couple of days impossible. This female was attracted to him. Looking at him with greedy eyes. She wanted him.

Sand wanted her right back, and there was fuck all they could do about it. There would be no running. No hiding. There was going to be plenty of suffering however. Mountains of that shit. Things couldn't possibly get any worse.

"My heart went a little nuts because I looked in that trunk." She pointed at the wooden chest. "You should go and see for yourself. I mean, I was expecting a nice change of clothes. A… pair of shoes… some socks, maybe. I was not expecting what is inside of that thing. That's for sure. Is she for real? I can't believe it…"

Sand listened to Macy go on. She sounded like she was in shock. He lifted the lid. *What?* Sand lifted out a red silk negligée. It was long, with a slit right up the side. Came complete with little straps. He dropped the garment, picking up the next one. A lacy number this time. Black and sexy as fucking sin. He swallowed thickly. The chest contained many more of such items. It also included undergarments. G-strings made from freaking dental floss they were so thin and barely there. The bras were sheer. Made for sex appeal rather than comfort.

"Holy shit," he pushed out.

"'Holy shit' is right," she muttered, sounding like she was about to panic or cry or something. "Did you see what else is in there?"

"These." He pulled out a pair of silk boxers. They would do fuck all to hide his erection. Then he took out a pair of tight briefs. They were white. He might as well walk around naked. "And these." He frowned. Two golden balls on a string. *What the fuck!* He picked them up, trying to decide what they were for, although, he could guess.

"Those are Ben Wa balls. She even threw in a couple

of sex toys. Can you believe it?"

Sand frowned, picking up a box with a U-shaped silicone item in it. "For his and her stimulation. It vibrates." He shook his head. "*The ultimate in g-spot stimulation,*" Sand read before tossing the item back in the chest. Next, he took out a disc-shaped device with a small silicone cup on the end. "Holy fuck! This is to stimulate a female's clit."

"You look unimpressed."

He looked up, noticing how flushed her cheeks had become. "I am. Human males suck big time if females of the species need items like this to get off." He dropped the disc thing in the chest. "How's about a good old-fashioned mouth... add in a tongue. Maybe a couple of fingers. Finish that all up with a basic understanding of the female anatomy and she will go off like a rocket every time."

He watched her throat work, catching her delectable scent, enhanced by her arousal. And just like that, his cock was back up. *Note to self, no talking about sex.* Even if it was at the forefront of his mind. Sand turned away from her and pulled on his jeans. It took some fun and games to get the zipper up without mutilating himself, but he finally managed.

"She's doing everything in her power to get us to... you know." Macy shook her head. "Like lingerie and sex toys will get us to fall in bed together."

"Imagine that!" he muttered. Sand hoped to god she didn't actually put any of that stuff on.

"The only problem is that... we have nothing else. I can't wear this for much longer." She wrinkled her nose.

Turned out that things *could* get worse. They could get

much worse. "I'm going to make us something to eat." He needed to get his mind off of sex.

"I'll help you."

"No." Sand shook his head. "You stay there."

She frowned. "Nonsense. I'll—" She stood up.

"You stay there," Sand said again. "Please. I won't be able to concentrate with you anywhere near me."

"That bad?"

He nodded once. "Yes." He cleared his throat, trying to shove aside the thoughts he had of fucking her with that disc device against her clit. He was so screwed. *Or not!* They couldn't give in to that crazy Feral bitch though. He had to find a way out of this place and soon.

CHAPTER 7

The next day…

Macy opened her eyes. The light was still soft. The sun would have just begun to rise. The room was still bathed in a fair amount of shadow. She'd slept through the night. Despite everything, she'd actually slept. It had taken forever to fall asleep, but she'd gotten a good night's rest in the end. She must have been more tired than she realized. Sand had been sweet enough to insist on her taking the bed. She turned onto her back, expecting to see him fast asleep on the sofa. She gave a shriek when she saw him standing at the foot of her bed. He was staring at her. Just staring. His eyes were narrowed. His brow furrowed. He looked seriously pissed. "Are you okay? Sand, what's going on? Did something happen?" She sat up, the covers pooling around her hips.

His eyes dipped down to her chest, and he groaned.

Sounding like he was in physical pain. He turned around and paced away. "Cover up!" His voice was gruff.

Macy looked down. She wore the silk red negligée from the trunk. It was long and did a half-decent job of covering her body. Especially since she wore a bra underneath as well. Still, though… shit! There was cleavage everywhere. Macy pulled the blanket up, even though Sand wasn't staring at her anymore.

The dragon shifter was breathing heavily. Still facing away from her. It sounded like he was breathing through his mouth. He cursed. "I'll be right back." He stomped off into the bathroom. He didn't quite shut the door.

Macy had known that her ovulation was going to be hard on Sand, but she hadn't expected this. He bristled with raw energy. The way he looked at her. She shivered. It was like he was going to give in and ravage her at any second. He'd said he would be able to control himself, but she wasn't so sure anymore. Fear rose up in her and adrenaline coursed.

She heard him groan softly from inside the bathroom. It sounded like he was trying hard not to make any noise, and failing. The groan was low and drawn out. She felt her cheeks heat, realizing that she was listening to him coming. There was no pleasure or satisfaction in the noise, just more frustration.

Macy tucked the covers under her arms, listening to the toilet flush and then water running. Sand appeared moments later.

"Are you feeling a bit better?"

Sand shrugged, still looking angry.

She would take that as a *no*. "Anything I can do to help?"

"A blow job would be nice." His voice was gruff and tense.

She choked on nothing for a few seconds before inhaling deeply. "That's a little rude of you, don't you think?"

He shook his head. "It was a bad joke. I wasn't being serious. Then again, maybe I was… without realizing it. You must be feeling horny as well. You're in your heat. Humans can't be completely immune to their own bodies' needs. Or are you?" Sand paced from one end of the room to the other. He was agitated. A bristling ball of pure energy and hormones. "There are a ton of things we could do without actually fucking." He stopped walking and turned to face her.

Was he being serious? "Okay, so you're not joking anymore?" It was a stupid question, since she could see in his eyes that he wasn't joking. She could sense it.

His eyes had a desperate edge. He shook his head. "No! Not joking. I would make it really good for you. I swear. I'm great with my mouth… really fucking good. I'll toy with your clit until you beg me to let you come." His eyes moved to her lips. "I'm sure you are amazing with that mouth of yours." He got a look of longing.

"Okay." She swallowed. "I'm going to pretend this conversation never happened."

Sand groaned. He swiped a hand over his face, squeezing his eyes shut. "I told you to ignore me earlier. Thank you for paying attention. Please keep ignoring me. I apologize for my behavior. This won't be the last time I try to proposition you. Tell me to fuck off when I do! I'm going to feel like the biggest asshole once this is over." He was looking down at the floor, looking defeated.

Macy felt sorry for him. "I take it I'm ovulating now? That's why you're so... bad?"

He shook his head, locking eyes with her again. They were almost fevered. His whole face was pinched. "Not yet but soon. You're highly fertile right now though. This is why we stay far away from females in heat. Far away. Especially when we're attracted to them." He clenched his jaw, looking at the ceiling.

"You're attracted to me?"

"Yeah." He nodded. "Big time. Red looks good on you. Holy shit." He groaned, putting a hand over the bulge in his pants. A bulge? There was a bulge? "You'll need to excuse me."

"Again? Already?" *He'd just...*

"Yes. Looks that way." He rushed into the bathroom, not even bothering with the door this time. It wasn't like she could see inside from this angle.

Not even ten seconds later and he was groaning, same as before. There was flushing and washing. Sand reappeared not looking any better. "I'll just go and stand over here." He headed to one of the exits, leaning against the wall, facing outside. He pulled the curtain open, which ruffled in the light breeze.

"Can I get you something to eat? Something to drink?" Macy tucked the sheet more firmly around her body. She didn't want to make things more difficult for him than necessary. Covering up was top priority.

"Maybe later." His voice was a deep rasp.

"I'll go and check on my clothes." She'd washed her things the night before. That's why she'd had to wear the stupid negligée in the first place.

"Yeah, I already checked and they're still wet." He

sounded like he was forcing the words out between clenched teeth.

Shit! That wasn't good. "I know showering helps, so I'll do that as well."

"Thank you." He didn't turn around.

"I'll go now," she mumbled. "Are you sure you'll cope with this?" She swallowed hard. This was bad. Really, really bad. "I'm getting nervous here."

Sand turned around. His whole body looked hard and ready. His eyes were narrowed. He looked all set to wage war. "Then you understand what's coming your way when that crazy bitch sends in a Feral male."

Her heart raced. Beating like mad inside her chest. Fear soured her mouth. "I-I'm petrified just thinking about it but…" she shook her head. "I-I can't… we can't…"

His whole stance softened. "I agree with you, Macy. I don't want whelps but if I did have them, I sure as fuck wouldn't hand them over to that crazy female. We'll find a way, but you need to understand the ramifications if I fail. I won't lay so much as a finger on you unless you ask. A Feral would not be as… controlled. I might get rude. I might get angry. I will get vulgar, but I won't hurt you." He shook his head. "You have nothing to fear from me."

"I appreciate it." She nodded once. "I might get scared. I might question you. If you get vulgar, I might get angry, but I will try really hard to trust you despite everything."

"Don't!"

"What?" That was the last thing she expected to hear. "You just said…"

"Don't trust any non-human in a situation like this. Kick me as hard as you can in the nuts if I come at you – which I won't – but…" His jaw tightened. "In fact," he made a face, "I might ask you to kick me hard at some point. If this gets bad enough. The kind of pain that comes from a kick to the balls might be more bearable than this kind of pain." He winced.

"You would rather I kick you in the balls than lose control?"

He nodded, looking uncomfortable.

Macy smiled. "I'm not worried then."

"What did I just tell you about trusting a shifter during your heat?" He looked pissed.

"I won't trust just any non-human. I will trust *you*, though. Thank you. Any guy willing to take a kick to the balls ranks high on my list. You're a good guy, Sand."

"Not really. If you could read my mind you wouldn't trust me for shit."

"Well, good thing I can't read your mind then. I'm not worried." She shook her head.

He nodded once. Macy turned to head to the bathroom.

"By the way…" Sand said.

"Yes?" She turned back to him.

"You snore."

"I know." She felt her cheeks heat. "I apologize. I had hoped you would be too busy talking in your sleep to hear me." Her ex had complained bitterly. It was one of the many reasons she hadn't wanted to fall asleep the night before. She hadn't wanted Sand to hear her.

"I thought it was cute as hell!"

"You're just saying that. You have no idea right now what's cute and what's not. How can you? I could scratch out your right eyeball and you'd still be attracted to me…

right now, that is." It was all the hormones talking. Sand had a pair of ultra-thick, rose-colored glasses on.

"It has nothing to do with your heat." He frowned, as if he wasn't sure. "You're cute when you snore."

"I'm loud for a woman. Cute?" She shook her head. "I think not! I'm going to take that shower. I'll be out in a bit."

"Take your time." Sand gave her a tight smile.

"Oh… would it help if I stayed in there?" She pointed to the bathroom. "I could close the door and—"

"No." He shook his head. "The bathroom is a space contained within a space. It wouldn't help at all. I need to get away." He looked outside longingly. "I could handle being around you better if it was in short bursts."

"What would you do if you were out in public and you ran into a female in her heat? It must happen."

"We don't mingle with humans very often, but to answer your question," he nodded once, "it does happen. Thankfully almost all human females are on some form of birth control. Females don't go into heat all that often. It's only for two days every few weeks, or so, that it gets this bad. It's nowhere near this intense either, unless we're attracted to a female." He bit down on his lower lip for a second, looking at her in a way that had her wanting to squirm or blush, or maybe both. It was just the hormones talking. She needed to remind herself of that. Macy preferred it when he was being vulgar. He was easier to deal with.

"The biggest thing is being able to get away. We can handle being around a female in her heat. One that we're attracted to even, as long as it's in short stints. This, though." He gripped the bars of the cage. "This is a nightmare."

Macy couldn't begin to imagine what he must be going through. What were they going to do when that woman came back? What about when some other man was thrown in there with her? Someone who wasn't as good as Sand? Fear immobilized her for a second. It clogged her throat. It filled her mind with terrible images of what her fate could be, and for a moment she was tempted to give in. Rather it be Sand than some monster. At the end of the day, she couldn't give in. Sand was being strong. She needed to be strong too.

CHAPTER 8

The next day…

S and physically hurt. It was a strange pain. No, not physical. It couldn't be, not with his healing abilities… and yet, it *felt* physical. It felt deep-seated. Every muscle, every limb. Even his eyes, make that his whole damned face. His senses were on high alert. His sense of smell, so much more acute. His vision as well. His whole body buzzed with raw energy and adrenaline. Need coursed through him every second, every minute, every hour.

It seemed to be getting worse. It was like his body could sense that the window was closing. Macy wouldn't be fertile for too much longer. *Thank fuck!* But then what? What would that Feral bitch say when she returned?

Macy was wearing her jeans and shirt. Well-covered. Not that it mattered. She may as well have been naked. Her pussy smelled so good. So fucking good. His balls pulled tighter and he groaned. He pulled his knees up higher and squeezed his eyes shut even tighter. *Ignore the fuck out of it!*

She turned to him. "Are you okay?" She frowned. Macy had asked him that question about a million times. "Of course, you're not okay," she muttered to herself. "I mean, look at you. You're in the fetal position on the sofa. You haven't eaten anything since lunchtime yesterday. I'm going to prepare something for you. Maybe there are ingredients for a broth. Something light is what you need."

"There's only one thing I want to eat." His voice was so gruff, he was sure she hadn't understood him.

"Ignoring," she said in a singsong voice. Macy was taking this well. She was a strong female. He respected her. This despite asking her to suck him off twice more after that first time. He'd even asked her if he could please fuck her. He'd promised to pull out before coming. Shame burned in him. At the same time, he was having to hold himself back. He was on the verge of begging. Getting on his knees and begging her to let him rut her. He was almost past the point of caring anymore. Not about whelps. Not about that crazy Feral female. Not about anything other than sinking his cock into something tight and wet. Not just something. He wanted Macy. He wanted her on her knees. On her back. Against the wall. On the floor. In the shower. Any which way he could get her. A part of him didn't care anymore if she was begging him for more or begging him to stop. It scared the shit out of him. It made his blood run cold despite the fire in his veins. Burning, consuming, raging. The need to fuck! He may as well be an animal. His scales rubbed him. It hurt. It all hurt. Sand wanted it to stop.

He'd jerked off so many times that his dick felt raw. His balls still ached. His cock knew the difference between hand and pussy. Although he'd come… there would be very little seed. No relief. He needed relief. *Fuck!*

Macy had been talking to him all the while. He had no idea what she was saying. Then she was there. Standing right in front of him. He could hear her heart. The blood rushing through her veins.

She put something on the table. It might have been the food she was talking about. He couldn't scent anything beyond the wet slit between her legs. It beckoned him. There had been stories of denied males who had died during a female's heat. "I don't want to die," he muttered.

"What?" Macy asked. Her voice was sweet. Like an angel. She was trying so damned hard. She'd showered so many times. "You aren't going to die." Concern was laced in her voice.

"I need you to kick me in the balls," he blurted. He couldn't hurt her. If this got much worse, he might. He'd give that Feral bitch exactly what she wanted. Macy would hate him. He wouldn't blame her. He would hate himself. What of the whelps? *No! Fuck!*

"I would prefer not to." Macy sounded appalled.

"Hard," he growled. "Are you wearing shoes?" His eyes were still closed.

"Yes."

"Good. Be careful not to hurt yourself but kick me as hard as you can, and square in the balls. No hesitation. Do it as soon as I stand up."

"But I don't want—"

He opened his eyes, looking up at her. "You need to do it. Please!" He said the last between clenched teeth.

Macy's eyes widened. He obviously looked that bad. She nodded quickly, looking freaked out.

"Good. You ready?" he growled.

"Yes." She nodded again, looking more composed. That was his girl. Strong and bold. "I am."

"Okay, then." Sand jumped to his feet. He was brimming with energy.

Macy narrowed her eyes with determination. Fuck but she was beautiful. Full, soft-looking lips.

She gripped his shoulders, preparing to knee him. Her hands tightened and all of his synapses fired all at once. "Stooooop!" he groaned the word, crouching. His balls exploded with an orgasm of epic proportion. All it took was her hands on him. That's how fired up he was.

Macy's grip tightened some more, helping stabilize him so that he didn't fall. When he opened his eyes, she was looking at him with concern. "Are you okay?" She asked him for the million and oneth time.

"I am now." He pushed out, feeling like a teenage asshole.

He had a feeling the pain would be back soon enough, but right then, at that moment, with Macy's hands still on him, he felt relief.

"In desperate need of a shower but…" He glanced down. Wishing he hadn't. It was a fucking mess. The whole front of his jeans were a disaster area. Heck, there was come on his stomach. That's how much had left his body. "Don't!" he warned Macy who looked down.

She let him go. "Oh… oopsie."

Oopsie!

Had she really said 'oopsie'? The look on her face was comical. The way her cheeks turned red was downright adorable. Sand burst out laughing. "I'm sorry," he said between chuckles. "I so damned sorry. Thank you, though. Who knew a shoulder squeeze was all it would take."

She smiled. "Glad I could finally help."

"I'm going to take care of this mess. Which set do you prefer?"

"Set of what?" She frowned.

"Set of underwear. It looks like it's black silk or tighty whities. I could even wrap a towel around my…"

"It doesn't matter. Whatever works best for you."

"Commando, but I'm guessing it would make you uncomfortable."

She nodded. "You'd be right."

Sand headed to the trunk and grabbed himself the boxers. "You're one heck of a female. Not timid at all. That happens to rank high on my list." He used the same words she had earlier.

Sand could already feel his balls tightening. He could feel his dick hardening back up, but he had a feeling he was over the worst. The pain would be bearable now.

Although, when the Feral came back, chances were good their real troubles would only just start. "We need to try to find out what her name is," he blurted. "That way, when she releases me, I can go to my kings. We can seek the help of the Feral royalty to track her down." He was thinking out loud. "Human females have several weeks between cycles. She will need to wait before bringing a Feral male. In that time, we could possibly find you."

Macy shook her head. "I don't want you to go. She could bring one of those Feral men immediately after you leave."

"I doubt it."

"No." Her lip wobbled. It was the first time he had seen her truly afraid. "What if you can't find me?"

"We need her name. If we manage to identify her, I'm sure we will be able to find you. Then I can get you out of here. That's first prize."

She pulled in a deep breath and nodded. "You're right. Of course, you're right."

"We'll figure out a plan B as well. I'm not just going to leave you here. I swear it."

"You might not have a choice."

Sand would find a way. He had to. He would do whatever it took.

CHAPTER 9

The next day...

Her eyes blazed. They looked like they were on fire. She opened her mouth, flinging her head back and screeched long and loud.

Macy and Sand covered their ears with their hands, trying to block out the noise. Sand staggered and dropped to one knee. He was panting hard, his face scrunched up with pain.

"What is wrong with you?" the Amazon woman raged. Her voice no longer melodic, but a high-pitched squawk. "I thought you would be a male and do the right thing."

Macy stepped forward. "It was my choice. Sand *is* a male. He was strong and—"

She set her teeth when Sand pulled her behind his back. "We are not going to give you what you want. The human does not wish—"

"Do you think I care about either of your wishes?" she screeched. "The answer is no! It's a couple of months of your life." She looked over Sand's shoulder, directing her anger at her. "I told you I would care for the whelps. I wanted this done the easy way. Now you might be injured. Possibly even killed during the rutting." She actually looked upset about the prospect. "Which will mean finding another suitable candidate. Not an easy task." She shook her head.

So, there it was. Macy was making her life difficult. That's why she was so upset. It had nothing to do with Macy or Sand's feelings. Heaven forbid that be the case.

"Don't do this." Macy had to try. "Please don't—"

"I'm going to have to find a male who won't kill you." The Amazon lifted her eyes in thought.

Sand snarled, his hands curling into fists. His muscles bunching.

"Don't try to be a hero," she casually addressed Sand. Her eyes lifted again. "I might need to find a healer." She tsked a couple of times, shaking her head. "This is all far more complicated than it ever had to be. Why couldn't you do as you were told?"

There was a loud crack and Sand went flying across the room. If Macy thought back, she might have seen the Amazon's arm move. She certainly had heard the crack as the palm of her hand hit Sand across the face. It happened lightning quick. If she had blinked, she would have missed it.

Sand was back on his feet a split second later. His back to her. His muscles roped. Scales visible in patches on his skin.

"I'm done with you." This time the Amazon addressed

Sand, who wiped his face, his hand came away bloody.

Macy could breathe again as she watched the non-human turn to leave. They couldn't just let her go. As much as Macy wanted to do just that, she needed to intervene.

She needed to try to change this woman's mind. "What is your name?" Macy blurted, her voice shrill. "I'm Macy and this is Sand. We are people. We have feelings, desires, emotions, families. Please!" She watched the Amazon's back stiffen, hoping to god she had gotten through to the woman, even just a little bit. "Please tell us your name. Please see us as people."

"My name is not important. Just as your names are not important to me. Nothing other than becoming a mother is important to me. With that in mind, you may call me Mother. I *will* be a mother. This is going to happen one way or another. Do not try to tell me anything about yourself again. I do not care. You are vessels to me. A means to an end. Nothing more." She turned, leaving their cage. The door chinked shut. The heavy lock clicked into place.

They watched her leave, standing like that for a good couple of seconds. Both of them were too shocked to move. "At least she didn't take you away immediately," Macy finally said, looking at Sand. "Oh no! Are you okay?"

"It's just a busted lip." He gingerly touched a finger to the open gash. It was leaking blood down his chin. "She may not have taken me yet, but she does still plan to bring a Feral male. She made that clear. She needs to plan her next move. She never expected me to be able to resist you and I almost didn't." He used the back of his hand to wipe up the blood.

She snorted.

"I mean it, Macy. I'm not sure I would hold up a second time."

She didn't say anything. Macy was sure he would. He didn't give himself enough credit. "What are we going to do? I don't think we'll find out her identity."

"I doubt it as well, but you never know, she could slip up."

"How many Feral women are there? Maybe not nearly as many as you would think. There are very few dragon women."

"I don't know." He shook his head. "She said their males were desperate, which indicates that there aren't that many, but we can't be certain."

"How many of them are stark raving mad, though?"

"She comes across as mentally unstable to us, but she might just be normal amongst her kind. I'm afraid we don't know much at all about these creatures. We need to find out more. That much has become apparent. I'm also not even sure her king would help us."

Macy nodded. "She brought us more food." She pointed at another canvas bag lying on the ground where the Feral woman had thrown it. Macy had never seen such anger before. For a few moments there, her life had flashed before her eyes.

"I could eat," Sand announced. "No clothing, though." He looked down at the black boxers he was wearing. The shifter could really rock the color black. It contrasted perfectly with his sandy hair and beautiful, light brown eyes. Then again, he could also rock silk. Not many men could pull it off. He could.

"Nope." She shook her head. "This outfit could use a

wash as well." She was still wearing her jeans and shirt from the day before. "At least I can put something from the trunk on without fear of you jumping me." She giggled.

"Yeah… of course." He ran a hand through his hair, squeezing the back of his neck.

"I noticed you didn't tell me how cute my snoring was this morning." She laughed harder. "You were funny when you were so… so…"

"Horny?"

"Yeah. You were so complimentary during my heat. Since when is snoring considered cute? I mean, come on." She rolled her eyes. He'd told her numerous times how attracted he was to her. All hormones, of course.

Sand smiled and nodded. He didn't say anything.

"So, what now? We hang around waiting for her to throw me to the wolves?"

"If only it was just wolves you had to worry about. Wolves still have honor. These Feral, though…" Sand's brow was furrowed. He looked really tense. "We have to find a way to get the bitch to keep me. As the seed donor. We need to tell her that you changed your mind. You won't resist this whole thing anymore. Maybe she won't send me away. It'll buy us more time."

"She'll see right through it. She was very clear about giving us one chance and one chance only. Nothing has changed."

"We have to try. She's so damned strong. She doesn't turn her back on me. Not for a second. I'll take my chance if it presents itself, but fuck!" He shook his head. "I didn't see that blow coming, and she didn't even try." He touched his mouth again. It had stopped bleeding. "We

need to figure out where the hell we are and who she is."
Sand grabbed the bars of their cage. "We're in the middle
of fucking nowhere. There are zero landmarks. How the
hell would I find this place again? That Feral isn't stupid.
She wouldn't move me while I'm still conscious. We need
time. If we have that, she might just screw up. An
opportunity might present itself."

"We'll have to figure something out." Macy couldn't
fathom what that something might be. She needed to
resign herself. That Feral woman was coming back. She
was most likely going to take Sand. Things were about to
get worse for her. Infinitely worse.

Unless.

Unless she could come up with a plan. Macy started
thinking.

CHAPTER 10

One week later…

S and put the pop tart on the side-plate.

"So that's it?" Macy asked, eyes glued to the tart as well. It was tiny.

"That's it." He folded his arms, staring at the treat.

"We have nothing left to eat after this?" she asked, even though it was a stupid question because she already knew the answer.

"I'm afraid not."

She'd been racking her brain the first few days and had come up with half a dozen reasons for allowing Sand to stay with her. She had to convince that Feral woman. The best reason so far was that she was attracted to Sand and would find it easier to make a baby with him than with a stranger.

Weak.

The excuse was incredibly weak. Amazon woman would see through it in a hot minute. Essentially, they had to come up with why things would be different next time or a plausible reason why they hadn't worked this time. *What had changed?* Another one was that she hadn't known Sand long enough before. That she had been shy. Since they began rationing food, she hadn't been able to think of anything else. It had to be something rational. Logical. That's how the Amazon woman was. It was all facts. No emotion. Her reason needed to come from that place. She didn't understand humans. Didn't care about either of them. The only thing they had going for them was that the Feral woman would prefer it if Sand stayed. She didn't want to have to find another guy to replace him. It would be too much effort with less chance of reward. These were all things the Feral knew already, of course.

Her stomach twisted in her gut. Her mouth watered just looking at the delicious tart. The center would be sweet and gooey. The outside crispy and delicious. They'd lived on crackers and peanut butter for the last two days. The measly amount of fruit and greens the Amazon had brought ran out quickly. Macy never thought she'd ever crave salad and yet, there she was, mouth watering just thinking about all that was green and crisp and juicy. "What I wouldn't give for a double cheeseburger and a huge salad. With dressing too." She licked her lips.

Sand chuckled. "You take it." Sand pushed the plate over. "Dragons can go without food for long periods." He shrugged like it was no big deal.

Take it, Macy! Take the pop tart! Take the offer! Do it! Macy forced herself to shake her head. "We should share it. We'll cut it in half." It was the best solution. The only solution that was right. She taught the kids about right and wrong on a daily basis. She needed to stick to her guns now that times were tough. "Sharing is caring," she added, thinking of a certain purple dinosaur.

He pushed his lips together for a few moments, gaze still on the tart. "Just eat it, Macy." He pushed the plate over to her. "You are a human. You need it more than I do."

"It's not fair if I eat the whole thing. You already insisted I take that extra cracker last night. Don't think I didn't notice the extra peanut butter either. It's not right." Her stomach growled noisily at the mere mention of food.

They both looked down at her midriff. "See. You need the food more than I do." He scratched his newly shaven jaw.

They might not have food, but they had plenty of toiletries. "Pity we can't eat shower gel, sex toys and lingerie," she muttered.

"We'd be stocked up for weeks," he grumbled right back. "I'm not sure what the hell she's playing at here." He pushed out a pent-up breath and touched the plate. "Eat… please." His own stomach grumbled loudly.

They locked eyes and laughed. It took a few seconds for her to gain her composure. "By the way, you were talking about food last night… in your sleep," she said as she opened one of the drawers, taking out a knife.

"That makes sense." He smiled. "I tend to talk about whatever is on my mind."

"It sounded like you were out to dinner or something. You were ordering food. Lots and lots and lots of food." Macy cut the tart in half. "Then you kept asking for people to pass you food items. Mainly steak or ribs… which makes sense, I would imagine shifters have a thing for meat."

She watched his throat work. "Don't even get me started. You'll just make us hungrier than we already are. I'm sorry I talked so much." He frowned. "I hope I didn't wake you up."

She shook her head. Her stomach had woken her up. Their predicament had woken her up. "No… it's this place. When do you think she's coming back? Surely, she won't leave us to starve? Could she be that angry with us for not doing what she wanted?"

Sand's jaw tensed and his eyes flared with anger. "She still needs you. Withholding food is a classic method used to make people more accommodating. More susceptible to suggestion."

"Do you think that's what this is about?"

He shrugged. "I don't know. It seems that way. It's the only logical explanation." He looked back down at the food. What little of it there was. "I thought you said you get hangry when you don't eat." Sand looked back up at her. "You haven't lashed out once and are handling this better than I would ever have imagined."

She nodded once, trying to smile. "I'm a mess inside."

"I doubt that."

"I am." She nodded, picking up her tart and taking a small bite. She closed her eyes and savored the flavor burst on her tongue. When she opened them, Sand was looking at her in a way that reminded her of how he had looked at her when she was ovulating. The look was gone almost immediately. His eyes flashed to the pop tart and he licked his lips. It was the food, she realized in the next instant. They both had food-lust.

He picked up his half of the tart. "You sure about this? We have no idea how long she plans on withholding food. It could be a couple more days, or more, before she comes back."

"Half a tart isn't going to make much difference either way."

"You're right, but…"

"No buts. We're in this together… at least for now." She shoved down the panic that rose up at the thought of Sand being taken away. Of being alone in there. Of not being alone… of some non-human—*No!* She couldn't think along those lines. Macy had to think of something. She *would* think of something.

"You okay?" Sand touched the side of her arm.

She nodded once. "Maybe we should have done it. Given her what she wanted. I'm scared, Sand. I believed I could handle it, but I don't know if I can."

"I won't let her take me. We'll find a way to convince her and I won't let her go through with this fucked up plan either."

"Thank you. What if we do convince her? What will happen when we still don't give her what she wants?"

He gripped the tops of her arms looking her in the eyes. "We need to take this one day and one step at a time. Right now, I need to stay. We can't have her throwing some other male in with you. All we have to do is convince her that me staying is the better option. It *is* the better option, so I'm sure she'll agree."

She nodded. He had a way of making things sound so simple.

"Eat your food." He looked pointedly at the tart in her hand.

They both ate in silence. Sand popped the entire thing into his mouth. He chewed a few times and swallowed. Washing it all down with a big gulp of water. Macy took her time with each bite. She savored them all, loving the burst of flavor. The tartness. The sweetness. The crispy outer crust. It was gone in less than a minute. Macy licked her fingers and just stood there, enjoying the taste that was left in her mouth.

She watched as Sand stepped out of his jeans. She wanted to look away. She really did, but she couldn't. Macy watched the glutes of his ass move up and down as he took the last few steps to the chest. The guy had become infuriating with his nakedness. He had no qualms about dropping his jeans, boxers or briefs. It was a natural and normal thing for a shifter. As far as Sand was concerned, she'd seen him naked a good couple of times already, so what was the big deal.

What was the big deal?

What was the…?

Unfortunately, she could not possibly tell him what the big deal was. Macy couldn't tell him how she got a funny feeling in the pit of her stomach when she snuck peeks at him or how her heart sped up just a little every time she ogled all the hard planes of his body. His abs were tight. His back was… could a back be called beautiful? His was. It was muscled and sculpted. His ass. Lord help her. He even had a great penis. It was still big even when he wasn't aroused. Long and thick. The guy was well-hung. He didn't have any hair down there either. By now, she got the impression he was like that naturally. That shifters maybe didn't have hair down there. His chest was also clear of any hair. All he had was that gorgeous tattoo. It glinted in the sunlight. It was bad of her to even notice Sand in the first place, given their predicament. But how could she not? There he was right in front of her. She was trapped here with him, for god's sake, and she had eyes.

The ironic part of the whole thing was that he seemed to be completely over her now that her ovulation had passed. It was a good thing, of course. He didn't look at her like he had done before. He hadn't tried to proposition her again either. Macy was glad about all of those things. If they had both been attracted to one another, it would have complicated matters. They had to stay away from complications. It was the last thing they needed.

The Amazon woman wanted her pregnant by him, so being attracted to Sand was a ginormous complication. Good thing he hadn't seemed to notice. Thank god… and she really needed to keep it that way.

He pulled on a pair of silk boxers. They hung 'just so' on him. His ass was almost better showcased in the shiny material than when he was naked. It clung to him… everywhere. He lifted his arms, stretching. She knew this routine. A couple of stretches and then he'd start working out. "You're still going to exercise?" she asked. "At a time like this. You're running on empty."

Sand nodded. "Yep." He began jogging on the spot, stopping to stretch his quads or his lats. Then he did some squats.

"Don't you need to conserve energy?"

He shook his head. "On the contrary. I'm buzzing with it. I'll go crazy if I don't move."

"Suit yourself." Macy did what she normally did every day when he worked out. She grabbed a magazine. Macy had found them inside the last food bag that was dropped off on the first day. How nice of the Amazon woman to have brought a couple of them. Especially since food would have served them so much better.

This was her making the most of a shitty situation. She positioned herself on the sofa, pillow at her back. Macy opened the dogeared magazine, pretending to read. She didn't have a clue what was between the pages. Not a cooking clue. It was riveting stuff, nonetheless. At least, she pretended it was. By now Sand was doing push-ups. She'd never seen anyone do them so well before. His body was completely straight from his heel to his head, and perfectly parallel from the ground. *Up... down... up... down.* So rhythmic. His biceps popped. He kept going... and going... and going. First using both arms and then using one.

One.

Lord help her. He put the other arm behind his back. *Up... down... up... down.* His breathing turned slightly ragged when he swapped arms. He just swapped by pushing himself up a little higher. No need to stop or anything. Sand put his other arm behind his back and carried on going like nothing had changed. It was mesmerizing. She tried to act all nonchalant and was sure she was failing dismally. *Magazine. What magazine?* She either paged too quickly from the start to the finish – all the while looking at him – or sat there like a statue, book in hand. Good thing he seemed too busy to notice. Sand gave a soft grunt as he moved to a sitting position. There was a light sheen of sweat covering his body. His face was slightly flushed. His muscles had muscles.

Shit! She quickly turned the page, realizing that it had been a while since she had pretended to read the magazine.

Macy forced herself to glance down but soon found herself lifting her gaze.

Sand had lain down on his back. Legs apart and bent at the knee. Feet flat on the ground. He put his hands behind his head and started doing sit-ups. He went almost to the ground and back up. Up and down he went. The guy had some stamina, that was for sure. Then he did them by pulling his knees up, opposite to opposite. His abs went nuts. Her eyes almost fell out of her head. This was followed by squats, lunges and more stretches. He bent over and grabbed his ankles. He leaned against the wall. Watching him work out and stretch like that was her only highlight of the day, hands down! Although she'd kill for food. That would be a highlight too. This was almost as good. If she wasn't starving, it would have been better. That was saying something.

She turned the page of her magazine, not even pretending to read anymore. Not really.

"You sure you don't want to join in?" he asked, making her heart stop for a second or two. Sand didn't look up though.

"Um… I… well…" she stammered. Maybe he paid more attention than she realized.

"You seem quite interested, that's all." He took up another stretch position, still not looking over at her.

"It's quite something to watch." She worked at pulling herself together. "You have s-so much stamina. You're so strong as well. Those one-armed push-ups are… well… you're definitely… most certainly… um… superhuman."

"I could give you some pointers." He looked her way. "Not right now, of course, you should preserve your strength."

"Yes, sure thing." Did he think she needed to exercise? Probably. "If the Feral lets you stay and she brings us some food, you can… help me work out, for sure."

"You're on then." He flashed her a grin before starting a set of burpees.

This time she did look at the magazine, even though she burned to watch Sand, she kept her eyes on the book still not reading a word. He didn't act like he had noticed that she was checking him out… but *had* he noticed? Her cheeks burned when she realized he probably had.

CHAPTER 11

The next day…

Macy grabbed Sand's hand, holding it tight. "It'll be okay," he said, nodding once. "I can scent food." He smiled at her and squeezed softly. "That's positive."

Macy nodded once, feeling sick to her stomach, and it had nothing to do with the organ being completely empty. "I guess so." Not if she was going to be forced into a meal for one.

"She's also alone." Sand smiled at her. She could see that he was tense from the lines around his mouth and by the way he clenched his jaw when he thought she wasn't looking.

The nails scraping on the rocks of the ledge reminded her of nails on a chalkboard. They made Macy cringe.

"We can do this." Sand squeezed her hand again. "I'm sure she'll listen."

The lock clicked open and the Feral woman entered. "Are you ready to leave, shifter?" she asked. The question made Macy's heart sink. Part of her had been hoping there would be a delay. That she wouldn't end up going through with it at all. Seemed like Macy was wrong.

"No." Sand shook his head. "I'm not going anywhere," he added. "You can leave me here. We've changed our minds." He looked down at Macy, squeezing her hand.

The woman put the bag she was carrying down. "We can do this the easy way, or we can do it the hard way. The hard way would involve beating you until you become unconscious, so that I can transport you. Although, I think it would all be over with one blow. It would hurt," she cocked her head, "so, I would suggest the easy way, which would entail a hug… same as I did with you, human." The Feral looked over at her. "It wasn't so bad, was it?" she asked Macy.

"You mean when you suffocated me until I passed out? Yeah, no, I didn't like that much."

"So dramatic. You should have allowed the dragon to rut you. All of your hardship would have been over by now."

"You're forgetting the part where I would be expected to grow children inside my body, give birth to them on my own," her voice hitched, "and then hand them over to you like I don't care. I would call that a hardship."

"I discussed my requirements with several males of my kind, and they are eager to meet with you, human. Too eager. I don't think you have any idea what hardship is. Whoever I pick will quickly point out your error in judgment." She sighed. "I am already on the lookout for a suitable female to take your place when you are torn apart."

Macy couldn't help the sob that escaped her. She put a hand over her mouth.

"Stop this!" Sand took a step forward. "Or so help me…" He let go of her hand. His whole body bristled. Macy clutched his arm. She didn't want him to do something that would get himself killed.

"Do not be a fool?" the Feral said to Sand before turning back to her. "Then again," she said. "I think you are stronger than you seem, human. Perhaps you will survive the breeding. I hope so. I like you."

Macy took back his hand and squeezed. If he tried something now, he would be squashed like a bug. The Feral was expecting it. It seemed that she wanted him to try.

Her freaky yellow eyes moved to Sand. "What is it to be, shifter? Would you like a hug?"

"I don't want to leave," Sand growled the words. "Macy doesn't want me to go either."

"It's getting tiresome saying the same thing over and over. What you want doesn't concern me. Not in the least." She paused, cocking her head to the side, her eyes lowering to where their hands were clutched. "I suggest you let the human go," the Feral looked at her, "and that you move to a place of safety, human."

"Don't do this!" Macy pleaded. "Please." Begging wouldn't help, so she forced herself to stop. She had to give the Feral something concrete. "I will let him have sex with me now. I changed my mind. I swear it. I'll let him… breed me." She used the Amazon's words.

"It's true," Sand tried. "Humans take time to get to know someone before they allow… rutting. They aren't the same as non-humans.''

"And you have had some time to," the Feral made a face, "bond? Is that what you are saying?"

"Yes!" she yelled. "That's it exactly. You just expected me to hop into bed with him so soon after meeting him. I couldn't. I *am* attracted to him though. Like you said before, he's a good specimen. How could I not want him… in that way? I just had to get to know him and… bond." *Please let this be working!*

"You know my feelings about the human," Sand said, sounding completely calm. "I would rut her from here until next week," he shrugged a shoulder, "but I couldn't do it without her consent."

It looked like the Feral woman was thinking it through. "I wish I could believe you." She sighed heavily. "It would make my life easier. You say that you are now bonded and enjoy each other's appearances?" She looked from Sand to Macy and back again, scrutinizing them.

"Yes," they both said in unison.

"So much so that you wish to rut?' she asked, cocking her head in that weird birdlike way. Why did it feel like they were walking into a trap? Sand must have sensed it too because he didn't answer either.

"You *now* suddenly give the male consent, human, is that correct?" she asked, looking at Macy.

"Yes, I do!" Macy nodded. "Give us one more chance." What they were really wanting was time. Time meant potential opportunity, which meant potential escape. There was always hope that Sand's people would find them, although he didn't hold out too much hope of that happening. They had discussed it and he was sure they would think the hunters had them, which was a far more logical explanation than a crazy, baby-hungry bitch.

The Feral woman seemed to hold her breath for a while. A long while. Macy had to stop herself from squirming and fidgeting and begging. *Don't forget the begging.* She wanted to do all those things. Sand held her hand tightly, almost trying to warn her against moving or saying anything. He seemed to be holding his breath as well.

"No," the Feral finally said, her voice flat and without any emotion. "You would have rutted by now if you were going to do the deed. I do not believe your reasoning. It makes no sense."

Sand stepped forward. "It's true. We—"

The Feral put up her hand, silencing Sand. "I have heard enough and have made my decision. Now do the right thing and step away from the female. I am giving you one last chance to come willingly."

"You can't—" Sand let her hand go. He ducked down and rammed into the Feral's stomach. She staggered back half a step. *Half a measly step.* Sand looked dazed from the impact. He pulled himself upright but lurched to the right, he shook his head as if to dispel dizziness.

The Feral woman stepped forward and slammed her fist into his face. Something crunched and he flew backward, colliding with the wall on the other side of the room. Plaster crumbled, exposing more silver bars. Sand fell down in a heap on the floor. Blood gushed from his nose.

"Stupid male." The Feral shook her head, giving what looked like an eye-roll. Macy watched as she walked over to where he lay unconscious.

Macy could see Sand's chest rise and fall. He would be fine. His nose was bleeding profusely and was sitting to the right instead of straight. *Broken, for sure.*

The Feral bent over, preparing to pick him up.

"Wait. I'm glad he can't hear us anymore." *Why hadn't she thought of this before?* "I don't want him to know what I'm about to say. I have a proposition for you."

The Feral turned, she looked bored. "You have ten seconds." She folded her arms across her breasts.

CHAPTER 12

Sand groaned, putting his hands to his face. To his nose. "Thank fuck!" he groaned as he felt up and down the bridge. Hurt like a motherfucker.

"I straightened it," Macy sounded panicked. "I hope that was okay? I wasn't sure what to do. Straightening it seemed like the right thing. It looked terrible before... still does. All swollen and purple."

Her eyes were wide. All four of them. He winced, closing his eyes. The motion hurt, so he groaned. He felt like a complete pussy. Put down by a female with one punch. Then again, said female was a Feral and she was strong and mean. "Am I still here?" he asked. "With you? Or am I concussed and imagining it?"

Macy laughed, sounding somewhat hysterical. "You are still here." Her eyes shone with unshed tears. "I was so worried about you."

"She's gone?" He half expected to hear the Feral bitch's

voice just then.

"Yes, she is. She left a few minutes ago."

"Wait a second." He carefully opened his eyes, feeling somewhat better. He winced, touching the top of his head.

"That was stupid," she chided him.

"I had to do something. I'm already healing. My headache should be gone in a little while." It hurt like a bitch, but she didn't need to know that.

"The swelling on your nose is already going down. Your healing capabilities are amazing." Macy touched the side of his face, her eyes focused on his nose. He was thankful there was only one of her.

"How? Why… What happened? Why did she leave me here?"

"I had to make her a promise or two and I lied to her about something." Macy bit down on her lip.

"Why are you so worried? Was it bad? What did you promise?"

"That's the thing. I can live with the lying. I mean, you have to do what you have to do sometimes. It was the promises that were the issue. Although I didn't *promise* promise. I kind of agreed more than promised, but still… We're going to have to live up to her expectations now." Her eyes were such a gorgeous blue. How could you not believe every word that came out of her mouth? No wonder the Feral had bought it all.

"What did you agree to?" He was almost too afraid to ask.

"It involves both of us. I should have discussed it with you first, but…" she made a face, "it's not like I could pull you aside, at the time, or anything."

"You had no choice, you had your back against a wall."

"And you were unconscious and bleeding against one."

"I've never been hit like that before." He touched his nose again and winced. "She's strong, hard as nails and—"

Macy laughed. "No need to explain. The Feral are strong. Even the females of the species. I've watched you work out. I know you're strong too. You tried, and for that I'm grateful. She could have killed you."

"I would do it again." Macy was sweet to try to bolster his ego. It didn't help. Seemed like his face and head weren't the only things that were bruised. "I'm one of the strongest of my kind." He felt stupid for saying it. Normally when people tried this hard… it wasn't true. In his case, though… it *was* true. All of it. It was hard to believe, after his attempted attack was so easily thwarted, however.

"I know. Relax about it, I'm not judging." She gripped her hands together so tightly her knuckles turned white. Then she chewed on her lip.

Whatever she had promised must have been really bad. She looked like she was struggling with telling him. Agonizing over what she had said. "Just tell me," he urged. "It can't be that bad."

"It is." Her eyes looked huge on her face. Her skin was translucent it was so pale. "I said we would have sex," she mumbled. "Tonight. She's coming back tomorrow to make sure it happened, and if not, she's taking you. There." Her eyes finally met his. "I said it. I'm so sorry," she gushed, looking distraught. "I would completely understand if you left tomorrow instead of… having sex with me. I know you'll do your best to find me after you go. I know—"

Sand couldn't help the laugh that burst out of him. "I'm sorry." He put a hand up. "You're making sex sound like a hardship. I would love to have sex with you." Now she was the one who looked horrified. Maybe he should dial it back a notch or fifty. "What I meant to say was… I understand. I get it. If we have to fuck," he shrugged, "then," he shrugged again, "we'll do what we have to do. That is…" Maybe her aversion was more for herself than him. "Unless you can't go through with it. We could possibly come up with a plan B otherwise."

"I can't get pregnant now, can I?" She looked panicked.

"No." He shook his head. "Not at all."

"Okay." She sucked in a deep breath, looking him straight on. "Then I think we should just do it. Make it quick and get it done. We can keep it clinical. In and out and… finished."

"No can do." Sand shook his head. "Ferals don't have a good sense of smell. I would need to make you come… a lot."

"What?" she squeaked.

"I would need to get a ton of my seed in you as well. We would need to do one hell of a good job. If we're going to do this, we may as well do it right. That way, that bitch and her bad sense of smell won't be able to take me away on a technicality. I want your system flooded with endorphins. There will be no showering."

"Oh." She chewed on her bottom lip. "I thought quick sex would do it."

Quick? Fuck that!

"I mean, you lasted ten seconds when you…" She stopped talking. Must have caught the look on his face.

"That was when you were in heat. I, assure you I can

last longer than ten seconds."

"Then the other time you just touched my shoulder and… boom. I was kind of expecting that. Wouldn't that be enough?"

"Let's go back to the part where we need your system flooded with endorphins. She won't believe us otherwise. The proof has to be irrefutable. I *can* last longer than ten seconds." *No fucking pressure!* His ego wasn't just bruised, it was bleeding. It might not actually survive.

"Oh, I see." She didn't seem thrilled at the prospect, which was weird since he was sure he'd caught her checking him out and on numerous occasions.

"Think it through, otherwise, we might do the deed and she won't be able to pick up on it. We would end up fucking for nothing."

"That would be terrible." Her eyes were so wide.

Not *so* fucking terrible! *What the hell?*

"Look," he leaned forward, taking her hand, "it's up to you. It's… not a big deal to me. I'm a shifter."

"You have plenty of casual sex." Not a question. She nodded once when she said it, even looked at him as if she pitied him.

"Not as often as I would like." He laughed, noticing that she didn't join in. It made him feel like a dick about making the stupid joke in the first place. He was trying to lighten the mood. "What I meant to say was that I think you are very sexy, and I would love to…" *How did he say this without sounding crass?* "go there with you… a good couple of times to be sure… if you're okay with it. It's up to you. All up to you." He was such a dick!

"Thing is… I was desperate when I promised that to her." She groaned and rubbed a hand over her face. "I don't do well with sex and emotions. I just don't. I become attached too easily."

He felt his palms begin to sweat.

"I fall for someone when I'm intimate with them. I don't cope well with 'casual.'"

"We won't be intimate." He shook his head. "I'll fuck you… that's it. We can have rules, like no kissing. No holding hands, or any of that shit!"

"Fucking, sex, intimate, they all mean the same thing to me. Sex is sex."

It wasn't, though. Was it? "Oh." He couldn't believe how deflated he sounded. He had really looked forward to sex with Macy. He wanted to bury his head between her soft thighs. Listen to her cries of ecstasy as he brought her over the edge. He had a feeling she would be noisy in the sack. He loved females who expressed themselves. "I see."

"That's just it, you don't. I had sex with Rock some months back."

Sand narrowed his eyes on her. "Rock? As in the dragon shifter, Rock?"

"How many humans do you think there are out there with the name Rock?"

"None, I guess."

"Exactly. It was dragon shifter Rock and I haven't been able to get him out of my mind. As I said, I'm bad at the 'no emotions' thing."

Relief coursed through him. "Oh, I get it. You still have feelings for Rock. You would feel bad sleeping with me because of him."

She lifted her eyes in thought. "Not bad, exactly. We aren't dating or anything. I just wanted you to know about my past and how I am and…"

"But you want to date him, and sex with me might ruin that? Especially now that your best friend is living with a dragon shifter? There will probably be an opportunity to see Rock again. To pursue things. Us fucking could definitely screw that up." Sand would hate it if a female he was interested in rutted another male. Shale had stolen enough of his females in the past, and vice versa. They had just been hook-ups, though. He couldn't imagine Rock's reaction if they were more. It was a valid point.

"I guess so." She nodded once.

Sand breathed out. Loads of the tension he had been feeling eased. "I can't say either way what the right thing to do here is. I can't give you any advice. The decision would be yours and yours alone. You can let me know what you want to do."

She nodded again.

Thank fuck she wouldn't become attached to him. "We have until morning then?" he asked.

She grimaced. "Yes. She will take you if she isn't convinced of our 'bond.'"

"Ball's in your court then."

"So simple." She shook her head. "You always make things sound so darned simple and they're not."

"It *is* simple." He smiled at her. "What else did you agree to? It sounded like more than one thing."

"That we would breed when the time came." She rolled her eyes and shook her head.

He nodded. "Hopefully we'll be long gone by then. This will buy us a couple of weeks… I think. It will take that long before your next heat, won't it?" He raised his brows.

She nodded. "Yes, it will. Every time that Feral returns

it's an opportunity. She might just slip up."

"Let's hope. I still don't get how you managed to convince her. She seemed dead set on removing me."

"I lied to her. She's cold and calculating. She's more about facts than emotions."

He nodded. "Anyone who insists that a female can have more kids to replace the ones she was forced to part with, is cold-fucking-hearted."

"Exactly. The answer just came to me when I saw you broken and bleeding."

"It wasn't that bad."

"I don't mean it like that. I think you had some nerve trying to go against that thing." She widened her eyes. "I remembered an earlier conversation we had. She believes humans are money grabbers."

He made a face. "A lot of humans are."

"A lot of us don't care about money."

"Absolutely." He held up both his hands, not wanting to argue. "I wasn't talking about you."

"Maybe you should have been." She snort-laughed at her own joke. "Anyway, I'm sure you remember how she mentioned making this whole plan of hers worth my while financially. She was shocked when I didn't show any interest. She offered a couple of pounds of gold per month if I stuck it out in here."

He nodded. "I remember thinking she'd lost her ever-loving mind."

"I told her I denied sex with you so that I would get an extra month's gold. That it was too good of an opportunity to miss out on."

He frowned. "You didn't."

She scrunched up her face. "I totally did."

"And she bought it?"

"In a heartbeat. She told me this was my last chance, though. Not to mess around this time… or else."

Sand grinned. "That's unbelievable. You're unbelievable. That was smart thinking."

Macy smiled as well. "I had to do something. Had to say something that would convince her."

"Well, it worked. Well done! Don't feel bad about any of it."

"I don't!" She shook her head.

"How's about we get some food? I just heard your stomach grumbling… again."

"Yeah, let's do that." She smiled, but still looked both tired and tense.

Sand took her hand as she was stepping away. Macy turned back. "You say the word and… it's up to you where we go from here."

She nodded once, her throat working.

"Let's eat first. Big decisions shouldn't be made on empty stomachs."

CHAPTER 13

Macy couldn't fit another bite of food into her stomach, which now protested. She'd never eaten so many grilled chicken wings in one sitting before. Ten of them. They also devoured mashed potatoes and gravy. As well as grilled vegetables. She'd eaten and eaten and eaten. Both of them had, and in complete silence for most of the meal. They had been that hungry.

"Maybe we shouldn't have eaten so much," she said, drying the plate Sand had just handed to her.

"She'll be back tomorrow. There'll be more food." He washed the next plate in the soapy water.

"I guess." She put the plate away and took the next one from him. "So, you really don't want kids? I mean, one day?"

Sand shrugged. "I don't know. For years I didn't think so, but it's hard to say for sure. My instincts push me in that direction but I'm too young to be a father. Too young to think along those lines, period."

"How old are you?" she asked as she took another plate.

"Thirty-two. It's young for a dragon."

"It's young for a human as well. Especially since you're a guy. Guys don't have ticking clocks like we do. I'm thirty." She made a face. "You would swear I was ancient by the way my mom carries on. She's always trying to set me up with someone. The manager from the store she goes to or one of her friends' sons. She once tried to set me up with one of her doctors." He had been fifty-one and completely grey. The worst part of it was that he had two ex-wives. Then there was that cheating lawyer. Her mom obviously thought she was desperate. "It comes from a good place, but it's annoying as hell."

"I'm sure. You're still young, Macy. You still have plenty of time."

"Most days I'd agree, however, I have the odd day where I buy into all that crap she sells me. My brother is gay. He and his husband have decided not to adopt or to try to find a surrogate. I'm her only chance at grandbabies." Macy sighed. "*I want to be a nana, Macy.*" She pretended to be her mom. "*You are our only hope at grandchildren, you can't let us down,*" she went on. "*Don't deny an old woman.*' She's not old at all. She and my father are still fit and healthy… thankfully."

He whistled low. "All that pressure…"

She packed away the last of the dishes, watching as Sand wiped the countertop. "Thing is, I want the same thing as she does. I broke it off with my ex two or so years ago because he didn't want to take the next step. We'd been together for four years and I thought it was time, but he didn't agree."

"His loss."

She smiled. "Thanks, I agree. I don't want to settle though. I want… the right person in my life. In hindsight, I'm glad Jim and I didn't settle down. We lacked something."

"Didn't you love him?"

"I did. We missed passion in our relationship. That spark you need in a healthy relationship. We didn't have it."

"Compatibility. Yes," he nodded, "it is important that both love and compatibility are present."

"Hopefully I find the right person before my time runs out. My mom would never forgive me otherwise."

"It has nothing to do with your mother. Besides, Rock *does* want kids. I can tell you that now. He's that kind of a male. He always goes on the Hunt."

"You're talking about the Bride Hunt, where your men hunt human women and the strongest, fastest win those women to mate with?"

"That's right." Sand nodded. "Rock always takes part. He has hopes of winning a female. Maybe—"

"Stop right there. That's good to know, however," she pulled in a deep breath, "I don't think that talking about Rock right now is a good idea."

"Why not?" Sand leaned back against the counter, his arms folded. He looked amazing. Truth be told, there were worse things than having to have sex with a guy as good-looking as him. She felt a little bad for him because, well, he got *her* in return. Not that she was bad or ugly or anything. She just wasn't… in his league. That's all. She wasn't being hard on herself. She was being realistic. They were worlds apart. He could grace any magazine cover. He had a face for the big screen. She was more of a plain Jane. She was a bit on the chubby side but wasn't giving up food for any man. She was happy in her skin but… just look at him. Sex god with the eyes of an angel… make that the devil. Maybe a little of both.

He narrowed his eyes. "Have you come to a decision?"

"That's just it." She wrung the dishcloth in her hands. "I think we have to just go ahead and do it." There it was out.

"You mean fuck?"

Her body reacted when he said the word. Fuck. Four letters had that effect on her. He was rude and arrogant, and he turned her on in a way nice guys could never do. It was something she hadn't known about herself and yet there it was. "Yes." She cleared her throat. "That's exactly what I mean. As long as you're sure you're comfortable going down that road… with me."

"I'm a male, Macy. I happen to enjoy fucking very much. I would enjoy fucking you." So clinical. So straight forward. He shrugged. Men were built like that. They could fuck just about anyone and still have a good time. Leagues be damned. "As I said before, I would ensure you enjoyed it too."

She nodded once and cleared her throat. "You said the ball was in my court. I think we could spend time thinking about it. Trying to come up with another plan, but," she shrugged, "I doubt we'd get anywhere. I don't see any other way out, at this time."

"Me neither, and quite frankly, there are worse things."
Indeed.

Her only worry remained the 'falling for him' part.

Then again, he was so not her type at all. She needed to tread carefully anyway. "We do this tonight and then I think we need to stay away from one another after that." She couldn't risk her emotions getting the better of her. She'd had sex with Rock three times during the course of one night – not even a whole night – and she'd thought of him far too many times afterward. She felt regret when he left. Macy thought back to her high school days. Namely, about Jeffery Butler. He'd kissed her during that game of spin the bottle at her friend's birthday party. Macy had been devastated when Jeffery hadn't asked her to go steady. To him, it had been a game. To her… so much more. It had hurt.

Yep, she needed to tread carefully. "No unnecessary sex. We convince her this once and then move on." She was shocked at how detached she sounded.

"I disagree," Sand countered. "That Feral female is cunning. She'll smell a rat if we don't fuck regularly. She'll know it was a set-up. She'll have no qualms changing her mind and removing me before your next heat. We need to keep her convinced. If we fuck… we can keep fucking for a while. It's not a big deal."

Not to him. Macy did like the sound of frequent sex. It had been a long time since she'd had frequent sex. In fact, her encounter with Rock was the only time she'd slept with a guy after breaking it off with Jim. It was dangerous. What if she fell for him?

"We'll need to have a clear set of rules."

"What kind of rules?" she asked. "Don't get me wrong. I agree with you." Something like this could be key.

"Like I said earlier, no kissing, no cuddling, no holding hands or any of that bullshit."

"Okay. Although I'm not sure how we'll get started without kissing." That was how sex had been initiated since the beginning of time. Or wasn't it? Was there another way?

He got this little half-smile. It was downright naughty. His eyes glinted. "I think we'll be okay, Mace, but let me get a little more detailed… no kissing on the mouth. Everywhere else is fair game."

Oh! That made her mouth a little dry and her palms a little sweaty. "Okay." She nodded, a little too crazily. Head bobbing like her neck was on a spring.

"Um… I'll continue to sleep on the sofa," he said.

Macy would offer for them to take turns, but she knew he wouldn't go for it. She'd tried that already. She nodded.

He looked up, clearly in thought. "I think we should avoid the missionary position. It could be considered the most intimate of all the positions. All that staring into each other's eyes bullshit. We should stick to doggy, you can ride me facing either direction. There are a couple of others I know you would like. It would all be about making you come."

"Me? Why me? It would be both of us. Wouldn't it?"

"Trust me on this one."

She just widened her eyes, not sure what he meant at all. It was the first time she had heard a man essentially deny himself where sex was concerned. That didn't happen ever. She was missing something here.

"You need to understand that when a female comes, everything is better for the male. The scent of her pussy is better, her channel tightens up and spasms around him…"

Her mouth had just fallen open and she couldn't seem to close it.

Sand went on, "the noises she makes will drive him insane. All of it. That is what it's about. That's what fucking is about. A male will have no other choice but to come as well. His pleasure that much greater with her tight, wet pussy clamping around him and her moans in his ears."

She nodded, eyes still wide, mouth still opened. "That makes sense," she said when she finally managed to close her mouth. Her voice had a husky edge as something tightened in the pit of her stomach. Her nipples were hard too. If they talked for much longer, she was going to jump him, and that would be embarrassing.

"Was there anything you wanted to add?"

"To what?" Her brain wasn't functioning so well anymore. "Oh yes. The list. Um…" She tried to think of something. Tried hard. "I think you covered everything. No kissing – on the lips," she quickly added.

"Mouth," he corrected.

She felt herself blush. "Mouth. No sleeping together in the same bed. It's all about me because it's then inadvertently all about you."

"Us," Sand growled, his voice low. "It's all about getting us out of here before your next heat."

"Of course." She had forgotten about that part. Already forgotten. Was there any other way around this without having sex with Sand?

"I guess the biggest rule is no falling for each other." He chuckled. "I don't think we have to worry since I'm not looking for any kind of relationship at this stage in my life and you having feelings for another male." He clapped his hands together. "I think we're good to go. When do you want to start?"

"I'd like to take a shower." She needed to shave. Everywhere.

"I could join you?"

She shook her head. "No... I need to actually wash and stuff."

"I could help with that."

"I'll manage."

"Suit yourself. One or two things, though." He walked over to the trunk, rummaging inside it. He finally pulled out a royal blue, silk negligée. "I want you to wear this."

She looked down at the garment in his hands, and then he handed it to her. At least it wasn't sheer. There were plenty of numbers in that trunk that were. It was thin and cut to about midthigh. There was no built-in support either. "I'd like a bra and panties as well please." She'd feel practically naked in this.

"Why?" Sand frowned deeply. "Did you miss the part where we're going to fuck?"

"I have big breasts," she blurted.

"I had noticed. Your breasts are great. I want access to them." He got a desperate look in his eyes that made her feel like maybe this wasn't quite as one-sided as she had initially assumed.

"They'll bounce," she added, her mind reeling. He thought her boobs were great.

"Um... about us fucking. Breasts are supposed to bounce during sex. At least they will when I fuck you, and you'll love every minute that I'm inside you. You won't even notice what your breasts are doing, but I most certainly will, and I'll love it. Now humor me and put that on. Don't shave your pussy hair off. That was the other thing I wanted to say. You can trim if you have to, but don't take it all off." He winked. "Humans have this terrible habit of taking most, or all of their hair off. Non-humans enjoy fur. I thought I'd let you know."

"Oh… I see," she squeaked. *No shaving then.*

"You sure I can't… help out? We can skip the negligée entirely." He smiled.

"Um… I'm just going to…" She pointed to the bathroom. "I won't be long."

"Oh, and, Macy…"

"Yes?" She wasn't sure she wanted to hear any more. Partly because he was a bit of an asshole but mostly because she loved it. *Loved!* What did that make her? An idiot, for sure.

"Don't touch yourself in there. You're saving all of that pent-up frustration for me. We clear?"

Macy frowned. *No way. No freaking way he could know.*

He nodded. "Yes, I know when you touch yourself." He answered her question so perfectly that for a second she wondered if she had actually asked it. "You masturbated three days ago and once during your heat."

She gasped.

"I wasn't trying to be a stalking, peeping tom. I swear. I can't help it. It's just really difficult for me not to hear and scent and," he shrugged, "I could tell. That's all. Don't do it again."

"You've become really bossy all of a sudden and I'm not sure I like it. Maybe we should add that onto the list of rules or something. We're fucking… or about to fuck, but that doesn't mean you own me. I don't own you either. There is no owning going on here."

Sand licked his lips. It was maddeningly sensual but at the same time, it was hugely masculine. He was so irritating. "I'm going to have to disagree on that one."

"What?" she snorted. "You can't disagree."

"Oh, but I can. I *will* own your body while we are fucking. I *do* have a say. Ultimately, you will always have the final say, of course, but… if I want hair on your pussy or," he shrugged, "if I want you in that shirt of yours and nothing else, or the lacy number… I *do* get a say. Just as you have a say as well. Do you want me naked? In jeans, maybe? You can tell me how hard you want me to fuck you. Where I should touch you. Name it. Demand it. Fucking own it. My dick is yours for the foreseeable future. You can't have anything else from me just as I don't want anything else but sex from you, but let's not take things off the table that need to be there for this to work."

Shit! He had a point. "Fine. I want you in the black silk boxers. I don't want us to have sex in the bed for the first time either. Too boring." If he was going to make demands, then so was she. She'd made up the one about the bed. Quite frankly she didn't care where they did the deed, but if he thought he was going to be the only one issuing orders, he was mistaken. "Lastly, let's try one of those *other* positions you mentioned." She turned and headed for the bathroom, trying not to run. There was nowhere for her to run. They were stuck in a cage. Even if she could run, Macy didn't think she would. Not now.

CHAPTER 14

What a huge surprise. The human wasn't as timid as he had believed. If he was honest, he had been trying to scare her off, and it hadn't worked. Apparently, she didn't scare easily.

He wore the black boxers. He was pacing. He was… nervous.

Macy expected him to last all of ten seconds and after being trapped inside this small space with her for going on two weeks, it might just play out that way. After all the big talk, he'd embarrass the fuck out of himself. He considered using one of the toys in the trunk to get her good and ready but decided against it. Sand had never needed help before, he was fucked if he was going to start now. Not that they couldn't use the toys, at a later stage. Maybe.

She showered for what felt like forever. Sand kept on pacing. The water finally stopped. It took another fifteen minutes before she finally stepped out of the bathroom. Sand turned towards the door and stopped in his tracks.

Fuck!

"Wow!" he ground out. "You look great in that negligée."

"It's a bit… small." She tugged on the hem and clasped a hand around her breasts, before letting her arms fall back to her sides. Her cheeks were a bright red. Her hair was still damp.

The silk clung to her curves, accentuating them. The deep blue brought out her eyes. The length was perfect, giving him a fantastic view of her lush thighs. "The table."

"Table?" Her eyes widened. "Are we eating?"

I sure fucking am! "Yes. I want you on it."

She giggled, sounding nervous. "I can't get on the table."

"Why the hell not?"

"It'll break."

It was his turn to laugh. "You're a tiny human. Now if we were both to get on that table, I'd have to agree but since we're not, it'll be fine. Just you are. I'm having you for dessert."

"I'm not tiny." She shook her head. "My mom took me to a dietician last year. I finally agreed to go, just to get her off my back, and my BMI is twenty-eight. It might have risen since then. The bakery down the road started making these—"

"What's a BMI? What does it have to do with anything?"

"BMI. Have you never heard of it? It's an acronym for Body Mass Index. I mean, look at you. You must know all about it. You're a gym fanatic. It's a tool to measure if a person is over- or underweight. It takes your sex, age, height and weight, and then spits out a number on the other side. An ideal BMI is between," she lifted her eyes in thought, "I think eighteen, could be nineteen and twenty-five. I hover at around twenty-eight… maybe even thirty." She mumbled the last, like she didn't want him to know. "Let's call it twenty-nine. I was probably being a little ambitious earlier. So yeah, I think we should steer clear of the table."

"That's the biggest bunch of bullshit I've ever heard." He closed the distance between them. Sand clasped her hips and picked her up. "You weigh nothing."

She gasped, looking down at the ground and then back up at him.

"Put your legs around my waist."

"I'm not wearing underwear," she squeaked. "I don't think I should do that. In fact, my negligée is riding up. You—"

"We're about to have sex, so I'm glad you're not wearing underwear. In fact, I'm about to stick my tongue into your pussy, so underwear would get in the way."

She made a strangled noise and put her legs around his waist, her eyes were wide. "When you put it like that…"

He smiled at her. "Let's see if that table can hold up, shall we?"

She got this panicked look that he found utterly adorable. "Maybe that's not such a g-good…" she stammered as Sand walked over to the table in question.

"I'm teasing you." He pushed some of the chairs aside, putting her ass on the wood. "For your first orgasm, would you prefer my hands, my mouth or my cock?"

He watched her throat work. Sand could scent her arousal. "Um, I… I don't mind. I'll leave that up to you to decide. You don't have to go down on me, though. I mean, that's pretty intimate, isn't it? Maybe we should add that to the list."

"No fucking way." Sand shook his head. "Shifters love oral sex."

"You do?"

He nodded. "I would understand if you weren't game when it comes to returning the favor. We could put that on the list if you like but I want to eat you out… often. Right now, in fact."

She sucked in a breath. "Now?"

"Yeah, now."

She swallowed thickly. "This is weird. It feels awkward. Are you sure we can't kiss to get us in the mood? I feel nervous. I'm not ready to just dive in."

"We can kiss. Of course, we can."

Macy seemed to relax a little. Sand moved in, like he was going to kiss her but turned his head at the last second. "Just not on the mouth," he whispered into the shell of her ear before sucking on her earlobe.

Macy made a little noise. Her breathing became elevated in that instant. He moved down to her neck, planting kisses there. Down… down… down… kissing all the while. Sand nipped the base of her throat.

Fuck! Her nipples were plump and pushing against the silk. Trying to bore holes through the fabric, which strained. "You can touch me back, Macy."

"Oh. Okay." She put her hands on his shoulders. His shoulders, dammit. He bit back a smile. This female was sweet.

He closed his mouth over one of her nipples, through the fabric.

She moaned with both shock and frustration. He

nipped softly before suckling her again. This time the moan held pleasure. She leaned back a little, placing one hand on the table.

Better. He sucked on her other nipple. Alternating between nipping and sucking. Sand pulled back. The fabric on both nubs was wet. He took one of the thin straps in his hand as he leaned forward, nipping at her tight nub. She moaned, louder this time. Her legs had parted slightly. The negligée was riding up on her thighs. He gently slid the strap down, giving her plenty of time to protest. Macy didn't. *Thank fuck.* He knew her breasts were full, but fuck. The sight that greeted him had his balls pulling up. Right up. Her tits were seriously fucking plump. Her nipples were a deep pink that had him salivating. He sucked on the tip, swirling his tongue around the tight nub until she moaned in earnest.

Sand kept working on her breasts. Macy was into it. By now she was arching her back and digging her fingers into his shoulders. He took her legs and wrapped them around his hips, opening her up to him. The scent of her pussy hit him full on in the snout and a low growl vibrated inside his chest.

He rubbed a hand on her thigh. Up and down, going a little higher each time. Making sure his thumb trailed on the inside. Up and down and up and down, all the while still working on her tits. She yelled when his thumb finally brushed over her slit. All out yelled. Sand couldn't help but smile. "I hope that was a good shout and not a bad one."

She was panting. He glanced up. Her eyes were very wide. Her cheeks flushed. She had a look of shock on her face. He was going to love every fucking minute of this.

She licked her lips and nodded. "Good," she pushed the word out. "I'm sorry I yelled, I…"

"Good to hear and don't you dare apologize. I want to hear it. All of it."

She nodded.

Holy crap!
Holy freaking crap balls.

He'd barely touched her, and she was ready to go off like a rocket. She was vocal during sex but normally only towards the end. During the end of the main event. He'd caught her unawares with that brush against her… down there. It had been a shock. It felt that good.

He nipped her nipple before sucking on it. It stung but she also felt it between her legs. A sharp, pulling zing on her clit. It was weird, like the two parts of her body were connected.

This time when his thumb rubbed against her, it was there. Right there, against her clit. She groaned… loudly. Whatever he was doing to her nipples was making her more sensitive down below. Way more sensitive. It was like every nerve-ending was on high alert.

He kept his thumb pressed against her clit. Sand squeezed her breast with the other hand, he suckled hard on her nub. She ground out this bizarre, animalistic noise as her pussy clenched. It clenched hard.

He stepped back a little and she almost fell off the damned table.

"Easy." Sand gave a pinched smile. He had one hand on her hip and the other was still on her clit. His eyes also seemed lighter and brighter. They were definitely hooded.

"You like my version of kissing?"

"Yes." A breathless whisper.

"You're about to like it a whole lot more." He turned serious. "Put your feet up on the edge of the table and lean back on your hands." He pressed his thumb a little more firmly against her clit and circled once.

Macy bit down on her lip to stop the moan that built in her throat. She lifted her legs, planting her heels on the edge of the table, scooting back just a little.

"Wider." He used a commanding tone, still rubbing on her clit. Softly, ever so softly. "I want a good look at that pretty, little pussy of yours."

Macy whimpered. Loudly. He was so vulgar. Disgusting really. All she wanted was more.

More.

More.

Please.

Macy widened her stance. She quite literally could not wait to come. It wasn't going to take much. Sand chuckled, the sound husky. "Let go of my shoulder, sweetheart, and lean back."

She realized she was clutching him there, hard. Her fingers digging into his solid muscles. "Oh." It came out sounding like more of a moan, especially considering he was still toying with her clit. His finger barely moving, but it was enough to have her arching her back and making needy noises.

She put both hands behind her, although she was breathing fast, she struggled to get enough air into her lungs. Sand had his eyes on hers. A smile toyed with the edges of his mouth. His thumb was still on her clit, rubbing softly, when he pushed a finger into her. She yelled. Again. What was wrong with her? She needed to stop doing that. Only, he seemed to like it. His eyes became more hooded and his jaw tightened.

"That's it." Sand's eyes narrowed and his brow furrowed. "Let it all out. Don't hold back with me." His eyes stayed on hers as his finger began to pump. In and out. Not fast but also not slow. He did this thing with the tip of his finger that had her feeling things. Good lord, what was he doing to her?

He bit down on his lower lip, that finger pushing in and out. His thumb stayed on her clit but otherwise, it didn't move it. Not once.

She moaned, closing her eyes. It was too much. She was going to come soon. She couldn't take how he was looking at her. Like he was taking notes or something. He pulled back, and then his mouth was hot on her pussy. It was so sudden that she yelled, much louder than the previous two times. This time, she didn't care. She was beyond giving a shit at this point. His hands had been amazing, his mouth was pure heaven.

He moaned against her flesh. "Delicious," he mumbled. At least, that was what she was sure she heard him say, but it couldn't be. He stuck his tongue into her a couple of times, the air catching in her lungs. Then he sucked on her clit.

She groaned deep, again the sound so primal she wondered if it had even come from her. Sand stood up. She was shocked at how angry he looked. His eyes narrow, his jaw tight. His muscles were bunched. "Let's get this off." He tugged on her negligée.

"I'd prefer it on." She sounded desperate. "If that's okay?" She didn't want to have to suck in her belly during sex. She liked that she wasn't completely exposed. She normally preferred sex with the light off.

"Fine, but we compromise," he growled. She wasn't sure what he meant.

Sand leaned forward, his eyes on her chest. He yanked at the garment and it slipped down, exposing her breasts. She realized that he'd broken one of the straps.

Sand growled low as he leaned forward and sucked on her newly exposed nipple. Her clit went nuts. Even more so than before. He slipped a finger inside her… make that two… and began to pump slowly. Just like that, she was back on edge, moaning with every slide of his fingers, which were doing that thing again. She normally hated being fingered. Jim had hurt her a couple of times. She'd eventually told him not to do it again. Sand was an expert. He probably had diplomas on how to do this. He'd probably attended a graduation ceremony and everything.

She moaned in frustration when he stopped, mainly because she was there… right there. Her stomach was coiled tight. Her whole body felt tight. Her skin as well. Tight. The air too thin.

"Lie back," he commanded. "Put your feet over my shoulders." He yanked at the boxers, his beautiful cock springing free.

"Your shoulders," she panted the words out. "I can't—"

"Now, Macy. This is one of those other positions I told you about. You're going to love it. It's designed for deep penetration and hitting the g-spot every time." He palmed his cock, her eyes tracing the movement. He was so sexy. Sand knew what he was doing.

"Oh… okay." She put her feet over his shoulders and

yelped when he lifted her ass off the table. "I'm not so sure about this."

"Good thing I'm sure enough for the both of us. Hold onto my wrists or put your hands back and clutch the edge of the table. Don't you dare hold back, Mace. Don't you fucking dare."

"O-okay." Her whole body bristled with need. She put her hands back, holding on tightly.

"You ready?"

"Yes." The word was barely out, and he thrust into her. It was both careful and forceful. She hollered. It stung. It also felt good. *Already?* Sex normally took a long time to feel good. It was normally over by the time it started feeling like anything other than... Sand snarled on the second thrust. The sound was terrifying. Goosebumps rose up on her arms.

He crunched over his middle just a little, his face had a twisted, anguished look. *What? Why...?*

"You're tight... fuck, Mace. And wet, so fucking wet." Something dribbled out of her as he said it. "I'm hoping I did a good enough job..." He said something else, but she didn't hear what it was because he was thrusting again. Hard and fast.

Holy shit!

His hands clasped her tighter. She had to work to keep her feet over his shoulders. Her boobs jerked up and down. If they'd been any bigger, she'd be in danger of knocking herself out. As it stood, her chin might be bruised if this got any wilder.

He'd said deep penetration. Check. Sand was hung like an ox and touching her every which where inside her. It didn't hurt, though... she was too turned on for that.

He'd also said g-spot stimulation. Double check. There was a whole lot of stimulating going on. Her throat hurt from the crazy noises she was making.

He put both of her feet over one shoulder, holding her legs closed. *Closed. Really?* He hugged them to his body. He snarled on the next thrust. She may have screamed or yelled or something. There was noise, plenty of noise. Thankfully they were both equally loud. It seemed that with her legs closed up there, almost perpendicular to her body, things got tighter, more intense.

"Tight," Sand growled, as if agreeing with her. "So good… so… fuck!" he snarled the word.

It hadn't even been a minute and yet… and yet… that tightness inside her reached a crescendo. Macy's mouth was wide open. As were her eyes. The air stuck in her lungs for a moment as everything seemed to become suspended. Sand's hands gripped her legs tighter as he thrust harder. Then everything let go.

She shrieked, gripping the table as hard as she could. Pleasure rushed through her. Sand roared as he began to jerk. He hoisted her higher up on his body, continuing to thrust into her… hard and fast.

Her orgasm lashed through her, it went on and on, seeming to grow and grow before finally subsiding. He continued to thrust into her, easing up, slowing down. Wringing every ounce of pleasure out of her. He finally lowered her, easing out of her. Both of them were panting hard.

She wanted to feel embarrassed that her negligée was bunched up just under her boobs. So much for being covered. She was humming with too many good vibes and hormones to care. Her whole body seemed to vibrate.

"That was better than I imagined."

"You imagined having sex with me?" His admission was a shocker.

"I'm a guy, Macy. Of course I imagined having sex with you. We've had lots of sex inside my head."

"Maybe during my ovulation. I guess." That was true.

"I imagined having sex with you just this morning. I jerked off to images of you on the end of my dick and I can tell you that the reality was better. That doesn't happen very often." He winked at her.

Her clit did that zing thing again. How was that even possible?

Sand picked her up. "Let's get you in bed."

"I can walk, you know," she sounded drugged. Her voice husky from all the yelling.

He smirked. "Doubtful."

She laughed. He was too much. At the same time, he might just be right. She was still feeling shaky. She was shocked when he slid in next to her. "I thought you said we weren't going to sleep in the same bed?"

"Oh, we're not going to sleep any time soon, Macy. I'm going to fuck you again in about three minutes. I thought I'd let you catch your breath."

"Three minutes? That's not very long, will you be able to go again in…?" She stopped talking when she noticed his very erect cock.

"Dragons have plenty of stamina. Besides, there's this position I think you might like." He winked at her. "Let me get you some water to drink." He leaned over to the side-table and began pouring her a glass. "You're going to need it."

Had she died and gone to heaven? Talk about making

lemonade when handed lemons. All she needed to do was to keep her feelings out of this and they'd be just fine.

CHAPTER 15

The next day…

The Feral female sniffed the air, sniffed again, louder this time. The two of them stood very still, facing forward. Macy's heart beat out of her chest. What if the Amazon still took Sand anyway?

The female moved a little closer, standing right in front of Macy. She sniffed at her, reminding Macy of a dog. Ten full seconds later, the Feral pulled herself up and finally smiled. It was wide and strange looking. Almost scary, like the smile the killer made in a horror movie just before slaughtering someone. "I am glad the two of you have come to your senses. I brought more food and some clean linen and towels. Do not disappoint me again. Do you hear me?"

"Yes," they both replied.

"We will do as you ask. We've learned our lesson."

Macy paused. "I have a question, however." She cleared her throat. "Will you have help raising these children? Forgive me, but I worry about them. They will be my flesh and blood even though you will be their mother." Bile rose up in her throat. They needed to find out who this woman was. They needed information so that when the time came for Sand to leave, he would be able to find her.

"I do not need any help. I will manage just fine on my own. I already love these children. You have nothing to fear for them."

Not the answer she was hoping for. They needed details about this woman. Something to go on.

"Another concern I have," Macy said. "Will they be accepted by your people? They won't be Feral like you. They might be shunned."

"That is not something to concern yourself with." She looked bored.

"I agree with Macy. It is important to think these things through. What kind of a life will these children have?"

"It sounds to me like you might be trying to convince me that bringing a Feral male in here would be the best thing to do after all."

"No," Sand growled. "That's not it at all."

"All that matters is that I will have my young. I will love them enough for a whole village." It was clear that she was pulling the wool over her own eyes.

"Have you spoken with your village leader about this? What about your king?" Sand asked. "Do you have permission to do what you are doing?"

That was a very good question. The Feral woman cocked her head. "It is always easier to ask for forgiveness than to ask for permission."

"You might be punished." Sand shook his head. "What of the whelps then?"

"Enough!" the Feral yelled. Her voice a screech. "I have things I need to do." For the first time, she sounded stressed. Not as together as it seemed. "I will be back soon. You have enough food to last for a couple of days. I have provided more than before. I did not realize this human would consume so much." She looked pointedly at Macy, who wanted to shrink away.

Sand growled low, like a cornered lion. If his tail had been out it would have thrashed from side to side. "Macy does not consume a lot. She eats very little, if you ask me."

Her body flooded with warmth. He was defending her. Not because he had to, but because he wanted to. It meant a lot to her.

The Feral cocked her head. "I have observed plenty of human females since I brought you here. It is merely my observation that this one," she nodded towards Macy, "eats more than the average human female. That is all. I'm stating facts. I miscalculated on the food rations before, as a result. It won't happen again. I was merely trying to reassure you that I understood what the problem was. It won't happen again. It is my intention to keep you happy and healthy."

"I simply needed to state for the record that Macy is perfect just as she is." He took her hand and squeezed it.

"It is touching to watch the two of you." She looked from Macy to Sand and back again. "It would seem that you have, indeed, bonded. I am glad." She turned and left. Just like that.

They watched in silence until she was long gone. Sand let go of her hand. "I wish to god she wasn't so powerful,"

Sand mumbled. "I'd have no qualms about punching her lights out. Female or not."

Macy looked at him feeling concerned. "Please don't try anything unless you are sure you have the edge. These Feral are stronger than I ever imagined. She swatted you the other day, like I would a fly, and you flew across the room, unconscious, nose pulverized."

He winced. "Stop, please. My ego can't take it." He chuckled; the sound didn't hold much humor. "I'm afraid I wouldn't stand much chance against her. It could even put you in danger. Chances are good we'll need to beat her with brains, not brawn."

"What happens when we don't give her what she wants?"

"By then we'll have something on her. We did good today. We'll do better next time."

"Yep, I agree, we did good." Macy nodded.

The next day…

Her eyes were on him, even as she paged through that magazine. The one that was falling apart from use, even though he doubted she'd ever read a word. The human liked watching him work out. He liked that she liked it.

Sand bit back a grin as he turned onto his back, preparing to do some sit-ups. He could still feel her eyes on him, could hear how her heart was beating faster. He was sure he could scent arousal. His balls tightened up in response. Blood started to migrate south. They hadn't had sex since the night before last. He wanted her, and by the way she scented, the feeling was mutual.

It was time to play. He needed to keep his scent on her just in case that Feral bitch came back and changed her mind about letting him stay. Their questions had been necessary but at the same time, he hoped he hadn't planted any seeds. The last thing they needed was for that bitch to change her mind about him being the father instead of a Feral male.

They needed something that could identify her. Some sort of a detail. Something. They just needed to keep at it. And by *at it* he meant, they needed to keep questioning her and by *at it,* he also meant that they needed to fuck often.

Sand couldn't recall another female he had been this compatible with. Not a human or shifter. If they needed to pretend to have bonded to get them out of this cage, then so be it. "Macy." He lifted his head, looking her way.

Her eyes were already on him and not the book in her hands. He couldn't help the smile that formed.

"Yes?" Her voice was high-pitched, like she'd been caught doing something she shouldn't. Like perving over him maybe? Could that be it?

"Is there something you needed?" she asked, eyes wide.

Yes.

He needed her to sit on his dick. The sooner the better.

"I'm ready," he said, trying not to smirk.

"For what?" She frowned.

"To help you work out, Mace. Get your ass over here."

"Um…" she stammered. "I was just reading this great article about…" She glanced down. "It's about…" She had no fucking idea. Sand watched her squirm, glancing down again. Clearly not wanting to look like she was trying to find out and failing. "'How to tell if he's the one,'" she blurted, her eyes going wide as she realized what she had just said. It was comical. He had to fight to hold back a laugh. "It's just that I've read everything else and so I thought I'd... read this." She fumbled over her words.

It was hilarious. "Tucking away the information for when we get back?"

She frowned, a look of confusion in her eyes.

"For when you see Rock again," he pointed out.

"Oh." She smiled. "Of course." She nodded. "That's it exactly."

"Put the magazine down. I promised to give you some pointers and you promised to let me. So, let's do this thing. It'll be fun!"

"I didn't exactly promise," she grumbled.

"Exercise is good for a person. Get over here." He waved her over.

"Okay." She grumbled some more, looking about as enthusiastic as a nun in a brothel. Macy wore a lacy, silky pink number that looked dynamite on her. The Feral still hadn't brought them anything else to wear. "Wait a minute, I don't have a sports bra. Or any bra." She clutched her chest, making him want to groan.

"You don't need one."

"I beg to differ. You have no idea how bad it can get." She widened her eyes, still holding onto her breasts.

He had a really good idea, only, he wouldn't use the word 'bad.' *Fucking amazing. Sexy.* Those were much better descriptions. "I'll go easy on you. I swear."

She brightened right up at the thought of him going easy.

"I'll even help you when you start to tire," he added.

"Okay, that sounds good." She smiled.

"Alright then. We'll start with some warmup stretches." They went through a couple of basic sets. He particularly liked the one where she had to bend over and clutch her ankles. Okay, her knees, since she couldn't get down low enough. They had to work on her flexibility. Sand stood behind her to make sure she was doing it right, eyes glued to her ass. *Fuck!* He was going to hell. Straight to hell.

"Okay, that's great. Now that you're reasonably warmed up, we can start with some basic squats. You need to put your hands together. Legs spread apart." He couldn't help but smile. "Then you drop down. Not too low to begin with. Like this." He showed her.

"I'm sure I can do that." She grinned. He felt like a bit of an asshole right then, but she'd thank him when she was coming on his dick. She did a couple more.

"That's great," he said. "Now get even deeper."

He watched as she went lower. The silk negligée riding up on her thighs. She was already starting to breathe heavily. Her cheeks were getting flushed. Her ponytail bobbed as she came up.

"That's it. That's great. Keep going." He encouraged, putting his hands on her hips and assisting her.

"Can I stop yet?" she asked.

Sand chuckled. "Stop? You've only just started. I was about to tell you to go a little lower."

"Lower?" she huffed. "If I go any lower, I won't be able to get back up." She sucked in air between words.

He chuckled harder. "I'll help you." He squeezed her hips. "Here, maybe this will help." He sat down, keeping his hands on her hips.

Sand helped lift and lower Macy, who was almost

completely out of breath. Her cheeks were a bright pink. She was so cute and sweet and insanely fucking sexy. Her breasts bounced every time she dropped down. The dress riding up high. His dick took note. "Here. Maybe this will make it a little easier." He pulled her onto his lap so that she was straddling him.

She squealed.

"There. That's much better." He grinned.

She laughed, still panting like mad. Then she felt his erection and her mouth rounded out in an 'O.' Her eyes widened.

"I know another form of exercise you might prefer." His voice was deep.

"Oh yeah?" She lifted her brows. "I think I might be all tuckered out. You made me work hard."

"Oh, really now?" he growled. "Not nearly hard enough. I think I might have to motivate you then. A good workout instructor needs to be a really good motivator as well."

"Is that so?" She was smiling broadly now. Her cheeks not as red as they were a minute before.

Sand turned her on her back, in one quick move. She squealed again. His eyes zoned in on her lips and for a moment he was irritated that her mouth was a no-go zone. Macy had a gorgeous mouth. She smiled so naturally. Her lips were plump and a juicy pink shade.

Oh well.

Sand planted kisses down her body, starting at her neck. He didn't linger anywhere for too long. He was after a certain honey pot nestled between her legs. Sand pulled her feet over his shoulders. He yanked at the thin strip of fabric barely covering her slit. It came apart easily. "There you are," he spoke to her pussy. "So damned pretty," he added, voice husky.

Macy giggled. The laughter turned into a moan when he suckled on her clit. Then he laved on the nub until she was writhing and panting. Sand went back to suckling. He fingered Macy a good couple of times, until she was soaking wet. By the deep moans, he could tell that she was getting close already. "Back to that workout," he growled, flipping them back over, putting her on top.

"Wait. What?" Her eyes were hooded. Her cheeks had that beautiful glow again, and this time not from exertion.

Sand sat up, he yanked at his boxers until his cock sprang free. "I said I'd help, and I meant it."

"Maybe I could get into this whole working out thing after all." Her eyes lit up as they lowered to his erection. "You look like you could do with some help with that."

"Are you offering to bounce on my dick?" He couldn't help but grin.

"I believe I am." Her voice was a husky purr.

"You go right ahead then. I'll lift you up." Sand put his hands on her lush hips and did as he said. Macy positioned his dick at her opening, and he slid in an inch, maybe two. Her mouth fell open and a breath was pulled from her. He rocked back and forth a couple of times until he bottomed out inside her tight as fuck pussy. *Damn, but she felt good!*

He grunted hard.

Macy threw her head back and groaned long and deep. She put her hands on his shoulders.

"Hold up," Sand grunted. He tugged on the straps of the negligée. It was a shame to ruin it, but not seeing Macy would be an even greater shame. "Wow! You're so gorgeous," he groaned when her gorgeous tits broke out of confinement. His dick twitched inside her.

Macy groaned again. Then she gave him a tight smile. It was sexy as sin. She lifted and then pushed back down on his cock. They groaned in unison.

Sand held onto her hips, guiding her up and down. He also thrust into her from below. Her greedy, little pussy made sucking noises that drove him insane. Slowly but surely, they picked up the pace until her breasts were bouncing hard with every thrust. He couldn't take his eyes off her. She was delectable.

Sand was looking at her chest like it was the most fascinating thing he had ever seen. Thing was, this *was* hands down the most fascinating thing he had ever seen. And the hottest. He could feel that he was frowning deeply. He was that turned on.

"See something you like," she pushed out.

"Hell yes!" He lifted his gaze, his eyes locking with hers. *Shit!* He was about to come. His thrusts had turned hard and insistent. Sand frantically reached for her clit with his thumb. He rubbed on it like his life depended on it. Not too hard. Not too… her pussy clamped down on him.

Macy pushed out a hard yell that sounded very much like his name. He put his head between her glorious breasts and jerked into her, grunting hard. He fucked her harder, his hands digging into her hips. She felt amazing. So soft. So tight. Couldn't care about anything other than what he was doing to her. About her pleasure… and by the noises she was making, she was in heaven. Sand finally slowed, his breath coming in ragged pants.

"So," she was out of breath, "I think I might like working out."

He chuckled, his face still buried in her breasts.

Probably the best place on earth to be. "We're doing this again tomorrow." He lifted his head, looking into her blue eyes. "I can show you a couple of really good exercises. I know quite a few."

"Sounds interesting." Her chest heaved as she tried to catch her breath. "Tell me more."

"There's this one where you go on all fours."

"Oh really?" She smiled.

"Yep. It's best if the person doing it is naked." He pretended to be completely serious. "You have to stick your ass out in the air and rock backwards and forwards, starting slow."

"Let me guess." She bit down on her bottom lip, pretending to think. "Ending really fast?"

"Not too fast but yeah… you get the picture." He swallowed down his need.

"Tomorrow seems like… a long time to wait for you to show me this move. I'm not sure I want to wait that long."

His greedy little human. Fuck if that didn't impress him a whole hell of a lot. Sand smiled up at her. "Right now, I'm going to make you something to eat."

She got a look of disappointment. He loved that she was disappointed. *Loved!* It almost made him flip her around and take her again.

Too bad he'd heard her stomach rumble when she came over to him.

"I'm going to feed you because I know you're hungry and that was an intense workout… and then we're going to test that table again." He looked over at the table in question.

Her eyes brightened up. "Oh, really now? So, you're feeling brave?"

"Very. Brave is my middle name… at least," he made a face, "when there are no Ferals about." He chuckled at his stupid joke. "Once we're done eating, I'm going to put you on that table and—"

Her eyes had this look. Not a good look. "Are you okay?" He pulled out of her. "Hey, Mace. What's wrong?"

Her eyes looked like they had filled with tears for a second. She blinked hard. He pushed some wayward strands of hair off her face, tucking them behind her ear. She gave a small shake of her head and smiled. It was a small, sad smile. One that ate at him. "I just get scared sometimes that things aren't going to work out. That—"

"They will." He put his arm around her. "You'll see. We have a plan. It might not be the best plan… yet… but we're working on it… together."

She nodded, sniffing. This time when she smiled, it was more real. More her. Warm and friendly and inviting. "I'm so glad you're here. That we're in this together." Then she hugged him, close. Real, real close. They should add hugs to that list of theirs. This was intimate and it… it made him feel something. He wasn't sure what, but it couldn't be good. *Fuck it!* He hooked the other arm around her as well and held on for dear life. Macy needed this.

CHAPTER 16

Two days later…

Sand stood up, his nostrils flared and he inhaled deeply. His whole body bristled. His muscles bunched.

"What is it?" She could guess. That Feral woman was coming, and something had changed.

Sand headed for one of the exits, still inhaling noisily. He was frowning deeply. "She's coming." He kept his eyes trained on the sky. "And she's not alone this time."

There it was. "What?" She felt her blood run cold as fear settled in her bones. "She's taking you anyway. I can't believe this." She felt adrenaline flood her system; anger followed. "What are we going to—?"

"No." He shook his head. "She has another human female with her." He narrowed his eyes.

Macy felt ice shards hit her veins. "What?" she practically yelled, the ice quickly turning to fire. "We had a deal. What the hell is wrong with her. She's replacing me?" Her voice was shrill. She felt pissed off at the idea when she should be thrilled. *Why was that?* Macy felt bad for whoever was coming. It could be that. She also felt… something else… something she shouldn't be feeling.

"We don't know that." Sand took her hand; he was acting like it was no big deal. "Try to stay calm."

"That's easy for you to say," she blurted.

"It could be worse. It could have been a male. Maybe this means you're getting out of here." She could see doubt in his eyes. Sand didn't think that was how this was going to play out.

She frowned. "You don't think so?"

"I didn't say that. They're almost here. Let's wait to hear what she has to say." He pleaded with her with his eyes.

"If she's not letting me out and bringing in another woman to take my place, that means—" She gasped as a new notion hit. "Oh, hell no!" She pulled away from him.

Calm down! She tried to force herself to keep quiet. To keep her thoughts and emotions to herself. The thing she was feeling was jealousy. She even sounded jealous, as well as irrational, and it had to stop. "I'm not into kinky shit. Just so you know." She had to get that out, if nothing else. Two women. One man. It didn't take a rocket scientist to figure this one out, and she didn't like it.

"Yeah, I know. Just so you know, I don't like this any more than you do."

"Yeah, right." She sounded sarcastic and very jealous. Like maybe she had feelings for Sand. *Shit! Shit! Why was this happening?* They had a plan.

The crazy Amazon landed on the platform. True as nuts, there was a human woman in her clawed grasp. The woman was unconscious. Her dark hair covered her face. It was glossy and healthy. It didn't look dyed, which meant that the woman was young. Of a childbearing age. Of course she was. This was the Feral's back-up plan to make sure that she got herself a couple of babies.

The Feral screeched as she shifted. A backpack thudded as it landed on the stones. It had been strapped to the creature's back.

The lady in her arms moaned. She looked tall and slim.

"What is this all about?" Macy couldn't hold back.

"Calm, human." The Feral had the audacity to smile at her. The Amazon cow unlocked the door and carried the woman inside, placing her on her back on the bed. Her curtain of hair parted. *Great!* Just as Macy suspected. She looked to be in her late twenties, and she was quite beautiful. It looked like she didn't snore. Or sleep with her mouth open. Or drool. The woman was quiet and serene and pretty. "What the hell is this?" Macy pointed at the dark-haired figure on the bed. "We had a deal. This was not part of that deal." She walked towards the bird-lady. Her blood still boiling. "If you think we're going to bounce him between us... you have another thing coming. That is not going to happen. I am—"

The Feral laughed. It was a melodic and quite beautiful sound. Pity it came from such a deranged source. "You have it wrong."

Macy frowned.

"It is good to know that you have indeed bonded with the dragon. You're jealous."

"I'm not into stuff like that. That's all. Most humans aren't. I doubt *she* would be." She pointed a finger at the sleeping beauty. "Take her back. You don't need two of us. You're just going to cause problems." Macy also felt bad for the woman on the bed. Here was another person ripped away from her life. As jealous as Macy was feeling, she could see that.

The Feral raised her brows. "I realize you might be feeling possessive, but that is a good thing."

What? A good thing? "Whatever," Macy muttered, rolling her eyes. She *was* jealous. She didn't want to be, dammit, but she was.

"The female is a healer. Not just any healer but one who specializes in young, and being with child. She is a gy… a gyna-logical-ist."

"A gynecologist. She's a doctor? Why would you bring a doctor?"

"I don't want to wait. I did my research and if you take certain herbs… healer drugs… you will reach your heat quicker and will be sure to become with child." Her eyes lit up. "That female will be able to help you with the task."

"I hate to break it to you, but this is a small space and three's a crowd."

"You really are very possessive, human. Do not worry, the female will only stay for as long as is necessary. Only until your heat comes. Unless, of course, you want her to stay, dragon?" She looked over at Sand, and Macy had to grit her teeth to keep from saying anything stupid.

Sand just clenched his jaw. He looked pissed. *What did he have to be angry about?*

Macy's attention was forced back to the bed, where Sleeping Beauty stirred again. Her eyelids fluttered. It looked like she was waking up.

"I am going to leave now. The human is petrified of me." The Feral rolled her eyes. She turned back to Macy, narrowing her gaze. "Explain things to the healer. I need this to go smoothly. Moreover, *you* need this to go smoothly."

Macy nodded, watching as the Feral left. The sound of the lock clicking back into place filled the small space. Macy turned to Sand. He was looking at the woman sprawled out on the bed.

Sand felt bad for the healer. Another person torn away from her life so that the crazy bitch could have whelps.

Macy was pacing.

"You should check if she's okay," he said.

"She seems fine," Macy replied, looking angry. She stopped pacing and pushed out a sigh, looking down at the female. "Her color is good and she's breathing alright. Maybe some water." She seemed to calm down some. "I can't believe that creature," she muttered as she walked to the kitchen. "She thinks she can take whoever she wants and toy with people however she sees fit," she went on, talking almost to herself.

"I know," Sand agreed. "This poor female."

"This moves up our timeline." She grabbed a glass out of the cupboard.

"You don't know that." Sand shook his head. "Just because the female wants something doesn't mean she'll get it."

"You heard that crazy Feral, she wants me to start taking fertility medication." She filled the glass.

"Sit down." Sand gestured to the bed. He could see that Macy was breathing too quickly. Her heart was going nuts.

"No, I'm fine."

"You're not fine," he insisted. "Sit."

For a second it looked like she was going to argue, then she did what he asked. First, she put the glass down on the side-table and then she sat down on the edge of the bed. Sand gripped her knees, going down on his haunches in front of her. "We can still make this work. Let's get all the facts. All it means is that we have to adjust course. Nothing has really changed. Maybe this can help us."

"Help us?" She snorted. "I doubt it. Everything has changed." Her eyes widened, he could see her trying to calm herself down. She breathed in and out a couple of times. "But you're right, let's get the facts…"

The healer moaned again; they both looked her way. Her eyelids fluttered and then cracked open. Her eyes widened, filling with shock and fear but she didn't move. Didn't breathe.

"Are you okay?" Macy asked. "That's probably a really stupid question."

The healer sucked in a breath and sat up. She blinked a couple of times, breathing strangely and looking dizzy.

"It's okay," Macy went on. "You're afraid and confused. I'm going to get you some water. This is Sand. He's a good guy," she quickly added.

The healer turned her big eyes on him, they widened up some more.

"I know he's big and a little scary-looking," Macy went on, "but he's… he's really nice… a total sweetheart, I swear. You don't have to be afraid of either one of us."

The healer kept her eyes on him. "Where is she?" she asked, sounding slightly hysterical but managing to hold it together. In Sand's opinion, only just.

"She's gone," Macy said. "You can relax. We won't hurt

you." He let Macy do the talking. "Are you hurt?"

The healer shook her head. "No. Where are we?" She let her eyes flash around the room before looking back at them.

"We don't know exactly. She has us locked up in here."

The healer's lips began to tremble, and tears welled in her eyes.

"We have food and water," Sand interjected. "We are safe."

"Safe?" Her eyes grew wild. "From that… that… thing? I don't know what that was." She shook her head. "That wasn't even human." Her lip trembled some more.

"I call her Amazon woman," Macy said. "She won't hurt us as long as we give her what she wants."

"What is she? I've never seen anything like it. It's like she's from another time. She speaks strangely and doesn't wear clothes."

"Excuse the way we look, as well," Macy mumbled, glancing down at the negligée she was wearing over her jeans. "She didn't give us much in the way of clothing."

Thankfully, Sand was wearing his jeans. It could have been worse. He could've been in those tight, white briefs. Humans weren't very partial to nudity.

"What did she say to you? What does she want you to do?"

"She asked me a ton of questions. Can I have that glass of water you offered earlier?" The healer glanced in the direction of the kitchen.

Macy nodded. "Of course. You didn't tell us your name."

"Oh." The female shook her head, squeezing her eyes shut for a second. "Sorry, it's Brittney Baker… Dr. Baker."

"I wish I could say I was pleased to meet you. I'm sorry the Amazon woman brought you here." Macy handed her the glass she'd filled earlier.

"Me too," the healer said. "I have so many people counting on me. Patients due to deliver any day now. Patients trying to become pregnant. One of my patients is waiting for a result on a biopsy I took. Mrs. Tailor will be so nervous right now. She might have cervical cancer. I need to get back." She pushed some hair behind her ear.

"That's terrible. To think I was worried because my kids will be missing me. I'm a pre-school teacher. I have twenty young minds in my class. I worry about what type of substitute they will have arranged." Macy seemed to catch herself. "Oh… sorry… my work concerns are nothing compared to yours."

The healer shook her head. "Those concerns are important to you, right? I'm sure you're valued by your students."

"Absolutely. I'm also worried about my puppy. He's eight months old but still such a youngster. I wonder where he is right now. Is he being looked after? Does my neighbor still have him? I can't imagine that Colin will have kept him all this time. Scout is incredibly spoiled. He sleeps with me. He's allowed on the sofa. He eats a lot and he farts even more."

The healer laughed. Sand smiled. Trust Macy to be able to get a person at ease in a situation like this. "What about you?" the healer asked him. "What do you do you do for a living?"

"I'm in production. There are several people who could take my place. I won't be missed on that front." He kept his explanation simple. He could expand if need be. They were fully trained to deal with this type of interrogation. He was glad Macy hadn't said anything about his identity. Sand needed to let her know that his true identity needed to be kept under wraps, if at all possible. It would most likely be necessary to confide that he was a shifter at some point, but he didn't want to scare her needlessly right then.

"Forgive me for asking but… are you guys together? And, now that I've calmed down some, I can ask the burning question of the hour, why the hell am I here? Why are *we* here?"

He answered *no* and Macy answered *yes* in response to the first question. "Not together, together," she quickly stammered, her cheeks turning a dark shade of red. "The Amazon lady kidnapped us. She wants me pregnant so that I can carry a baby for her."

"What? Look, she said… a couple of things that didn't make too much sense at the time, but I never expected this. How did it… she capture you?"

Macy explained the situation surrounding their kidnapping and confinement, saying only what was necessary. "If we don't go along with her sordid plan, she will throw a male version of herself in here with me to do a proper job."

"One of those creatures?" The healer's eyes were popping out of her skull and her mouth fell open.

"Yes, only, she's worried that I might not make it out alive if one of them tries to breed me. She's afraid he'll rip me apart. Her words," Macy added. Sand could see that she was trying not to let it get to her. He wanted to put an arm around her to comfort her but refrained.

"Oh my god." The healer covered her mouth. "That's just awful."

"What did she say to you? What does she want exactly?" Sand asked, growing impatient. The healer seemed more composed and able to provide them with some answers.

"She wanted to know a whole lot about fertility. About…" She scrunched up her nose. "She used strange terminology, but I got the gist of it."

"What kinds of things?" Macy asked.

"She was thorough. She wanted to know all the ins and outs of a woman's menstrual cycle. She wanted to know how we could manipulate that cycle using drugs. In short, she wanted to be able to make a woman ovulate more quickly in her cycle. She also, and most importantly, wanted to ensure that the woman did indeed ovulate. That she was in the best possible position to become pregnant. Now I know why." She sighed. "It's sick. I can't imagine how the two of you must feel. You're strangers. Strangers who might not think of one another in that way." She was speaking more to him than to Macy, which made him feel uncomfortable. "And you're expected just to get into bed together."

"What's even worse," Macy piped up, drawing the healer's attention back to her, "is that we would be expected to just give up our child were I to become pregnant." Her eyes took on a faraway look. "I would have to carry to term and hand my baby to that psycho bitch."

"That's not going to happen, Mace." He clasped her hand for a second. "I told you that. And I meant it. We'll find a way out of this."

She gave him a ghost of a smile. Then she looked at the healer. "What happened next? Did she give you one of her hugs?" Macy grew angry. Her jaw tightened.

The healer made a choked noise and shook her head, her lip trembled again but she bit down on it. "Don't get me started on the hug," she finally said, "It was terrifying." She visibly shivered. "No, she told me to talk her through a treatment plan, as if she were the patient needing to get pregnant. She wanted to know everything, step by step. Then she made me pack the bag. She told me to take everything I needed to perform the procedure, as well as secondary, fall-back drugs. I told her I needed an ultrasound machine. I told her I needed to be able to perform blood tests, that I would need to check if a patient was a good candidate for fertility treatments, but she wouldn't listen." She took a sip of her water. "Certain individuals should not be on fertility drugs. Also, there are various options, so we should choose drugs based on the results of the tests." She frowned. "Anyway, there was nothing I could do to convince her, so, I packed a bag, like she asked. Then, I got myself a hug." She shivered again, her face pale. "I thought I was dead, for sure. Then I woke up here."

"Amazon woman wants you to kickstart my ovulation and to ensure that I get pregnant." Macy looked pale as well. She sat down on the edge of the bed.

"We'll find a way out of this," Sand said. His words sounded hollow.

"Just before she hugged me," the healer swallowed thickly, "she told me I had better get the job done or that she would kill me. That she wouldn't hesitate. She told me she has a good sense of smell and that she will be able to tell whether or not the drug regime is working. She told me not to try anything. By the look in her eyes… I believed her."

CHAPTER 17

Two hours later…

D r. Baker put her hand on the bag next to her. "Are you sure you want me to do this?" she asked, eyebrows raised.

"It's not like we have any choice," Macy said. "If you don't, she will kill you. I believe it. You looked into those eyes. You said you believed it too. Do you want to die, doctor?"

"O-of course not, but—"

"But nothing." Sand stepped forward. "If you don't do it, Macy will die as well. If one of those creatures is thrown in here with her, she's dead. Her death will be agonizing. We need to do this."

"Okay, okay…" Macy felt the icy tendrils of fear slide their way through her, threatening to take hold. "That's enough. I don't want to think about that right now, but only because you're right. Sand is right." She directed the last at the doctor.

"I'm sorry." Sand drew her attention back to him, and it was probably her imagination, but his eyes softened when they landed on her. "I just need the... doctor to understand the ramifications if we don't do everything the Feral requests."

"Feral?" The doctor frowned.

"It's my name for her," Sand responded.

"Oh... okay." She nodded. "It actually works. She *is* rather feral, although, at the same time, it's a little unnerving how intelligent she is. I definitely got that from her. She may have limited knowledge of our society, but she's no fool."

"Yes, that's why we have to do what she says," Macy said. "She'll know if we don't."

"So, you're just going to roll over and give her what she wants?" the doctor asked.

"No," Sand said. "Not at all. Don't be alarmed but," he paused, "I'm a shifter," he admitted.

Dr. Baker sucked in a breath. "A shif... oh... I see..." She gave him the once-over, taking her time about it.

Not getting jealous!

Not!

Then she went on. Finally. Her eyeballs were probably getting tired from all the perusing of his body. *Not going there!* "Oh... a shifter... How will that help us? I take it you can't overpower her, or you would have done that already?"

"I tried and it didn't work out so well. Not only is she strong, but it's like she was carved out of granite or something." Sand shook his head. "The Feral are much stronger. They are the strongest of the non-humans. Look, we've been down this road of thinking before. Based on conversations with this creature, we have established that the majority of her species most likely have no idea what she's up to. We need to identify who she is. We need something on her. A name… something personal… anything along those lines… anything." He pulled in a deep breath. "I'm not sure where we go from there, though. It's up to Macy as to how we proceed. We'll either have sex while she is in heat, or…"

"There's a strong possibility she'll become pregnant if you do. Both of you need to understand that, and the implications."

Neither of them said anything. Macy didn't know what to say. She'd always wanted a child so badly. Thing was, she wanted a family as well. She wanted it all. Not like this. Never like this.

"I would be removed once you were with child. I would hopefully have something on that bitch by then. Something to take to her people so that they could help me find her. I'm sure her king would not accept these actions. This could result in full-scale war against the Feral."

"You just said they're stronger, though," the doctor responded. "Why would they care about a war?"

"I doubt it would come to that. I am sure they would care, since all of the non-humans would band together in an instance like that, in which case they would be greatly outnumbered."

The doctor nodded.

"The other option is *not* to have sex during your cycle," Sand went on. "I would be removed fairly quickly.

Hopefully, I would find you again before she did something rash."

"Yep. Throwing a guy version of her in here with me could be termed 'rash.'"

Sand folded his arms. "It's definitely the riskier route." He shook his head. "I don't like it. I'm all about minimizing risk."

"Wait just a minute," the doctor said, clearly deep in thought. "We just need to make her believe it. What if we could make it seem as if you were pregnant."

"What?" Macy asked.

"I have hCG hormones in the bag as well. They're the same hormones your body would make if you were pregnant. I could give you the hormones and we could fake your pregnancy. You'd get a false positive response on a test. No sex, no baby, no—"

"That wouldn't work." Sand shook his head.

"Why not?" the doctor said, frowning.

"She'd be able to smell if we were having sex or not. She'd be able to scent whether or not Macy was in heat. She'd know we weren't actively trying for a baby." He ran a hand through his hair, looking frustrated.

"That's crazy!" The doctor looked bewildered for a few moments. Then she grinned. "That's easy to rectify, you could use condoms during sex. I have those." She tapped the bag. "I help out with a local outreach program."

"There's a good chance she'd smell it," Sand interjected. "Human coverings stink to high heaven. She'd go berserk if she found out we were trying to trick her."

"So, condoms are out." She scratched her chin. "I wouldn't recommend any kind of oral contraception, not after manipulating your body into ovulation. It would be too risky. Also, most of those would *prevent* ovulation, which she would smell." She lifted her eyes in thought, making a humming noise. "There is one other option if you're dead set on the having sex route."

"We don't have a choice in the matter. If we want to keep the Feral calm and happy, we have to have sex, bottom line."

It shouldn't hurt, but his words stung. At the same time, it was a good reminder. Sand was having sex with her mostly because he was being forced into it. Chances were good it would never have happened otherwise.

She noticed how Sand had leaned in, waiting to hear what Dr. Baker had to say. "You could take the Morning-After pill after having sex."

"That would kill the baby."

Macy was shocked at the level of animosity in Sand's voice.

"Um… no… not technically. I'm not getting into religious discussions here. We're going to stick to the facts. You would take a pill like that within seventy-two hours of having unprotected sex. In your case, you'd take it much sooner." She paused. "There's a good chance the sperm and the egg will not have even met yet, and if they do, no division will have taken place. It's too early on in the conception for it to be considered—"

Sand held up a hand. "Okay, doctor… thank you for the explanation." He didn't look convinced.

"You can call me Britt." She smiled at Sand.

Sand didn't say anything.

"The doctor is right," Macy said, watching as Sand scrubbed a hand over his face.

"I'm sorry, I just… it felt… it felt wrong to me. We're

wired to protect. To preserve."

"To procreate," she offered. It was what he had told her when they had first found themselves in this predicament.

"Yep." He nodded. "I guess so. More so than I imagined. I guess you learn new things about yourself all the time. Especially in situations like this."

"We don't have to decide yet," Macy said. "I need to take those drugs, and then we need to figure out who this Amazon bitch is, so that you can get back here to rescue me." She worked hard at staying strong. She believed in Sand. She knew he would do everything and anything to make that happen.

"So, back to my original question, are you sure about this?" the doctor asked.

Macy nodded.

"Okay then." The doctor rummaged in her bag for half a minute, taking out an inconspicuous box of drugs. She removed a small white pill from the blister pack and placed it on Macy's palm.

"So," Macy said, looking down at the drug, "this is going to make me ovulate… yesterday."

"No," Dr. Baker shook her head, "that's going to bring on your menstruation. I have a drug call Clomid in my bag of tricks, that's going to make you ovulate. We'll discuss that part of the process when the time comes. I don't want to overwhelm you."

"You don't happen to have any pain meds in that bag of yours, do you? I normally get quite hectic period pains." Macy made a face. "I don't mean to come across as a baby or anything."

The doctor nodded. "Yes, no problem." She tapped the

bag.

Macy pushed out a sigh. She put the pill in her mouth and drank it down. "That one wasn't so bad then."

"It's the…" Dr. Baker began and then sucked in a breath. "I have an idea. Why didn't I think of it sooner?" She rummaged in her bag, pulling out a cellphone from one of the side pockets.

Macy wasn't so sure what she was so excited about. "There is no reception all the way out here. That's useless."

"No, it's not," the doctor smiled broadly. "It has a perfectly good camera."

CHAPTER 18

The next day…

The lock clicked open. Macy's heart raced. She glanced at Sand, who was lounging on the sofa reading one of those magazines. At least, that's what it looked like he was doing. When he noticed her watching him, he winked, looking back down at the magazine.

Macy looked over at the doctor, who was standing next to her. She could see that Britt was having a mild panic attack inside. "It's okay," she mouthed to the other woman, who nodded once.

The Feral stepped into the enclosure. She sniffed the air.

Sand turned a page and folded the magazine in half, his eyes shifted to the Amazon woman before going back to the book. "No more prisoners today then?" he asked, sounding bored.

"Do as I ask and there will be no need for more prisoners," she said, her eyes narrowing in on the doctor.

Britt took a step back, putting a hand to her chest. "I did what you asked me," she blurted. "I started her on the medication."

"How soon will she be ready to breed?"

"In roughly two weeks' time, but it's not—"

"That is not soon enough, healer." Her voice took on this angry edge. "You need to do more."

Britt stepped back. "I'm not some kind of miracle worker. I can't make anything happen. I can help the body along, but that's it."

"The female," Amazon lady glanced at Macy as she spoke, "will have her heat and will become with child! It must happen! Do you understand?"

Britt nodded. "Yes! There is a very good chance of that happening."

"Good chance?" The Feral cocked her head. "Good chance isn't good enough!" she snapped.

"It's the best I can give you. Bring me an ultrasound machine and I'll give you more decisive answers. I'm flying blind here, which means I do the best I can with what I have." Macy liked that she had grit.

"The female specimen is perfect for breeding." The Feral looked her up and down. "Nice, wide hips. She had a good, strong heat before. The male will have good seed. With your help and *them actually doing as I ask*," she threw Macy a dirty look; Macy, in turn, had to bite her tongue, "this breeding will be successful. Your lives depend on it."

"They are good candidates," Britt stammered, telling the Feral what she wanted to hear.

Britt wrung her hands together and licked her lips. "I

can leave the medication for Macy. I wouldn't need to stay…"

"No!" The Feral screeched. "You will remain here. You will make this happen, or else."

Sand shifted on the sofa. "We will do as you ask," he muttered. "We didn't need the healer."

"This is going to happen. Do you hear me?" she screeched. "You will make it so." She pointed at Britt who cowered, tears streaming down her cheeks. "The two of you will rut during the human's heat. I am giving you one last chance!" she screeched.

Sand jumped up, still holding the book. "We've told you that we're on board. None of us want to die. You are scaring the females."

Britt was breathing heavily. She was going to need a paper bag soon if she didn't calm herself down.

"We'll do it," Macy said. "I will make sure everything happens as discussed. No one needs to get hurt."

She watched as the Feral calmed down. Her chest slowed its rising, and her hands unfurled. "Don't disappoint me. I brought more food. I will be back."

"We need clothes," Macy said, stepping forward. "You can't expect the three of us to walk around half-naked." She took a deep breath, realizing that what she had just said meant very little to the creature. "Humans prefer to be covered. We are more comfortable that way. The healer will be able to work better, and I will be less stressed. Females who are stressed have less chance of becoming pregnant."

The Feral's eyes narrowed and for a second she was sure she would tell her to go to hell. Instead, she nodded once. "I will see what I can do." Then she turned and left.

No one said anything for a while. When she couldn't wait anymore, Macy turned to Sand. "And?"

"That was perfect." He grinned. "I'm sure I have it all." He handed the phone to Britt. It had been between the folds of the magazine.

"Let's have a look." Macy noticed that the other woman's hand shook as she held the phone. "We don't have much battery life left, so I really hope this worked." She was swiping the screen.

The sound of their earlier conversation came out of the device. Macy looked around Britt, at the screen, and there she was. The Feral, nice and visible on the device.

Sand punched the air. "We have her!" he yelled. "I'm going to need to keep that though." He gestured to her phone.

"That's fine," Britt sighed loudly. "I don't care about the phone. As long as that… thing is taken to task over this. I'll buy a new device. I don't care."

"Thank you," Sand said. "I'll take it with me when I go." He turned to her. "They'll know who she is, and the clip is damning. She threatens us all. Her leaders will have to help us find her, and then we'll find you."

She smiled back at him.

"Have the two of you decided what you want to do?" Britt asked. "Not that you need to make a decision just yet."

Macy felt everything in her tighten. She felt nauseous at the thought of sleeping with Sand and actually becoming pregnant. She felt just as sick at the thought of taking those pills to stop herself from becoming pregnant. Macy wasn't sure she could go through with it. She might have to. Like Britt had said, it wasn't as if a baby will have formed yet.

It wasn't taking a life, or in this case, two lives.

Two lives.

This was a terrible situation. Sand cupped her chin, lifting her face. He let go. "Are you okay, Macy?"

"It's a terrible predicament we're in."

"I'll do whatever you tell me, Mace." His eyes got that soft look again. "You decide. It's your body…"

"No," she shook her head, "it's your body too. Those pills might not work, Sand."

"They are about ninety-five percent effective," the doctor interjected. "So, chances are…"

"Ninety-five means that there is still a chance, and you're a shifter, so chances are that percentage would be lower." She had spoken extensively with her best friend, who was a mother to shifter babies and had a shifter boyfriend. Shifters were not like humans. They were stronger, faster and much harder to kill. She had a feeling his sperm would be no different. Even if it was five percent. Five percent was five percent.

"You're right." He nodded. "There is a chance they might not work."

"You might end up being a father to children you don't want," she added. "You don't want to be a father."

"That's harsh," the doctor interrupted again. "You're putting words into his mouth."

"How would you know that?" Macy pushed back. "Sand and I have been locked up in here for a couple of weeks already."

"Exactly." Dr. Baker put her hands on her hips. "You hardly know one another."

"We know each other just fine. We've discussed this—"

"Yeah, but you can't possibly…" She shook her head dismissively.

Sand must have seen something flash in Macy's eyes—murder maybe—because he stepped forward. "I think we should talk about this in private." He directed the comment to her.

"Private? How the heck do we get that one right?" She asked, feeling both flustered and at the same time, thankful he had suggested it. Dr. Baker could go suck eggs.

"The bathroom." He pointed in that direction. "It has walls and a door. You understand, Brittney? This is between Macy and me."

The doctor nodded. "Of course, I'm here for advice if you need me." She smiled sweetly at Sand.

"Thank you," Macy managed to push out. She didn't think that the other woman was trying to be difficult. It was just a case of all of them being stuck in each other's faces. Also, she had a feeling Dr. Baker had a little crush on Sand. As much as she wanted to, Macy could not blame her, since she had one too. In a big bad way.

The door clicked shut behind them. The bathroom wasn't big, especially when shared with a massive dragon shifter.

"We don't have to make any decisions yet. We have two weeks, or so, before we're forced into that," he whispered.

"I know, but two weeks isn't as long as you think." She shook her head, feeling anxious.

"I don't think that avoiding sex during your next heat is the way to go."

"Oh, really now?" She raised her brows, trying not to smile.

"Not because it would be agony." The sides of his

mouth twitched. "I think she'll check on us this time. She won't leave us alone for a whole heat cycle. She's far too desperate for a whelp." He scrubbed a hand over his jaw. "She'll replace me with a Feral male before the end of your cycle and I won't make it back here in time. She needs to believe that you're with child, only then will you be safe enough to leave. Think about it."

Shit! He was probably right. The thought of him being replaced with one of them...

He grabbed her hand and squeezed. "Your heartrate just went crazy and I can scent fear."

"I don't like the idea of one of them anywhere near me, especially during that time in my cycle."

"Okay, so we agree that I'm seeing you through your heat. That we're having sex. We just need to decide on whether or not we take that medication that prevents pregnancy."

"We also need to understand that I might get pregnant." Her voice was more than a touch shrill. Her eyes filled with tears.

"You also might not. We can talk about this. We'll talk about it a lot more." He kept her hand in his. It felt good. Britt had slept in the bed with her. Sand stuck to the sofa. She missed him. Missed what they had. Not that they had anything real, but she still missed it anyway.

"Okay." She nodded.

"If you don't want us to have sex, then we take our chances."

"No, I think you're right. I think we have to do the deed to keep her off our backs but... it's the rest I'm having a tough time with."

"Okay, so we have step one. We just need to decide on

step two." He pulled in a deep breath through his nose and gripped her hips. "We have time though." He got this look in his eyes. This smoldering look. Maybe she was just imagining it.

His eyes dipped to her cleavage. She wore the long red number with a bra and panties. Um… was he was checking her out? His hands tightened on her hips and his nostrils flared. "Sand… what are you… what are you doing?"

"I'm getting turned on by talk of sex with you." His beautiful golden eyes lifted to hers. "I happen to enjoy sex with you very much. I miss it."

Her sentiment… not exactly… but she'd take it anyway. "I miss it too."

He leaned in, his cheek almost brushing hers. His breath hot in the shell of her ear. One hand slid around to clasp her ass. "I think we should… make the most of our private time."

She giggled. "Are you suggesting…?"

"Shhh… we would need to keep it down, but… that's exactly what I'm suggesting. I can make you come in under two minutes."

"Two? You're slipping."

He chuckled softly. "I don't want it to be over too quickly," he walked her to the door and put her against it. "You game?" He tugged on the hem of her negligée.

"I think I just might be." Macy sounded all breathy, but that couldn't be helped.

Sand ran a hand under her silky negligée, his fingers brushed against her mound. He pulled her g-string to the side and circled her clit, making her catch her breath. His eyes stayed on hers, holding them captive. "I love the way you feel." Using a single finger, he pushed into her. "Wish I had time to taste you." He licked his lips, actually looking disappointed.

She groaned softly as he picked up speed, his thumb stroked her clit. Her breath was coming in sharp pants.

"Keep it down," he whispered with a tight smile. His thumb still stroking on her, Macy's core was tightening already. Her mouth was open, the pants becoming harder, almost turning into groaning.

There was a distinct sound of a zipper. Sand pulled away slightly, yanking his pants down to mid-thigh. He bunched her negligée up around her waist. Macy loved how desperate he looked. The big shifter picked her up easily. Even that was a huge turn-on.

"Put your legs around my hips," he whispered.

Macy did as he asked and he anchored her against the wall, entering her in one easy thrust that had her throwing her head back with sheer pleasure. He grunted softly.

Leaning forward, Sand closed his mouth around her earlobe as he thrust a second time. Nipping at her neck as he picked up the pace.

She moaned. The sound reverberated around the small room.

"You need... to be quieter... than that." He kept pushing into her. His hands were tight on her thighs, his breath coming in hard pants. His chest was pressed against hers.

"Too good," she moaned, struggling to catch her breath. She groaned again, despite trying to keep her lips pressed together. Her body was tightening.

"Shhhh," he warned.

"Oh god," she groaned. "Oh..."

Sand chuckled as he closed his mouth over hers in an unexpected move, she had not seen coming. The kiss was hot and wild from the start, drowning out the noises she was making. At least, for the most part. His thrusts picked up pace in insistent strokes that had her mind turning to mush. She dug her fingers into his shoulders.

When her orgasm hit moments later, it hit hard and fast. She half-yelled into his mouth, whilst everything inside went nuts.

"So much… for keeping… quiet," he snarled into her mouth, jerking against her as he came.

He fucked her in hard, deep strokes with less and less movement. Their kiss became searing. The pleasure that rolled through her was so intense that her eyes flew open and her back bowed.

He finally slowed. The slowing, too, becoming… something else… something… He pulled away, still rocking into her. "For the record," he whispered, moaned the words, his eyes hooded, "that wasn't a kiss."

"It wasn't?" She frowned, still panting like she'd run a marathon, even though she technically hadn't done anything, since her feet were off the ground.

"Nope." He shook his head. "That was me keeping you quiet, and since I didn't have any hands…" He shrugged.

"I see, and yes, I agree." She shook her head. "It wasn't a kiss at all."

He pulled out of her and put her down. Then he went and fetched a warm towel for her to clean up with.

CHAPTER 19

Nine days later…

Britt placed a yellow pill into the palm of her hand. "That's the last one."

Macy put it in her mouth and swallowed it down with water.

"You're looking at five to eight days for your ovulation to occur. My job here is pretty much done, unless she makes me wait for it to actually happen. Just in case she removes me, I think I should hand over all the necessary drugs now."

"I think that's a good idea." Sand walked over and sat down next to Macy, even though there was an open seat next to Britt. She loved how he always hovered near her. That if there was an option to sit near her, that was the choice he made. He stood up for her if there was an argument. Macy caught him looking her way more times than she'd care to admit, only because, this wasn't going to go anywhere. *It wasn't!* They were in a terrible situation. Once they were out, things would change. Sand would change. They would be over.

Britt had cooled down where Sand was concerned. It had happened right after their first 'private talk.' Thing was, they went for private talks often. He kissed her every damn time, which didn't help her emotional situation concerning Sand.

"Okay," Britt said, drawing Macy's attention back to her. "This is the Morning-After pill." She tore two pills off of the card. "Effective for up to seventy-two hours. One pill should remain active for up to five days, but I recommend taking the first pill twenty-four hours after sexual activity during a period where you are receptive to conception. Are you sure I can't leave you a couple of ovulation test kits?"

"Not necessary… I have an excellent sense of smell." Sand leaned on his thighs.

"Okay then. So, take one after twenty-four hours and another one three days later. That should cover you over the entire risk period. Important to note," she turned to Macy, "you might experience some side-effects. It's nothing to be concerned about and they'll wear off once the pill leaves your system."

"What kind of side-effects?" Sand asked before she could.

"Nausea, fatigue," she lifted her eyes in thought. "headaches, breast tenderness, you might bleed vaginally."

"I didn't get any of the symptoms you said I might get from the fertility drugs, so hopefully I'll be okay after taking these." Macy picked up the pills, examining them.

"I'm just warning you that it's perfectly normal, just in case it happens. I'm sure you'll be just fine. Next is the hCG or Human Chorionic Gonadotropin hormone." She placed, a couple of syringes and a box on the table.

"Oh boy." Macy squeezed her eyes tightly shut for a few moments.

"You'll need to administer these," Britt spoke to Sand.

"No problem. I can do it." Sand nodded, looking serious, nervous and adorable all at the same time.

Britt spent the next few minutes explaining all of the ins and outs of injecting Macy in the ass every day. Sand asked loads of questions. He nodded every so often, clearly taking his allotted job very seriously. Just when she thought they were done, he asked one more question.

"Will this drug," Sand tapped the box, "affect the unborn child?" His Adam's apple worked. "We might not decide to use the pills." He shrugged. "The pills might not even work," he mumbled. "I guess," he cleared his throat, "I need to be sure we aren't going to harm… the baby." Britt still didn't know that Sand was a dragon shifter. He had blurted a couple of things in his sleep but she'd assumed he was dreaming. So, Britt also had no idea that if Macy became pregnant, that she would have twins.

Britt smiled. "You're so sweet. He's sweet, isn't he?" she asked Macy.

"Yeah." Macy forced a smile.

"Okay, no," Britt shook her head, "the body naturally makes hCG hormones during pregnancy. I have them in my bag because we sometimes use this hormone in the case of an emergency to try to prevent miscarriage."

"Okay." Sand visibly relaxed. "Good to know."

"So, you can quite safely use the hormone. We just need

to work out when you should start taking the drug, and determine the necessary dosages." Macy could see that she was thinking it through. "The body starts creating hCG naturally six to twelve days after implantation of the embryo. That would mean—"

"Females who get pregnant by shifters are only pregnant for six months. The whole process happens more quickly with us."

Britt nodded. "Important to note. So, we're looking at four to eight days then." They talked it through for the next ten minutes. Britt grabbed her prescription pad and wrote out basic directions for administering the injections, together with the dosages.

Then she pulled out a handful of pregnancy tests. "You should get a positive result as soon as you start administering the hormone, since the pregnancy tests test specifically for hCG."

"So, we won't know if I'm really pregnant or not?" Macy clutched her hands together on her lap.

"I'm afraid not." Britt shook her head. "The test will pick up hCG. We won't know whether it's the administered version or hCG your body is producing because you're pregnant."

Macy felt her shoulders slump. There would be no way of knowing.

"Once you test positive, I'll be released," Sand said. "I'll have your phone, Britt." He looked Macy's way. "It might take me a few days to find you. I hope not but… it could." His eyes moved back to Britt. "How long before these hormones wear off, after I won't be there to inject Macy? That crazy Feral might want to conduct further pregnancy tests despite an initial positive. What if a test came up negative?" He was frowning heavily. "She might also scent a hormonal change, although I doubt that."

"I wouldn't put it past her retesting me," Macy agreed. "As you said before, she's desperate and she doesn't trust us at all."

"She might suspect if you're not actually pregnant. Her senses are not as developed as ours, but they're a damn sight better than any human. She might also just suspect that something is off." Macy could see that Sand was thinking out loud. "I worry, that's all."

"You could try doing the injecting yourself. It would…" Britt must have seen a look on Macy's face because she stopped there. "You've gone as white as a ghost. It's safe to say that option won't work. It can take up to two weeks for the hormones to properly work out of the system, but I wouldn't leave it for longer than five days, just to be sure."

"I'll have five days to find you then." Sand pulled in a breath through his nose.

"I'm betting you find me in under two."

His jaw tensed and his throat worked. She watched as Sand schooled his emotions. "You're on, Mace. Less than two days. I enjoy a challenge." He winked at her.

"I'll be waiting right here. Won't be going anywhere."

"I'll find you." He put an arm around her and pulled her in. She felt something press against the top of her head and realized that he had just kissed her. It made her feel odd. It also made her feel uncomfortable. The lines were getting blurred, just as she suspected they would.

Right now, she needed comfort, so Macy leaned into him, breathing in his scent. It was warm, soapy, masculine…

"You two should get a room," Britt piped up. "Make that… a bathroom!" She giggled.

Sand chuckled, he left his arm around her. "That's a good one, Brittney."

"I wonder if it's going to become a thing for the two of you once you get out of here. Bathroom sex!" Britt laughed. "At this rate, it's becoming a habit. You'll want more of it when you're free."

"There are better places," Macy answered. She couldn't wait to have sex in a bed again. Or lying down for that matter. Not that she was complaining. Their bathroom sex was off the charts hot, despite the location.

"Nope." Sand shook his head, letting her go. "I guess it hinges on whether or not Macy is pregnant in the end, but we're not actually together, so no more sex when we get out of here." He scrubbed a hand over his face, looking tired.

Ouch!

Ow!

She tried not to react. Macy knew this of course. They'd discussed it in-depth and yet, it still stung hearing him say it. Lots had happened and things had changed. She had been sure that there was something between them. That feelings had developed. Maybe that was true for her but clearly not for both of them. She was such an idiot. Such a fool!

Breathe slower!

Calm down!

"You're kidding me." Britt looked shocked. "I know you weren't together before, but surely…" She shook her head. "You guys go for your 'private talks' all the damn time. I'm sorry, I try not to listen in, but," she widened her eyes, "you sound like you're having a good time in there."

Sand shrugged. "You don't need to be in a relationship to have good sex. We explained about the Feral and—"

"Yeah, yeah… you need to have sex regularly so that she doesn't get worried about you not doing the deed during Macy's ovulation, like before." She smiled. "Thing is, regular sex and sex all the time, are two different things. You don't have to have as much sex as you're having. I assumed you were into one another. That it was more than just sex."

"I like fucking Macy and she likes it when I fuck her. End of story." Sand looked completely relaxed. The picture of calm.

"Well, that puts me firmly in my place," Britt mumbled.

'*You and me both,*' Macy thought to herself.

Nothing had changed.

Nothing had changed at all.

Nothing.

Shame on her for getting ahead of herself. *Shame! Shame! Shame!*

Her eyes stung. Her chest clenched tight. It hurt. It really hurt. She couldn't become pregnant. She had to take those pills. The last thing she needed was to be pregnant with twins and no partner at her side. No real family. It sounded like Sand would try to make a relationship work with her *if* and only if she was pregnant. She didn't want a guy who would only be there out of a sense of responsibility. She really needed to do everything to keep from becoming pregnant. If it happened anyway, there would be no 'them.' No family. No dream. It would be him, and then her and their kids. Not at all what she wanted. Not a healthy situation.

Her eyes stung but she managed to blink any tears away. She even managed to smile. "Enough about our private talks. It's just something we have to do. More importantly, let's focus on the near future. With that in mind, let's go through all of this one more time." She touched the prescription note that had the directions written on it. Macy was thankful of how strong and together she sounded when the opposite was true.

"Good idea." Britt picked up the blister pack with the two pills. "This is your Morning-After pill…"

Macy's chest tightened just a little more.

Four days later…

Candied apples. The tangy kind. Sweet and tart and fucking delicious. Then there was the scent of pussy. Hot, wet and enticing. There was a familiar throbbing in his dick and tightening in his balls.

Things were about to get uncomfortable, and fast. It was just the start of Macy's heat, and yet her scent was already driving him batshit crazy.

There was a scraping on the ledge. *Shit!* He'd been so busy sniffing at the human he hadn't been paying attention to their surroundings.

Both the females jumped up and went to stand by the entrance. Their eyes were wide, their heartrates spiked.

The Feral appeared, she unlocked the padlock on the door and stepped into the enclosure. She sniffed the air and then looked over at him, her eyes moving down the length of him. Yep, if she looked close enough, she'd see one times erection and scent a good dose of testosterone.

It was apparent enough for even a Feral to smell. In fact, the humans might even pick up on his musky, needy scent.

The Feral smiled, her eyes took on a look of glee. "Well done, healer!" She rubbed her hands together. "It looks like your pills worked."

Both Macy and Britt looked over at him, their eyes filled with confusion.

"It won't be long now," he said, as his eyes locked with Macy's. "Your heat. I was going to tell you." He hadn't wanted to worry her. Truth was, they still had no idea about that pill. He hated the idea of her taking it and yet he wasn't sure about having whelps. Just thinking of being a father, of being tied down, made his chest tighten and his eyes widen. His heart began to pound inside his chest. *What the hell were they going to do?*

"I left a couple of pregnancy tests," Britt explained motioning to the table. He noted that although her breathing became a touch elevated, at that moment, her outward appearance was calm. "It will make it easier to test Macy for pregnancy." This was important if their plan was going to work. They had to convince the Feral early on that Macy was pregnant.

The Feral cocked her head, narrowing her eyes. "How does it work?"

"The body produces a hormone when a woman is pregnant. That," she pointed at the box, "tests for that particular hormone. If it is present in the urine – Macy would need to pee on the item inside the box—then she is pregnant. You would need to look for two pink lines. One line means negative, but I do need to caution about the possibility of a false negative," Britt raced on. "If a test shows negative – so only one line – wait a day or two and then try again. If a test is positive – two lines – then that means Macy is pregnant. No doubt!"

The Feral's eyes were bright with excitement. "How soon can we do this test? How soon?" she repeated, looking eager.

"Normally I would say to wait until after menstruation is missed."

The Feral frowned. "I do not understand."

"The bleeding. Normally I would say to wait until after a female misses her bleeding."

"Oh." The Feral nodded. "That makes more sense to me."

"In this case, I don't think you would have to wait as long, since shifters have a shorter gestation period. I might be wrong, so it is important to retest every couple of days until you get a positive, or until Macy bleeds."

The Feral screeched, seeming to grow in size. The females shrank back. "I am almost sure she will be pregnant. I used good medicine," Britt tried, her voice shrill, "good human healing herbs on her," she added, eyes wide, heart racing.

"How long, healer?"

"A week. You sh-should try in about s-seven days," Britt stammered, looking fearful.

"You are leaving now, but if the human is not with child, I will find you and bring you back. I might even throw you in too, with that one," she pointed at Macy, "and one of my males. That way there would be two of you to keep him company. Maybe he would be less inclined to do irreparable damage to either of you."

Britt blanched. Macy made a sobbing noise and clapped a hand over her mouth.

Sand wanted to rush in. He wanted to have at the bitch. He did none of those things since they would only serve to incense the creature. "I will get the human with child," he boomed, trying to defuse the situation. They had a plan, fighting with this bitch wasn't going to do them any favors at this point. He did keep his gaze locked with the Feral's though. He bit back a snarl.

"Best you do that," she spat. "It's time for your 'hug,' human."

"No... no... please." Britt backpedaled. Her face looked stricken.

"Why not blindfold her," Sand suggested. "Humans are timid. You don't want to accidentally hurt her. What if you need her again?"

"We just conducted a whole conversation about that not happening. I don't want to have to see her ever again."

"I get that." Sand spoke in a soothing voice. "Humans are clueless creatures with very little in the way of senses. That includes sense of direction. Sense of smell, hearing... all of them. They live a dulled existence. Even if you left her eyes uncovered, I am sure she would never be able to lead anyone back here. Eyes covered, you can forget about that happening. It doesn't seem like you wish to harm any of us."

"I do not care either way but," she snorted, "if the human is that afraid of a little hug, then I suppose covering her eyes... no, her whole face... would be acceptable."

"I wouldn't be able to breathe... I..." Britt looked panicky.

"We could use a pillow cover," Macy suggested. "The fabric is thick enough that you won't see anything and thin enough that you could breathe."

"Tie her hands behind her back as well," the Feral insisted.

"You'll be fine," Macy said, facing Britt.

The healer nodded. "Okay… yes, it's better than the whole 'hug' thing."

Sand noted that she looked pale. Macy removed a pillow from its cover. Sand ripped a strip off the bottom of the sheet and tied Britt's hands. "Will you be okay?"

"Yes." Britt looked pale and scared.

"Take care of yourself," Macy said.

Britt nodded. "You guys too."

"Ready?" Macy asked.

Britt nodded and she put the cover over her head. "I'm going to tie it off at the bottom so that it doesn't come off."

"Okay." Britt's voice was muffled.

"You good?" Sand asked.

"Yes." Her voice was small and childlike. Sand felt so bad for the female.

Then they watched as the Feral hoisted the female over a shoulder. Britt yelped, but then she was silent. The healer was tough, she would be okay.

The Feral locked the cage, shifted and left. Sand reached over and squeezed Macy's hand. He could feel how she was shaking.

CHAPTER 20

Something hard pressed against her lower back. Sand rubbed his hand up and down her arm. He clasped her hip, pushing himself a little tighter against her. "Do you need to rest some more?" he asked, his voice husky and deep.

"No, I'm…"

Sand kissed the back of her neck, running his hand down her thigh. "Are you hungry or thirsty?"

"No, I'm good, I—"

"Are you sore?" His voice filled with concern. "I think I—"

"I'm okay, Sand." She sounded a little exasperated.

He pulled away, turning to lie on his back. His member jutted from his body. "I'm sorry, I'm coming on too strong. We don't have to do anything more until you're ready. I could control myself before, I'll manage again."

"That's not it." She sat up as well, the sheet gathered

around her hips. "It's not your fault—"

There was the familiar scraping sound on the outside ledge. Both of them turned towards the sound.

Macy grabbed the sheet, pulling it around herself. Sand made a noise of frustration. He sat up, not bothering to cover himself. They watched as the Feral let herself in. She sniffed the air, a satisfied smile spread across her face.

"Happy now?" Sand asked, sounding irritated.

"I would have preferred if I had caught you rutting, but…"

"Macy is a human," Sand growled. "She needs plenty of rest between bouts."

"I am glad you listened. I would not have enjoyed scraping what was left of you off the floor," she spoke to Macy.

"We made a deal and I plan on sticking to it. I don't want to die, thanks," Macy said.

"I'm glad! I am excited for the future." The Feral held up a hand. "I will leave you now. You have yet to reach your full heat." Her eyes gleamed. "Not long now." Her smile turned into a wide grin.

"Don't let the door hit you on the way out," Sand muttered.

"I am careful, dragon," she said as she shut the door behind her. "I would never let a thing like that happen. Have fun!" She set the lock and left, her nails scraping on the stones as she pushed off the rocky surface.

"We were right." Sand lay back down a half a minute later. "She will be checking on us… on you… every step of the way."

Macy sighed. "I think so too."

Sand looked her way. His eyes had that look. His face

was pinched. His gaze drifted to where the sheet had slipped. "I think I'm going to work out while you rest. Maybe I'll take a cold shower." He sat back up.

"What I was trying to tell you earlier, was that it's been twenty-four hours," she blurted. "I need to take one of those pills now." It felt like her throat was closing. "I would appreciate it if you could bring me a glass of water and the drug. You know where we stashed them the other day?"

His chest rose and fell in quick succession. Sand's eyes were fixed on the bed. "Are you going to take it then?" He paused. "You've decided?"

"I think I must." Her chest also heaved, and yet she felt like she could hardly breathe. "No, I *know* I must."

"But what if…" He clenched his jaw for a few moments. "What if you are with child?"

"I'm not *with* anything. Right now, there's an egg and there's sperm. That's all. It's stopping this thing from happening before it even begins."

He groaned. "It doesn't feel right, somehow. I'm struggling with it."

It made no sense. It had to be his instincts talking. He would regret this. "Do you want to be a father?" She looked him in the eyes, feeling tears well.

"You know the answer to that question." He sounded agitated.

"Answer me. Do you want to be a dad, Sand?"

"It's not always about what a person wants or doesn't want. It's not always as simple as that." He shook his head.

She laughed. "That's rich coming from someone who always finds everything so simple. It *is* that simple. Either you want to be a parent – you want these babies – or you don't. Which is it?" She knew she was being hard on him, but he would thank her in the end.

"I… I…" He ground his teeth.

"Are you ready to be a dad, Sand?" she pushed. "It's a simple question."

His face was filled with anguish. His eyes were stormy and dark. "No." He shook his head. "No, okay? One day… yeah… maybe… but right now… no, Mace. I'm not ready. The possibility makes me feel out of control and it just doesn't feel right. Having you take that pill though…" He ran a hand through his hair. "It feels just as wrong."

"You don't want to be a father right now?" She looked him in the eyes.

"No," he choked out the word.

"Bring me the pill and some water please." Her lip trembled.

"What do *you* want? You've always said you want children. That you would die for a family. Why wouldn't you want these babies? Surely this feels wrong for you too?"

"I want a family, Sand."

"I would step up." He nodded, looking resolute. "I would be there."

"I want a family unit with a mom and dad who are together. I know that's not always possible, but I'd like to at least start out with the best chance of it happening. That isn't the case with us."

"I'd be there, Macy." He took her hand. "We could make a go of it, if," he squeezed her hand, "if it came to that."

A go of it. She pulled away. "I want love, Sand. I don't

want someone who settles. Someone who's there just for the children. I deserve more than that."

"We need to think of the whelps—"

"There are no whelps, Sand. There's you and me. We're fuck buddies, remember? We're not together. It's just good sex, right?" She used his words. It hurt her to say it, since she felt strongly that there could be something between them, but a one-sided relationship would never work. "You get that, don't you?"

"I can't get over how wrong it feels."

"Well, I can," she pushed. "Bring me those pills."

He just sat there, his beautiful golden eyes piercing hers. "Now, Sand." Before she lost her nerve. "Go!"

He sighed as he stood up. Sand disappeared into the bathroom. She heard him open and close the cabinet door. Then he reappeared, the small blister pack in hand. He headed for the kitchen, yanking the cupboard door open and taking out a glass. Then he filled it to halfway and headed back to her. "Are you sure about this?"

"Yes." She took the pills from him.

Sand placed the glass on the side-table.

She pushed the pill through the foil. It fell onto her palm. So inconspicuous. This was the right thing to do. *It was!* There was no other option. She could be strong and do it. It wasn't a big deal at all. Just sperm and an egg. Sperm and an egg. Not an embryo even. No babies in sight.

"Macy." Sand sounded concerned. "Hey, Macy," he clasped a hand around her upper arm in a tender hold, "you don't have to take them."

Shit!

Holy crap but she was crying. Her cheeks felt wet and

she was sniffing. *What the hell?* This was the right thing to do. She lifted her gaze from the small white pill and looked him in the eyes.

They were soft and filled with concern. "It doesn't feel right, does it?"

"This is stupid, Sand. There is no baby... or babies. There are *no* babies." Her voice was stern. "There's nothing yet. Why am I even crying?"

"It feels wrong, that's why. It feels wrong to both of us. Don't take the damned pill." He shook his head.

"I have to." Tears ran even faster down her cheeks. "I really have to." She'd find the right man. A great guy. A sweet guy. Someone who cherished her. They'd try hard at making babies. She'd pee on a stick. Her heart would beat as she waited to see the result. Her husband would be pacing. Then she'd relish the look of excitement and sheer happiness on his face when the test came up positive. They'd laugh and cry and he'd pick her up and swing her around. Then they'd laugh some more.

That's what she wanted.

Yet. Yet... She couldn't make herself put that pill in her mouth. "I have to. I must."

"No, no you don't." He put his hand over hers and closed it. "We'll tackle whatever comes our way. If it's meant to be, it will be. We'll figure it out."

"That's irresponsible." She used her other hand to wipe her face.

"Then we'll be a little irresponsible. At least we'll be doing what feels right."

"More like, what doesn't feel wrong."

"Semantics." His jaw tightened for a moment. "Please don't take it. Trust me on this one. I know you. The kind of person you are, and this won't sit right."

Shit! She only wished that Sand felt the same way about her. This decision would be a no brainer then. He was right though. It wouldn't sit right. She could do this. She was a strong woman. "Okay," her voice hitched, "I won't take it."

He pushed out a heavy breath. "Okay then. It's going to be fine."

"I hope so."

"It will." He leaned in and kissed her. It got hot and heavy quickly. Before long he was yanking the sheet away and putting her on her back. Macy expected him to turn her onto her knees, but it didn't happen. Sand pulled her legs up over his hips and gently nudged into her. Slowly and carefully. Nudging his way into her. His eyes were on her. They burned with intensity. He covered her mouth with his and proceeded to help her forget about everything that was going on. He made her feel like it was just the two of them. That it would be that way forever.

A lie. A bittersweet lie.

CHAPTER 21

Six days later…

Macy lay on the bed, on her stomach. "Are you sure you know what you're doing?"

"I have no idea whatsoever." Sand was deadpan.

"Don't say that," she sounded panicky. Of course she did. How could she not in this situation? "How can you say that?" Her voice was shrill.

"Because it's the truth. I've never done anything like this before." At least he sounded calm. That was something.

"You have the instructions, right?"

"Yes, I do. I've read them four times. I know what to do." He seemed distracted. Then again, he was busy.

Macy pushed out a sigh. "Oh good. Earlier you made it sound like you had no clue."

"I don't have a clue."

"Don't say that!" she hollered, turning and looking over her shoulder. Macy wanted to run away or to hide. This was an important part of the process, so she could do neither.

He chuckled, standing up. "You're cute when you're worried."

"Cute, my ass," she mumbled.

"I happen to think you have a very cute ass." He grinned at her.

All she could see was the syringe in his hand. Moreover, all she could see was the needle. It was covered with a cap but, it was there, and it was long and sharp. Sand walked over to where she was lying. He had already placed the alcohol swab next to the bed. "Are you ready?" he asked as he sat down next to her. The bed dipped.

"No," she shook her head, "but since I'll never be ready, you may as well do this."

"That's the spirit. Now, remember what Brittney said, stay as relaxed as possible. This is a shot into the muscle. If you're tense, there's more chance you'll feel it."

"Don't say that." She was breathing more rapidly, her fingers white-knuckled in the tangled sheets. Macy felt like a big ninny but couldn't help it. "I can't relax and that makes me even more tense. It's a vicious circle."

"Britt said that it isn't a bad shot. You shouldn't feel much, if anything at all."

"Only if I'm relaxed," she practically yelled. Her eyes felt big. "If you're tense it hurts, and I can't seem to make myself calm down."

Sand chuckled, he quickly cleared his throat, forcing himself to stop. "Sorry!" He cleared his throat again. "I'm not going to hurt you, Mace. It's just a little prick."

"You don't know what you're doing though."

"That's true but it will be fine." She heard him put the syringe down. Then he ripped the packet.

She jerked when his hand touched her ass. Just his hand. It was warm.

"I'm not doing anything yet," he said as he rubbed her skin in slow easy circles.

"I know," she looked up at the ceiling, "but I can't help it."

"Lift your hips a little." She did as he said.

Sand pulled her silk nighty up. It was still morning. Even though the Feral had brought them clothing, Macy hadn't changed yet. He continued rubbing, directly onto her skin. "That's it," he said. "Breathe in and out. In and out." His voice was soothing.

Then he wiped an area on her ass with the swab. It was cold from the alcohol. Sand pressed his finger down onto her skin. She grit her teeth and squeezed her eyes shut. This was it. *Relax. Relax! Stay calm! Breathe. In and out and in and out.*

Sand chuckled as he wiped her skin with the swab again. Then he—*What was he doing?*—He pressed a kiss to the area he had just swabbed.

"You're kissing my ass?" she asked, sounding as shocked as she felt. "Just do it already, I'm dying here."

He laughed harder. "You're all done."

"I'm all done? What?" she bleated, filled with both excitement and sheer relief.

He gripped her hips, preventing her from turning over. "That wasn't so bad was it?"

Was it her imagination or had his voice dropped a couple of octaves? She looked back over her shoulder. His eyes were locked onto her ass. They were intent. Sand bit down on his lower lip. It was a look she recognized.

The bed dipped as he moved in behind her.

"Um… what are you doing?" she asked as he lifted her up, onto all fours.

"I'm kissing you better." No doubt about it, his voice was a deep rumble. He kissed her butt cheek a second time and then leaned over her, kissing her between her shoulder blades.

"Are you initiating sex?" she frowned. "We don't have to have sex anymore, Sand." They shouldn't have sex. It wasn't a good idea.

"I know that." His hands stayed on her hips. His boxer-clad erection bumped against her ass as he moved. "I meant what I said before, I enjoy fucking you." His hand dipped between her thighs, zoning in on her clit.

She gasped. His touch instantly set her nerve-endings on fire. No fair. Need surged through her and she moaned. "We shouldn't," she managed to push out.

"Why not?" A husky rumble.

Because she had feelings for him. Because he didn't feel the same way about her. Because things were about to get complicated.

She groaned. That finger though. Her belly had tightened up, her hips rocked forward. "Because we don't have to anymore," she mumbled, her breathing picking up.

"I want to, Macy. You want me too, don't you?" She was shocked at how vulnerable he sounded.

She wanted to stop him. Wanted to, but that finger… She licked her lips as pleasure coursed through her, as her nipples tightened up some more, rubbing against the silk nighty. Her ass lifted, almost of its own accord, her body preparing to take him inside it. "Yes," she groaned.

Sand stopped and moved back, his hot breath on her upper thighs. Before she could speak, his tongue traced the seam of her pussy, making her cry out instead.

"I love the way you taste." Sand lapped at her clit, his tongue moving fast in firm strokes that had her clenching her teeth to keep from screaming out. He knew her body so well. He knew how hard, or soft he needed to be at any given moment. He knew where to touch her and just what she liked.

Seconds later, she lost the battle, screaming his name as her pussy clenched with an orgasm so fierce that it had her eyes watering and her pulse racing. Good god, but he was good. It had also been a couple of days since they had done this.

His hands were still on her hips, luckily, they held her in place, or she would've sunk into a boneless heap as soon as he let up on her clit. Her cheek rested against the cool, cotton sheet. Her breath came in hard, ragged pants. Her hands fisted the sheets.

Sand groaned. "You have the best ass." He palmed one of her cheeks. "I'm afraid that this prick is going to be significantly bigger than the last," he said as he crouched over her. "It won't hurt, though. Not at all." He pulled his boxers down.

She laughed. It quickly turned into a moan as Sand pressed the tip of his cock against her opening. He leaned over her, caging her body with his, his chest covering her back. "I love being inside you, Macy," he growled, nipping at her shoulder.

"I love you… inside me." She was panting. The

pressure increased as his thick head breached her opening. It stung a little.

His finger found her clit, which he circled with the tip of his index finger. It felt incredible. She could already feel the beginning of another orgasm. Sand pushed in deeper, he groaned. "I'm going to miss this," he ground out.

This.

Not her.

Loved fucking her.

It was the fucking he loved. Not her!

Sand bottomed out inside her. His finger slipping and sliding over her clit. Softly, ever so softly. Sand began to move using hard, easy strokes. He grunted hard a couple of times, her mind turned to mush. Her body giving itself over to him. Every part of her. Not just sex.

Sand picked up the pace, his balls slapping against her ass. Her body sucking him in. She was groaning and whimpering and moaning. She was falling… falling… falling. Falling in all ways. Macy whimpered, "I'm going to come… again… soon."

Sand eased the pressure off her clit. He slowed his strokes until he almost stopped moving. "Want it to last," he grunted, still deep inside her.

Macy turned to look over her shoulder, her eyes zoning in on his thick, long cock as it moved in and out of her. He was crouched over slightly at the waist. His eyes were focused on where they were joined. "I fit you perfectly."

Utter per*fucking*fection.

Her ass was magnificent. As was the deep curve of her hip and the elegant length of her back. Her glistening pussy was swollen from her earlier release. It stretched tightly around his girth. A deep delicious pink. Her slit was covered in fur, which was dripping with her juices. Her clit was swollen beneath his finger. It was wet and easy to toy with. He needed to go really easy. This felt so fucking good, he never wanted it to end. The idea of her carrying his whelps made him scared fucking shitless but it also turned him on. *How was that possible?* Must be an instinctual thing and his instincts were riding him. Which was normal. He couldn't panic about it. He tried not to think too much about it either. He was just going to enjoy the moment and take things as they came

His finger stayed right there on her clit. Continued to play with the tight bundle of nerves, loving the way her breath came in pants and hard groans.

His balls had pulled up, already tight inside of him, ready for release.

"Oh, my…" she groaned. "Oh god… oh." Macy was really close. He wasn't going to be able to keep this up for much longer. Sweat dripped down his brow. She pushed back against him. That glorious ass of hers bounced a little with each thrust. Perfection. All of it.

He snarled as he picked up a steady pace. It wasn't long and her pussy walls fluttered.

"Oh, my… oh… I'm going to…" Her back arched up against him. Her pussy clamping down as she came. So freaking tight it almost hurt. He could hardly move. Could hardly breathe as the first spasm of his own orgasm hit. It pulled the air right out of him. Instinct took over as he clamped his mouth on her shoulder and bit down. Holding her in place. His hands closed on her hips.

Mine.

Pleasure coursed through him. Macy squirmed beneath him, screaming his name again as her pussy released and clenched in time with her orgasm. Her hands clawed at the sheets. Her back was bowed. He held her in place. Just when he thought he was done, another spurt left him. His eyes rolled back. Sand growled fiercely, letting her shoulder go. He rocked into her, riding the wave, drawing out her pleasure at the same time.

He finally slumped over her, careful not to put too much weight on her. Then he realized what he had done and pulled back. "Are you hurt?"

Macy moaned.

"Mace?" He touched her shoulder. There were teeth marks, but he hadn't actually broken the skin. *Thank fuck! What the hell was wrong with him!*

"You can bite me anytime," she mumbled, sounding drunk.

"Yeah, I probably shouldn't do that again." His mind was reeling.

"Why not?" She turned back. Her eyes were hazy. She looked sated. Completely and utterly sated. Beautiful. Her gorgeous blue eyes were hooded. Her lids at half-mast. Her cheeks were flushed red. Her hair was an adorable mess.

"It's mating behavior. It must be my instincts. That's all, just my stupid instincts. This whole pregnancy thing." He pulled out of her, pulling up his boxers. "It's messing with my head. It won't happen again."

Her eyes got this look. He wasn't sure what it was exactly, only that it wasn't good, and he didn't like the way it made him feel to see her like that. "You okay?"

"I'm good. Make that great. I did enjoy it. You're right

though, that can't happen again. We probably shouldn't have sex again either. It's too complicated now."

"I won't bite you again, Mace." He rubbed a hand down her back. "But I'm going to try my luck when it comes to the sex part of the equation. We're so damned compatible. My dick does a happy dance every time I'm inside you."

She didn't say anything, which he didn't like either. Why couldn't they keep having sex? It wasn't that much of a big deal.

"I'm going to shower quickly and then I'm making you breakfast." He kissed her shoulder. "You stay right there. Take a nap. I'll bring you breakfast in bed."

"Sounds good." She nodded, giving him a smile. He didn't like the way the smile made him feel either. Like he had done something wrong. Maybe it was just nerves. Macy was most likely pregnant. His own gut churned.

CHAPTER 22

Three days later…

"I'll be right back." She started to turn.

"No!" the Feral shouted. Macy turned back again. "I will go with you." The creature nodded, then cocked her head in that strange way.

"What?" Macy frowned. "Um… it's a little private, don't you think?" She widened her eyes.

"No. It is a bodily function. Natural and normal. Besides, I *must* be there." Macy realized that the female was worried. She was frowning and her eyes were narrowed. She looked tense in general.

"Okay," Macy said. "Suit yourself." She glanced over at Sand. He gave a nod.

She'd already had three hCG injections. This test would be positive whether she was pregnant or not. They had orchestrated it that way. Her breasts felt a little tender this morning and the thought of having milk with her tea earlier had made her feel queasy. All normal when using hCG *and* when pregnant. She had no way of knowing which one was the true cause of her symptoms.

Sand had pointed out that all dragons were averse to lactose. That it wasn't just a preference for him but a characteristic of his kind. He'd thrown the fact out there, where it simmered between them. Could she be pregnant? She most likely was pregnant and she wasn't sure how she felt about it. Part of her got excited at the idea. She couldn't help it. The bigger, rational side of her grew afraid. It was that side of her that prayed it hadn't happened. Sand had warned her that most heats *did* result in pregnancy. Most, but not all. They hadn't talked about it much, aside from skirting around the topic. They would face whatever came their way when the time came.

"Are you alright, human?" the Feral asked, dragging her out of her own head.

She nodded. "I'm fine."

"Do you have it?"

Macy held up the box. "Right here."

"Good. Let us go."

"You do know that it might not show up positive yet?" Macy mentioned, just in case the drugs somehow hadn't worked yet.

"I remember exactly what the human healer said. It could take a couple of tries. That we should keep trying until your bloods come in before giving this up as a failure. That is why we have a couple of those boxes." She looked pointedly at the pregnancy test in Macy's hand.

"Alright, let's go then." She glanced at Sand. He looked tense and was pacing. Macy wasn't sure if he really felt nervous or if he was just putting on an act.

She had a knot in her stomach, which churned. This needed to play out in the right way. Hopefully, everything worked out for the best. Macy touched a hand to her belly as they entered the bathroom. *Please let this work out!*

"Do you know what to do?" the Feral asked. She clutched her hands together and then seemed to realize she was doing it and let go, dropping her arms to her sides. She wasn't normally one to show such outward emotion, and clearly didn't like it.

"Um… let me just read…" She opened the box and took out the insert, quickly reading through the important parts. It was pretty straightforward and even had pictures as well. She handed the insert to the Feral, who took it, frowning heavily.

Her face instantly brightened when she realized she could get an idea of what to do from the diagrams. She nodded. "I can't wait anymore. I want you to do the test." Her eyes gleamed.

"Okay." Macy sat down on the toilet, taking down her underwear. "This isn't my first pee of the day. You realize that the test would be more accurate then?"

The Feral nodded. "If the test is negative, I will come back as the sun is rising so that we can try again." She wrung her hands together.

"I don't want you to get your hopes up yet."

"Don't worry about me, human. Do the test!" the other woman snapped.

Macy uncapped the end of the stick and held the absorbent end of the device between her legs. She had to breathe and to try to relax before anything happened. It took a full half a minute before she was able to pee. The

Feral watched her the whole time. It was off-putting. It finally happened though, and she counted to ten before removing the stick and recapping the end. Then she put the test on the end of the cabinet and finished up on the toilet.

By now, the Feral was pacing. Macy flushed the toilet and washed her hands with soap. Then they waited. "It said to wait five minutes but that a positive result might show up as soon as two minutes in. Should we check it? It's been about that."

The Feral stopped pacing and turned to her. The female's eyes were wide. She swallowed thickly. "Maybe we should wait," she finally said, looking unsure.

"I think we should look," Macy countered. "If it's one line we wait longer, if it's two… it means I'm pregnant."

The Feral swallowed thickly again. "Okay… do it!" She nodded.

Macy picked up the test. It was exactly as she expected. She handed the test to the Feral who screeched so loudly Macy had to hold her hands over her ears for fear of them bursting. The other woman then dropped to her knees in front of Macy, when she looked up, her eyes were filled with tears. "Thank you." A single tear rolled down her cheek, even though she was smiling. "You have given me the greatest gift."

Macy couldn't help that a teeny tiny part of her felt guilty. Despite this being wrong on every level, she felt bad for the creature.

"Is everything okay?" Sand asked from the doorway.

The Feral jumped to her feet. "The human is with child." She wiped her face. "Prepare to leave. I no longer have need for you."

"You are welcome." Sand clenched his jaw. "I'm ready when you are." Sand spread his hands. "It's not like I need to take anything with me, unless, of course, you'll let me take Macy."

The Feral grinned. "That is funny, dragon. Let us take our leave." She walked out, Macy followed behind. "Do you wish for me to knock you out or would you prefer a hug?"

"What about a blindfold? I promise not to look." He raised his brows.

The Feral laughed. "You are full of jokes today." She turned serious. "Unfortunately, that won't be possible. I cannot have you finding us. I'm sure you understand." She didn't wait for a reply. "I will take you far enough away from our territory and you will need to make the rest of your way home. I cannot risk being caught."

"Give me a minute to say goodbye, and then I don't really care which method you use," he growled, frowning all the while.

"I will wait a few minutes, but do not dilly dally." The Feral moved to the main exit.

Sand walked over to where Macy was standing. He took her hands, locking his eyes with hers. They were solemn. "Look after yourself."

"I will." She nodded, trying hard not to cry. He was coming back. It would be soon.

"I mean it, Mace. Drink plenty of fluids. Eat healthy food."

"I will bring—" the Feral began.

"Can you stay out of this," Sand snapped, turning to the Feral.

"I was only trying to be helpful."

"If you want to be helpful you can let us both go, otherwise keep your beak shut," he growled, his eyes bright.

"You do not have to be so testy." The Feral cocked her head, looking irritated.

Macy gave a tiny shake of the head, silently begging him to stay quiet. He tightened his jaw and pulled in a deep breath through his nose. "Just take care of yourself. Of them too." He squeezed her hands.

Her heart sped up. It was an act. The Feral was watching and listening in.

"I'll miss you." It was more acting.

She nodded. "I'll miss you too." Her eyes stung. It was getting harder and harder not to cry.

"Fuck it!" Sand cupped her face in both his hands and kissed her. It was soft and tender, slowly blossoming into something passionate and yet still… tender. She couldn't help but be swept away. Macy gripped his biceps, closing her eyes with a tiny whimper. She gave… she took… she fell some more.

"That's enough," the Feral said. "We need to leave."

Sand broke the kiss. He kept her face in his hands and his eyes on hers. Then he nodded once. She knew what the nod meant. It was a reassurance that he was coming for her.

She nodded once as well. He slanted one last kiss over her mouth and walked away.

"I'm ready for my h—"

The Feral bitch hit Sand square in the jaw. He flew back about seven feet and landed hard on the stone floor.

Macy ran over to him. "Why did you do that?" she yelled, crouching next to him.

"It is the easiest way to render a being unconscious," she countered.

"I heard a crack." Sand's jaw was already swelling. "You didn't have to hit him so hard, damn you!"

"I hardly even touched him. Dragons are such frail creatures," she snorted. "To think they are the next strongest species to us." She picked Sand up like he weighed nothing. "I will be back often to check on you. I will take good care of you, human."

Like she was a hamster, or a house plant, or something.

"You will be well rewarded at the end of this," she added. All Macy could do was nod and blink. Again, trying to hold back the tears. This had to be over soon. It had to.

CHAPTER 23

Later that same day…

How fucking far was the Feral territory from their own? It seemed like he had been flying for years, when in reality it was hours. He was close to home, but his reserves were almost done. Sure, he'd worked out inside that tiny cage. He'd even shifted a good couple of times when the urge had become too great, but he hadn't done this in weeks. He hadn't spread his wings and taken to the skies and he could feel it. Sand was dog tired. His limbs felt heavy. Every flap of his wings was a hardship. He struggled to get sufficient air into his lungs, which burned. Everything hurt. All he wanted to do was stop. To rest. Instead, he pushed on. He had to. Macy was counting on him. Sweet, kind, beautiful Macy. She would be afraid, and she was alone. Sand picked up the pace with renewed energy. It wasn't too far now. Did he go to the main balcony or straight to one of his brothers? As their king, Granite was the obvious choice. *No!* He didn't want to scare the male's children. What of Shale? His brother's children were still whelps. There was a good chance they would be home. Yes, his twin would know exactly what to do in this type of situation.

He aimed for Shale's balcony. There was no need to slow down since he was going so damned slow. He worked to keep his wings flapping. If he had been in his skin, his body would be covered in sweat. Now to slow down and to—He realized how quickly the ground was coming at him. His body wasn't reacting quickly enough to the signals his brain was sending. He was just too tired. There might not be much in the way of forward momentum but there was nothing in the way of breaks. *Fuck!* He tried, at the last moment, to divert, afraid of hurting someone, but there was no reaction from his muscles. Impact was imminent. He clenched his jaw, trying to make himself as small as possible. Less chance of hitting Georgia, or the whelps. There was an almighty crash as he hit the apartment bay windows, smashing through them. Glass splintered and he rolled head over heels a couple of times before coming to a stop.

"You okay?" He heard Shale asking his mate, Georgia.

"Y-yes," she muttered, sounding confused but unharmed.

"You're not hurt?" Shale growled.

With a huge amount of effort, Sand turned towards them. Shale had used his body to protect the female, who shook her head. *Thank fuck!* He breathed out in relief. They both turned to what had caused the ruckus. Namely to him. He was lying in a heap on their living room floor.

One of the sofas was on its side next to him and he was lying on something hard and splintered. Sand was pretty sure it was the coffee table but he couldn't be certain.

"What in the—?" Georgia began, her eyes wide.

"Sand!" Shale boomed, his arms still around his female.

Sand needed to tell Shale what had happened. He lifted his head, but it was too heavy for his neck to carry. He suddenly felt dizzy, his head was spinning. Sand felt his eyes roll back in his skull, his head crashed back down. All he wanted to do was sleep but he held back. *Macy... Had to save...*

"By claw!" Sand heard Shale yell. His brother sounded far away "Sand!" he shouted, closer this time. His ears felt like they were stuffed with cotton wool. He needed to tell Shale what had happened. They needed to rescue Macy. She was counting on him.

Using what felt like every last ounce of strength he possessed, Sand shifted. He felt his scales pull back. Same thing with his wings and tail. He felt his muscles shorten. The process seemed to take forever. It sapped him. By the time he was done, Sand was panting heavily. His mouth was dry. His body ached.

"I can't believe it," he heard Georgia whisper. "It's him!"

Sand felt his brother shake him. "Sand." Then Shale rubbed his back and shook him again. Harder this time. "Brother, please!"

Sand had to work hard to respond. Thankfully, he could feel some energy slowly return. He lifted his head, still panting hard. He felt dizzy and struggled to focus. *Fuck!* Maybe he should have taken it easier on the trip there. Sand had been frantic. Now that he was there, he calmed some. The plan was going to work. *It had to.*

"He's exhausted," Shale said. "Where were you?" He squeezed Sand's shoulder.

"Macy," Sand muttered. "Mace..." he said again.

"Where is she?" Georgia yelled, crouching next to Sand. "What happened to you?" She paused. When he didn't answer she went on. "What can I do to help him?"

"Need a team of males..." Sand pushed out. He kept his eyes closed for the moment. "Need to go back..." He sucked in another breath, opening his eyes. When the dizziness stayed at bay, he sat up, moving slowly, feeling like a day-old whelp. His brother visibly relaxed, even though Shale's eyes were still filled with concern.

One of the babies cried over the monitor. "That's Gossan," Georgia looked behind her. "I'll go..." she began.

Gossan. They'd called the whelp Gossan. "Gossan, after father." He shook his head "The old man must be thrilled." He could just picture his dad. The male would be beside himself with happiness. What would he and Macy call their whelps if—*No... fuck!* He couldn't think like that right then. He needed to rescue Macy first.

"He is quite." Shale nodded, a hint of a smile on his lips. It was gone in the next instant. "You still haven't—"

"And my other nephew?" Sand asked, just as both boys began yelling over the monitor.

"Granite," Georgia said. "We named him after your brother. He stuck his neck out and gave permission for my mom—"

"What?" Sand scowled. "I thought I was your favorite, Georgie. I'm hurt."

"Stop with the bullshit!" Shale growled. "You should

lay back down. I'm calling for a healer."

"No." Sand shook his head vehemently. "Assemble a team of males. We need to rescue Macy. She is safe, but not for very long."

"Those hunters!" Shale snarled. "We can't just head off to god knows where, to—"

"It's not the hunters who have her." Sand shook his head, a deep frown marring his forehead.

Then the babies began screaming in earnest. Georgia looked wistfully at him and then got up and left to tend to her whelps.

"It's the Feral who have her," Sand blurted.

"The Feral?" Shale frowned. "Why would the Feral want to take the two of you? What could they possibly gain?"

"Let me rephrase that," Sand said. "One specific feral took us and the crazy bitch still has Macy."

"Explain," Shale pushed.

"I need water." Sand's mouth felt dry. His tongue stuck to the roof of his mouth. His lips were cracked.

Shale nodded once. He headed for the kitchen, returning with two bottles of water. Sand opened and downed one of the bottles, his hands shaking. He wanted to drink the second bottle as well but held off. "She took us because she wants young." Sand went on to tell Shale everything that had happened, touching on all the main events and sticking to the facts.

"So, everything hinges on the healer's phone. Where is it?" Shale swept his eyes over Sand's body.

"I didn't take the whole device, just the memory stick. There was less chance of being discovered that way. I also didn't want to lose it while in dragon form, so I left the stick in my jeans pocket and hid the garment back where the Feral dropped me off."

"And you definitely didn't see anything after leaving that cage?"

"She knocked me out cold. Broke my jaw." He rubbed his chin. "They are very strong. I was no match for even a female of their species. I tried to retaliate against the female but got knocked out then too. Resistance was futile."

"We need to assemble a team and head back to where you left your jeans. We need to get our hands on that memory stick."

Sand stood up; his legs felt weak, so he swayed. Shale gripped him by the arm. "You need to get stronger."

"No time, we must leave now."

"Easy! I know you are worried about Macy." He pushed out a heavy breath, looking like he was deep in thought. "Especially since she is most likely pregnant with your whelps, but we can't rush into anything. Blaze and Granite will reach out to the Feral king. I will contact Storm, perhaps he can take you, with his helicopter, to the site where you left that memory stick. You will need to take a large contingent of guards."

"Yes. That's a good idea. There is no time to waste." He wouldn't have to wait until he felt stronger if they took the chopper.

"You said that we have five days until those drugs wear out of her system. Let's face it, the chances of her not being pregnant are small. We have time."

"She is locked up in there. Frightened and alone. No!" Sand snarled. "I told her less than two days and I am sticking to my word. I will go by myself if—"

Shale gripped his shoulder. "We are going to move right now. I will brief Granite while you get cleaned up and get some food in your belly. You can leave as soon as Storm gets here. I will put in a call to the male as soon as Granite grants permission, which he *will* do. We'll get your female and we won't make you wait any longer than necessary."

Sand wanted to set the record straight about Macy not being *his* female but couldn't bring himself to do it. Not right then.

CHAPTER 24

The next day…

Did she feel any different? Were her breasts any less tender? She didn't think so. She still felt queasy at the thought of drinking milk. It was too soon for the drug to have worn out of her system. It had just been one day. That was why she felt the way she did. Maybe it wasn't that, though. Maybe there was another reason for the symptoms. Macy was driving herself nuts.

Am I pregnant?

Am I pregnant?

The same question swirled around inside her head on an endless loop. It was also the *what ifs* that were driving her mad. *What if I am pregnant? What if I'm not?*

She pulled a pillow over her head, trying to drown out the noise inside her head because there was another *what if* doing the rounds as well. *What if Sand didn't come back?*

All of the answers to her questions changed, depending on how she answered that one. What if Sand didn't come back? It made her blood run cold and her heart beat faster. It terrified her. She groaned, the noise muffled beneath the pillow.

There was a loud screeching noise that broke through the pillow. The Feral... and she sounded angry. Macy jumped out of bed. She was prepared, wearing jeans and a blouse that fit her a little too snugly. Macy wanted to be ready when Sand got there.

There was the sound of metal protesting and then a ripping noise, followed by a crash. The Feral entered, she was in her half-shifted state, reminding Macy of all those weeks ago when she'd first appeared. There was murder in her eyes.

"What's wrong? What happened?"

The other woman ignored her. She walked up to Macy, who couldn't help but backpedal. "Wait!" She put up a hand, trying to ward the other woman off.

It didn't help. Next thing she knew she was being hoisted up. There was no hugging or blindfolding. The Feral moved so quickly, her stomach lurched. For a moment, Macy thought she might vomit down the creature's back. Then the Feral jumped off the ledge. Macy screamed, feeling the creature shift and change beneath her, even though it took a split second. Her hair must have broken loose from its ponytail because it whipped about her face. The air streamed past, making her eyes water.

Macy squeezed her eyes shut but not before she saw them. They were being pursued. The Feral screeched, grinding to a halt and hovering. Macy opened her eyes. There were more of them ahead of them. They were closing in. More Feral… but wait… if she looked into the distance… dragons too. Macy sobbed in relief. She also clutched onto the Feral's scaly, clawed hands. This wasn't over yet.

The creatures began screeching at one another. The Feral's claws clasped her even tighter as she screeched back. By now the dragons were surrounding the outer band of birdlike creatures.

The Feral woman gave an almighty screech. There was anger in the sound but there was also sorrow. A plaintive screeching wail filled with hurt and anguish. Then she let Macy go. Her clawed hands opened. Hard as she tried, Macy couldn't hold on. The yellow scales were slippery. There was just no purchase.

Macy screamed as she fell, looking up at the Feral woman's belly as it seemed to get smaller and smaller.

It happened quick as a flash. One second she was freefalling and the next, she was in another clawed grasp. There were iridescent scales though. She looked up to see a dragon. They headed for the cage. Whoever had her, landed and entered the cage. There was a cracking noise as the dragon folded in on itself.

She watched in fascination, still trying to catch her breath. Still trying to get her heartrate under control.

"Hey, Mace." It was Sand, in all of his naked glory. She'd never been happier to see a person in her whole entire life. *Never.* "Sand!" she yelled, jumping up and throwing her arms around him. Hugging him as tight as she could for a good long while. Until her heartrate returned to normal.

"I told you I'd come back." He finally murmured, lifting her off her feet and twirled her around.

Macy laughed, instantly feeling safe and secure.

"Are you okay?" He put her down, still holding onto her. Then began to run his hands up and down her body.

She pulled away, keeping her hands on his shoulders. "I'm fine. I didn't get hurt at all. What happened? I take it the Feral king helped you. Or did you find some other way?"

He nodded. "Yes, he did. First, sit down." He led her to the sofa. Macy did as he said, and Sand sat down next to her.

"Tell me what happened already." Macy kept her eyes on his. She could hardly believe he was there. That they were finally free.

The Feral dropped me just outside the furthest border of our territory. I had to stash the memory stick out there. With such a long trip ahead of me, I was afraid I might lose it in my dragon form. My brother, the Earth king, Granite…"

"Oh, yeah." She made a face. "I forgot you are royalty amongst your people. Sorry, go on."

"Yeah, and there I was expecting curtseys every five minutes." He half-smiled.

"Good thing you lowered your expectations." They both laughed.

"Anyway, Granite and the dragon king, Blaze left to see the ruler of the Feral species. He had no idea about what had happened. He did not know of any females amongst his people who would do such a thing. It's a good thing we gathered evidence because Granite said that King Leukos was reluctant to believe any of it."

She gasped. "Please tell me you found the memory stick and showed it to this king. Then again," she laughed, "you must have since you're here."

He smiled. "Yes." Sand's eyes brightened. "He became angry when he saw the proof. He knew the female. Her name is Leola. She is an unmated Feral female. One of the many infertile non-human females. He had only good things to say about her and was distraught at what he saw on the video clip."

"I must say," Macy thought back to the previous day, "I thought I hated her. Leola." Macy let the name roll off her tongue. "I thought she was a terrible person. When I saw how happy she was yesterday… it… it made me feel guilty. I know it's stupid but it… it did. I realized in that moment that she does have feelings. It doesn't matter how callous and cruel she may have seemed, she is a person at the end of the day. Am I crazy for feeling that way? After everything she did, and the way she dropped me out there…" Macy shivered. "I could have been a splatter on the ground."

"Leola… it feels weird to call her that." Sand shook his head once. "She was told to drop you. If I hadn't caught you, there were many others ready to do so. You were quite safe as long as you were away from the female." His whole stance softened. "And you're not crazy to feel sorry for her. It's definitely not stupid, Mace. That's you being a good person. You care. This whole thing has got me thinking as well. What about *our* females? What about *them?* We are so busy organizing our breeding programs with the humans. All orchestrated for our males. We're so hung up on continuation of our species that we have forgotten about them. What of the unmated, infertile females longing for families? Like Leola, they are just as driven to have children of their own. It needs to be addressed across the species."

"Yes, that's it exactly." Macy nodded. "I mean, we're not excusing what she did, but something could have been done to prevent this."

"I have no idea what that something is, but yes, we need to come up with a solution."

Macy hoped it actually happened. That something was done. "What happened after Leukos was forced into believing what you had to say?"

"He acted quickly after that. Leola must have caught wind of the whole thing. I think she expected us to arrive on Feral territory, but she never expected us to convince Leukos of what was going on. I'm sure she never anticipated that we'd create that video clip. Leola got spooked and raced to you, hoping to grab you and to get away. Fortunately we had someone watching her who sounded the alarm. We all then pursued her. The rest you know." He shrugged.

"That was scary." Macy felt her eyes widen and her heart race. "What will happen to her?"

"I'm not sure. They are already on their way back to their village now. That will be for Leukos to decide."

"She needs to be punished but… I don't know… I hope she gets help more than anything."

Sand nodded. "Me too." He pushed out a breath. "There's a group of dragons waiting outside right now. We need to get ready to get going."

She nodded. "I'm almost sad to be leaving, even though I really want to get back to my life."

"It wasn't all bad in here." Sand grinned.

"No, it wasn't." She smiled back.

"Talking about your ass…" He gripped both cheeks.

"We weren't talking about my ass." She giggled.

"Then I must have been thinking about it. I've missed it." He winked at her.

They both laughed. Then, together, they seemed to realize where they were and what they were doing. Things had changed. At that moment, things shifted between them. They both sobered and moved away from one another. They were no longer caged in. No longer being forced into anything.

"What do you say we get you out of here?" Sand asked.

"That sounds great."

"As much as I'd love to take you dressed like that." He pointed at her chest. "Because, don't get me wrong… you look…" He whistled low.

Macy glanced down. She gasped. The snug blouse had popped all its buttons and was gaping open. She wore one of the sheer bras from the trunk. It was light pink with a little black bow between her breasts. There was cleavage and nipples everywhere. "Oh shit." She made a face.

Sand chuckled. "Oh yes! I think all the males might get an eyeful." She was sure she caught a gleam of something that looked like it might be jealousy. His jaw definitely tightened. It didn't mean anything though. It had just been the two of them, or mostly the two of them, for so long. They had been fuck buddies, for lack of a better term.

"I'll change." She climbed off the bed.

"Storm should be here any minute. I thought you would prefer to take the chopper. It would be more comfortable, and we have to be careful…" He glanced down at her belly. "It would be more comfortable," he repeated, then seemed to think of something. "Unless you want me to take you back, or Rock maybe?" His eyes seemed to darken. "He is here too."

She was shocked to hear him mention Stone. "I don't think so. Too much has happened." She shook her head.

He nodded once, looking relieved, but maybe that was just her hopeful imagination. "I think you should go in the helicopter. It would be better for…" he glanced at her midsection again, "for you right now." He paused. "I'm sorry things didn't work out with Stone."

"Honestly, you can stop. There was nothing between Rock and me. Please drop it already."

Sand nodded. "Okay, then you get dressed and let's get you home."

"That sounds great. Are you taking me home? As in *home* home? Back to Dalton Springs? I need to find my dog. My puppy…" She stopped when she caught the look in his eyes that told her it wasn't going to happen.

He winced and shook his head. "We can't." He shook his head. "I'm sorry, not until we know whether or not you're with child."

"But that could take a while. A test would be unreliable and—"

"There is a way to know sooner." His eyes narrowed in on hers. "We need to perform an ultrasound."

"But they don't work on… Oh… I see." She licked her lips. "If an ultrasound machine doesn't work on me, then…" She widened her eyes.

"Then that would mean you are pregnant."

"What will happen if that turns out to be the case? Would you force me to stay on dragon lands?"

Sand shook his head. "We wouldn't force you to do anything, Mace. I meant what I said while we were locked up in here. I will be there for you… for them…" He looked down at her belly. "We can make this work."

Macy had to know. "If I'm not pregnant, you'll turn around and walk away?" She couldn't keep the hurt from her voice.

Sand pushed out a breath through his nose. "Let's wait and see," he said simply.

"But if—"

"Please, Mace." He pleaded with his eyes, scrubbing a hand over his face. "We have ordered an ultrasound machine. It will arrive by lunch-time tomorrow. My brother's mate, Louise, is a doctor, she will perform the ultrasound on you. It is all organized. Let's get back. Let's get you comfortable for the night and we'll find out what's going on tomorrow. We will plan further then."

Sand didn't want to commit if he didn't have to, and he'd brought up Stone. Tried to pawn her off on the guy. It told her everything she needed to know about their relationship. There was still this crazy part of her that didn't care. Macy had fallen for this shifter. She had fallen big time. That crazy part wanted him, no matter what. Thankfully, most of her was guided by logic. It was going to be tough to walk away, particularly if she was pregnant, but she would do it. She had to. Macy wouldn't stand in his way when it came to being a father and being there for the kids, but there was no 'them.' There was no relationship. Even after all they had been through, he still didn't see her in that way. Macy headed to the bathroom to change. She needed to wash her face with cold water and try to pull herself together.

CHAPTER 25

The next day...

Macy sipped her tea. She had a mug in one hand and a baby in the other. The little guy was sleeping soundly.

Georgia held out her arms. "Let me take him so that you can drink your tea in—"

"Don't you dare." Macy widened her eyes at her friend. "I'm loving my cuddle time."

Georgia bit down on her bottom lip for a few seconds. "I can't believe you might have a couple of your own in six months. Less than six months."

"Let's not even go there." Macy shook her head.

"Sand is a really great guy. He comes across as all macho, but I think he's just a big softy. I told you what he did to help get Shale and me together?"

Macy nodded. "Yes, you did." She forced a smile,

putting her mug down so that she could reposition the baby in her arms. They were both so perfect. Little bow mouths. Sand's... make that *Shale's* eyes. Georgia's red hair. Cuteness overload.

"He pretended to be interested in me and flirted with me. It drove Shale nuts. It worked, in the end, to get his head out of his own ass. Although, my head was up my own ass as well." She rolled her eyes. Georgia laughed softly.

Macy smiled. "You certainly can't blame all your earlier issues on poor Shale."

"Yep," her friend gripped her mug in both hands. "It takes two. It's the same with you guys."

"I know that," Macy interjected. "I know that only too well. I have feelings for Sand. I'll admit it, but it doesn't matter."

"What do you mean? Of course it matters." Macy shook her head. She briefly explained what had happened the day before. About how Sand had placed himself firmly in no man's land. Georgia looked like she was thinking it through, she asked a question every now and then.

"I haven't seen him since he brought me here yesterday." Macy took a big sip of her tea, trying to swallow down her hurt.

"He's hiding from you, from the situation. Maybe he's trying to figure things out?"

"Maybe, but I know where I stand on this. I also know that if he truly cared about me and truly wanted to be with me, he would have said something yesterday. He would have at least checked in since we arrived here. I might be pregnant with his children." She sniffed, her eyes stung, and she felt emotional. There was a huge lump in her throat.

"I'm sorry." Georgia moved to sit next to her. "Guys can be so stupid. They're not like us. They don't always know what they're feeling. They run and bury their heads sometimes. They're bad at dealing with emotions. I'm sure he has feelings for you."

"Feelings," she snorted. "He enjoys having sex with me. I think he enjoys my company, but I don't think there's more. Not out here." She looked around them. "Everything has changed. We're not the same people anymore. Not the same people who were initially locked in that cage, and not the same people as the ones who were forced into staying in there. Forced to be together. What if I'm pregnant?" Her voice hitched, and a tear escaped.

"It will work out." Georgia squeezed her shoulder. "You'll see. Even when you think it can't possibly… it will. Look at what happened with me."

"You were lucky." More tears leaked out, rolling down her cheeks. "That kind of thing doesn't happen often. You found your person after a night together." Macy smiled. "I'm so happy for you, but stuff like that doesn't happen in real life. That's why it's so darned special."

"You know you have me, right? You have Shale and me, we're right here for you. I know how it feels. I was alone for my entire pregnancy. Sand will be there, maybe not in the way that you want him to be, but he *will* be there."

"You're right." Macy sniffed, working hard to pull herself together. "I need to stop crying." She wiped at her face. "You said that Sand was coming to fetch me. He'll be here soon to take me for that ultrasound."

"You have every right to be emotional. To be scared

and to feel out of sorts. No one will look at you strangely for crying. Do you want me to go with you? I can…" Just then, Gossan gave a yell over the monitor. Someone knocked on the door.

"I think you might have your hands full." Macy smiled.

"Let me take him," Georgia said. "You get the door, if you don't mind. It's probably Sand."

Macy handed little Granite over to her friend. "That would make him ten minutes early," she said, glancing at her watch, feeling sick to her stomach.

Time was a weird thing. On the one hand, it felt like it had flown since arriving there the day before. On the other, it felt like it had dragged on endlessly. She desperately wanted to know what the outcome was going to be, but at the same time, she didn't want to face up to whatever the result was.

"Exactly. That means I have ten minutes to pack a bag and to settle Gossan." The little one yelled again, louder this time. There was another knock at the door. It was like baby and man were in sync or something.

"I'll be fine." Macy plastered a smile on her face and headed to the door. She didn't want Georgia offering any more support or making any type of kind gesture, in case the waterworks turned back on.

"Hey." Sand smiled at her as soon as she opened the door, but it looked forced. It probably matched the smile on her own face. "How are you feeling, Mace?" He leaned forward and hugged her.

She put her arms around him for a second. It felt stilted and awkward. "I'm good," Macy said as she pulled away.

"Did you sleep okay?"

"Fine, thanks." That wasn't true. Macy had hardly slept

at all, but this felt like polite chatter. Everything was always fine and great when a person made polite small-talk. Next, they'd be talking about the weather.

"You ready to go?" he asked, looking over her shoulder into the apartment.

"Come in for a sec." She stood to the side so that he could enter. "I just want to say goodbye to Georgia. We still have a few minutes."

Sand walked inside, looking around. "Where is my gorgeous sister-in-law?" He smiled, it looked genuine for the first time since he'd arrived.

"Here I am." Georgia walked out of the nursery. She was carrying Gossan. "He messed his diaper. Must have happened soon after I put him down. I need to get him back to sleep ASAP or their routine will go to hell in a handbasket." She looked a bit frazzled.

"Shale will be here soon," Sand offered. "Do you need me to help you with anything right now?"

Georgia smiled and shook her head. "Not unless you have a milk-filled breast."

He held up his hands. "Can't help you there, I'm afraid."

Georgia giggled.

"I'll manage. You guys go on, I'm sure you're both eager to find out." She looked at Macy. "Come straight back here, please. I want to know."

Macy swallowed thickly and nodded. "Okay."

Gossan wriggled in her arms, kicking his little legs.

"Please excuse me." She looked down at the baby in her arms. "My son needs me."

Macy felt her chest tighten. That could be her in the not too distant future. She forced another smile. "We'll see you in a little while then."

Her friend clasped her hand before she could turn away. "I'm thinking of you."

"I know. Thanks." Macy quickly headed out before her eyes could start prickling. Before her throat clogged up again.

They walked in silence for a few moments. She followed Sand, who glanced her way. "Are you warm enough in that thin sweater?"

She nodded. "I'm fine."

"It's rainy and the temperature has dropped some."

There it was… talk of the weather. That hadn't taken long at all. She realized that she had her arms tightly folded, so it probably seemed like she was cold. Macy forced herself to relax, or at least to make it seem like she was calm. "I'm perfectly fine. This top has long sleeves and I'm in closed shoes." She wore sneakers.

"I must say," he grinned, "I miss running around in boxers."

"Or naked."

"Yep, there were some upsides to our… situation. I enjoyed seeing you in those negligées."

He missed her ass.

He missed seeing her in a negligée.

They were all sexual reasons. None of them held any weight whatsoever. Hearing him say it hurt her, but Macy didn't say anything. There was no point.

"Are you okay, Mace?" His eyes were filled with concern.

She nodded. "I'm just nervous. I can't help thinking that I should have taken those pills." Even though she said it, she knew she wouldn't have been able to, regardless of what would have been the logical thing to do.

"No, you shouldn't have. You made the right decision. *We* made the right decision." He said it with conviction.

"Look, you said yourself you didn't want to discuss it until we knew the outcome of this ultrasound. Let's stick to that, unless, of course, anything has changed. Unless you have something to say to me before we go in there."

Panic. It rose up in him. She could see it in the way his whole body tensed up. She could mostly see it in his eyes, how they flashed from her to the ceiling and then back to her. Slightly wild. Sand was definitely in the middle of a panic attack. One which he couldn't show. His throat worked more than once as well. She almost felt sorry for him.

"Look, don't worry about it." She sounded a bit defeated but at least she wasn't crying. Macy wanted to cry right then, she wanted it so badly. Instead, she pulled her shoulders back. She could do this. She was strong.

Sand calmed right down as soon as the pressure was off. She wanted to hate him for it, but she couldn't. Thankfully, they arrived at their destination just then.

Sand knocked once on the door, even though it was slightly ajar.

"Come on in!" a woman yelled.

Sand pushed on the door and gestured for her to go in first. He put his hand on the small of her back. His touch both soothing and rattling. It was so confusing.

"Hello and welcome." The woman who greeted them was not at all what she expected. This was the queen of the Earth dragons. She was also tiny, with a head of curly red hair. Her smile was wide and her whole demeanor was warm and welcoming. "I'm Louise. I'm Granite's mate. It's so good to meet you."

Macy introduced herself and they shook hands. Then Louise and Sand hugged. They made small-talk about Granite and the kids and the weather, of course.

Macy struggled to pay attention. She was too nervous. She actually felt nauseous but that could also be from the hormones which would still be in her body. Could also be because she was—*Not going there!*

Louise touched her on the side of her arm. She realized that Sand and the doctor were looking at her. "Sorry, what was that?"

"I said that we should probably do the procedure. I'm sure you are both eager to hear the results. Or in this case, to see them."

"You are right, Doctor." She nodded.

The other woman laughed, her eyes were a beautiful, bright green. They twinkled. "No need to be so formal. Please call me Louise."

She nodded once. "Sorry, I guess I'm a bit nervous."

Louise handed her a gown. "You can go into the bathroom over there to change. Take off all your clothing from below the waist. We are going to do a transvaginal scan. We most likely won't be able to see anything, but just in case we can, I want to be a hundred percent sure that you're not pregnant."

"Okay." She took the garment and headed for the bathroom. Macy changed quickly. Her heart raced and her palms felt sweaty.

Sand smiled as she reentered the room. He also looked tense and even slightly pale. "You okay?" he asked.

She nodded, not trusting her voice.

"You can lie down on this bed." Louise gestured to what looked like a hospital bed.

Macy did as Louise said. The doctor pulled on some rubber gloves and held up an instrument that was attached to the ultrasound machine. "This is a transducer or wand." It looked like a thin dildo. It was even covered in a condom. "I need to insert this into your vagina."

Sand cleared his throat, looking distinctly uncomfortable. He stood by her legs on the other side of the bed. He shifted his weight and then moved to the head of the bed, his eyes on the black screen.

"It won't hurt," Louise continued, squirting some KY Gel onto the wand. "But it might be a bit uncomfortable."

"Okay, that's fine."

Louise moved a little down the bed, she laid a thin blanket over her lap. "You can bend your knees, placing your feet on the bed and then open your legs a little for me."

Macy did as she said, trying to clear her head.

"That's it." Louise was really sweet. "I'm going to insert the transducer now, if that's okay?"

Macy nodded. "That's fine." She pushed out a breath. The wand thingy was colder than she expected.

A picture immediately popped up on the screen. She couldn't really make out what everything was, but it was clear that they were looking inside her.

"Is that Macy's womb?" Sand's voice was deep and gravelly.

"Yes, it is."

"Does that mean…?" He sounded gruff.

Louise had her eyes trained on the screen, she seemed to be concentrating. "I just need to be sure, but I don't think you're pregnant."

Macy's heart sank. It didn't just sink, it plummeted. Like a rock into the ocean. A deep dark ocean at that.

Louise moved the wand a few times. "You're definitely not pregnant, I'm sorry." She glanced first at her and then Sand.

"I'm sorry, Mace." Sand squeezed her shoulder.

"No," Macy shrugged, "it's no biggie… it's fine…" *Shit!* Although she sounded upbeat, she realized she was crying.

"Oh fu…! Shit, Mace… I'm so sorry. I know you wanted this."

She did.

He didn't.

"I said it's fine." She wiped her face. "It's not a big deal at all. It's better this way. Much better. It's just been very emotional. That's all! I'm tired as well. I haven't slept well for the last few days."

"Okay." He let her shoulder go. "I'm here to talk. You can stay as long as you want and—"

"I'm leaving today," she blurted, wiping her eyes.

"Mace, you don't have to, we—"

"I want to." She swiped another tear as it hit her cheek. "These hormones are a nightmare. Hopefully, they'll be out of my system soon." She realized that Louise was still looking at her uterus. That she was still looking at the screen with intense concentration, a frown on her face. "Is everything okay doc… Louise."

The redhead smiled and look up at her. "All good. It's nothing to be concerned about but I'm pretty sure you have endometriosis."

"What's that?" Sand barked. "Is it bad? Is it—"

"There's nothing to be concerned about," Louise repeated. "It would need to be confirmed with an MRI but I'm ninety-five percent sure that you have it. You should have become pregnant by Sand. Non-humans and shifters have a particularly high pregnancy success rate. This will have been higher after taking fertility drugs."

"What is en-do-metri…?" He was frowning heavily.

"Very simply put, endometriosis is when the lining of the womb grows outside of the womb as well. It normally ends up covering other parts of the reproductive organs like the ovaries – where the eggs are produced – and the fallopian tubes, which are the pathway for the egg to get to the womb. These areas become inflamed and even damaged."

"How do you know I have it?" Macy asked.

"You have quite a few cysts on your ovaries and there are dark spots on both your fallopian tubes which, in my opinion, could be lesions associated with the condition. Do you have quite bad pain during your menstrual cycle?"

"Yes," both she and Sand answered.

"Sorry." Sand looked sheepish. "Go on."

"Yes, as Sand would know." She gave him a smile.

"It is treatable, and, with intervention, you should be able to get pregnant in the future." She spoke to both of them. "I suggest you go and visit your gynecologist." She removed the wand. "All done. You can get dressed now."

"I will doc… Louise. Thank you." She bit down on her lip to keep from crying any more.

CHAPTER 26

Later that day…

A breeze ruffled his hair. "I mean it," he folded his arms across his chest, "you really don't have to go just yet. Take a few days to… to decompress after what happened. Your best friend is here, I'm sure you want to spend time with her."

"I really need to get back to my own life. I've been gone for weeks with no explanation. I'm probably going to lose my job. My parents and my brother will be out of their minds with worry. Then there's Scout."

"Your puppy." He gave a half-smile.

She rolled her eyes. "Yeah, my puppy. I need to find out who has him. Hopefully, he wasn't taken to the pound and adopted out. I'd be devastated. I'm sure he misses me."

"I'll miss you as well." His eyes bore into hers.

Tell me to stay then.

Sand stepped forward and gripped her hips. His touch felt so right. "Is there nothing I can say to change your mind about going?"

There were so many things, but since he wasn't going to say them, she shook her head. "I'm afraid not. The time has come to go our separate ways, it would seem." As much as she wanted things to be different.

"I can't believe this is it, Mace." His hands gripped her tighter. "After everything. This is it."

It doesn't have to be. She tried to tell him that with her eyes.

Then he leaned in, his gaze locked onto her mouth. One of his hands slid around her back to pull her in.

"Um…" She turned her head a little to the side. "That's not a good idea, Sand. We should have stuck to our rules a whole lot more."

"That's just it, we didn't, so what's one more—"

"No, I'm going to have to insist. Those rules were in place for a reason and we were stupid to have ignored them. I was stupid." She reached up and hugged him tightly, like she would a close friend. Wishing for so much more, which tossed the friendship thing out the window. Macy swallowed thickly. "I will miss you too," she whispered.

Sand hugged her back just as tightly. He buried his head into her shoulder. On some crazy level, maybe he *did* feel something for her, just obviously not enough to try to get her to stay for the right reasons. "I'm sorry this all happened. That things had to end this way."

"Not your fault," she said as she pulled away. "Thank you for saving me."

"Anytime, Mace, and I mean that. I would drop everything." His eyes told her that he meant it. That it wasn't just hot air.

Tell me to stay then.

She nodded. "Duly noted." She pushed out a laugh. "Okay, then. Take care of yourself."

"You too. Oh and," he frowned. "Go and see a doctor. I'm sure you'll be just fine, but do it anyway just to be sure."

"I will be fine, but I do plan to go and see one." She shrugged. "You heard Louise. It is treatable. I'm not too worried." That wasn't entirely true. She'd googled the condition and wished she hadn't. The chances of her conceiving without intervention weren't great. Only half of women suffering from endometriosis went on to become pregnant. Half. Terrible odds, in her opinion. She pushed that thought out of her head right then. It wasn't like she was trying for a baby. She needed a partner for that. A husband. A lover. A friend. She needed Sand. Macy wanted to get angry with him for pushing her away. For throwing away what they had. He could deny it all he wanted, but they definitely had something. Something special. She couldn't bring herself to get mad, he *had* warned her. He'd been honest with her every step of the way. He'd never bullshitted or sugarcoated. Somehow, she'd believed that he would open his mouth when the time came. That he would somehow realize what was right in front of him and yet... *crickets.* She got nothing.

"I guess it's goodbye then," Sand said.

It didn't have to be. He could beg her to stay... with him.

It didn't happen. She nodded, not trusting her voice.

"I'm going to kiss you—"

She sucked in a breath, preparing to argue.

"On the cheek," he blurted. "On the cheek, Mace." He leaned in and kissed her, his lips lingering for a moment.

Then she turned and walked away. Not looking back was the hardest thing she had ever done, especially when she could feel him watching.

"We need to get one of those." Granite stood next to him, they both stared at the chopper as it disappeared over the horizon. "It looks like it would come in handy. Maybe Storm could teach you or Stone how to fly."

"Sounds like a plan."

His brother gave him a man-hug. It lasted all of a second. "Are you okay? You don't look okay."

"I'm fine. Keen to get back to work." He clapped his hands together.

"Are you sure you made the right decision?"

"What do you mean?" He frowned. Granite was referring to Macy. "It was her decision to leave. I tried to talk her into staying for a while, but she didn't want to."

"From what I heard, you've been keeping her at arm's length."

"Not true!" Sand shook his head. "I've given her some space. She's had enough of my ugly mug." Sand choked out a laugh that didn't hold much humor.

"You could have been a father. How do you feel about that?"

Sand shrugged. "I feel like I dodged a bullet."

"But you *sound* like you're about to go to a funeral. You don't look happy at all. I'll ask you again, was letting Macy go the right decision?"

"I'm not ready to settle down, so, yes, it was." Sand folded his arms.

"Why do you look so cut up over it?" Granite asked, not letting up. Why was his older brother coming at him like this?

"I happened to like Macy. I enjoy her company. I wish she would have stayed a bit longer… that's all."

"*Is* that all?"

"Yes," he growled, getting irritated. "That's all. End of story. Why are you giving me such shit about it?"

"Because I think you have real feelings for this female. I think you are refusing, for whatever reason, to face up to them."

"I just told you that I like her. That I like being with her, so, I guess you're right about me having feelings for her. I'll admit it."

Granite narrowed his eyes at him. "Real feelings, Sand. I think you might love this female."

Sand pushed out another laugh. "That's ridiculous. I don't… love…" he whispered the word, "Macy. It's not like that between us. She left, didn't she?" Granite had no idea what he was talking about.

"I had a chat with Louise, and we think that Macy is in love with your sorry ass. Personally, I'm not sure I get what she sees in you," he slipped in some sibling ribbing designed to try and make him feel better. It didn't work. "I'm pretty sure she left because you won't admit to your feelings for her."

"Macy doesn't… she… Okay, maybe she *did* develop feelings for me, but I wouldn't go so far as to use the L-word here. Humans don't fall that quickly."

"They do when they meet the right person. When they

meet *their* person. I think Macy is *your* person. Forgive me for overstepping the boundaries here, but I think you guys are perfect together. You should go after her before it's too late. Before you fuck things up even more than you have already."

"You're right." Sand clenched his jaw for a moment or two. "You *are* overstepping the boundaries. You have no idea about Macy and me. You hardly even saw her."

"I saw enough, Louise filled me in on a couple of things and I know you, Sand. You've changed."

"I was locked in a cage and forced to breed. Of course I've changed," he all but snarled, feeling as prickly as fuck.

"It's more than that, and you're tougher than to let something like that get you down." Granite's voice grew agitated. "You've changed for different reasons. You—"

"I feel like I lost my whelps," Sand blurted. The admission was a shock to him. "It's the stupidest damned thing. Macy wasn't even pregnant and yet I feel like I lost them." His voice hitched. "I feel like I lost—" Sand stopped there. He wasn't sure what he had been about to say but it was a path he needed to stay clear of.

His brother's whole demeanor softened. He put an arm around Sand and pulled him into a man-hug again. "I'm sorry this happened, Sand. You need to know that you *did* lose. You lost big time. I don't want you losing any more than you have to. My advice would be to fix it before it's too late. Get on your knees if you have to but win her back." He tapped Sand on the side of the arm and left.

Work.

It was getting late, but he was going to get started. All he needed was something else to focus on. Macy was gone and it was better that way.

CHAPTER 27

Four days later…

H er mother stirred her coffee even though she didn't take sugar. "You are lucky, Macy. Very lucky, my girl," her mom said for the eighth time since Macy had arrived ten minutes earlier.

"I know, mom." She added sugar to her cappuccino and stirred as well.

"I still can't believe they kept you on. And I still can't believe you won't tell me where you were." Her voice became animated.

"Let's leave it alone. I don't want to talk about it. Sit boy." She pushed on Scout's rear, trying to get him to sit back down. "I'll take you for a walk in a minute."

"I don't know why you insisted on bringing that—"

"Scout is my dog." Macy used a warning tone. "He missed me like crazy. He cries now when I try to leave him."

"It's not healthy for a dog to be so attached to a human." Her mother looked down at Scout, scrunching her nose and shaking her head.

"Please, mom, can we just have a nice cup of coffee and maybe a pastry? Can we not argue?"

"Of course, darling, although I don't know if you should be having the pastry, dear, your BMI is—"

"I don't give a shit about my BMI! If you can't be nice about my waistline and my dog, then I'm leaving." She pushed her chair back and Scout jumped to his feet, tongue lolling.

Her mom's eyes got panic-stricken. Macy knew she meant well but it sometimes hurt her when she acted this way. "No, please don't. I'm sorry." Her whole demeanor changed. "I didn't mean to… to…"

"Hurt me?"

Her mom's face dropped. "No, Macy. I'm sorry. It is never my intention to hurt you. I only want the best for you."

Funny, she knew it was true, but she wished her mom would find some other way to show her love. "Okay, we'll stay, but only if you're nice." She pushed on Scout's butt until he sat back down, looking disappointed. "We'll go soon." She petted his neck and he tried to mouth her.

"Good, because…" Her mother's expression grew sheepish.

"What?" she asked, not liking where this was going. "What have you done, mom?"

Her mother scrunched her face up. "Don't get mad."

"Mom! Tell me already." Scout whined, sensing the tension.

"Okay, but you can't get mad. I love you very much. That's where this is coming from. All of it."

"Who is he?" Macy huffed, still petting her dog.

"He's gorgeous, Macy, and really sweet." Her mom's eyes glinted.

Macy clapped a hand over her face. "No… please tell me you didn't."

"He's tall and did I mention gorgeous? I can't remember what he does for a living, but he does have a decent job. He drove a really nice car. And he was so cute and polite too," her mother gushed.

Macy kept her face planted in her hand for a few seconds longer. "Why, mom?" she spoke into her hand, her voice muffled. "Why do you keep doing this?"

"I hate seeing you alone," her mom said, sounding concerned. "I love you, Macy. I want you to be happy."

"I know you do, and I know you're just trying to help, but you have to stop doing this. You really have to stop already. I don't want you to set me up. How long do I have to make a getaway? When is he getting here?"

"Too late," his voice was deep and resonating. It was a voice she knew well. *No! No way! It couldn't be.*

Her eyes flashed to his. A beautiful golden, honey color she had drowned in many times. He smiled and they crinkled at the edges. "Too late to run away," he added, winking at her.

It had only been four days and yet she had forgotten how gorgeous he was. He could be wearing anything and still look good, but he'd chosen a white t-shirt and a pair of blue jeans. *Not fair!* She'd also forgotten how devastating his smile was. Right then, it was aimed at her.

Her mother laughed. "I'm so glad you came. Macy, you

must meet—"

"Sand?" Her voice was filled with shock and confusion. "What are you doing here?" She stood up.

"Wait a minute…" Her mother sounded just as confused. "You two know each other?" She stood up as well.

"I'm sorry I stalked you, Mrs. Stevenson," Sand began.

"Rhonda." Her mother flapped a hand. "You can call me Rhonda. How do the two of you know each other?" She frowned.

Sand narrowed his eyes. "You didn't tell your mother about our—?"

"Of course not!" Macy widened her eyes, trying to shut him up.

Her mother's frown deepened. "Wait a minute," she gasped. "Those weeks you were away. You met Sand then, didn't you?" Her eyes widened.

"She sure did." Sand folded his arms. Was it her imagination or did his chest look even better covered in a cotton shirt?

At that point, Scout got sick of being ignored. He'd been lolling his tongue and wagging his tail excitedly for a full minute and no one had acknowledged him. He jumped up, paws landing on Sand's chest. "Oh!" He grinned. "You must be…" Then he frowned. "Is this your *puppy?*" He made a face.

Macy couldn't help smiling. "Yep. Sand meet Scout." Her dog licked Sand's hand as he petted him. "You should get down, boy," Macy tried but Scout stayed right where he was.

"This," Sand rubbed Scout's fur, "is your cute little doggykins? Your 'pup,' I believe you called him on plenty of occasions? This is him?"

"Yes. He is still technically a puppy. He isn't even a year old yet."

"He's huge, and not at all what I expected." Sand rubbed on Scout's neck and her dog lapped it up. It seemed the guy had good hands, even when it came to dog-petting. "I mean that in a good way. He's gorgeous." There was more stroking of fur. "I was expecting a little… lap dog."

She laughed. "I think he's cute too."

"Are either of you going to tell me how you met and why you stalked me?" A voice interrupted their exchange.

"I think that's obvious, Mrs. Stevenson. I'm here to save your daughter," Sand said.

"Save her from what?" Her mom frowned.

"I need to save her from y—"

"Um… mom, can we finish our coffee date some other time?"

"What? You're not going to tell me?" Her mom raised her brows. "I'm curious to know about what the heck is going on."

"I will tell you, just not right now. Sand and I need to talk. We're going to take Scout for a walk."

Her puppy finally jumped off of Sand's chest and bounced around them, tugging on the lead. "Okay, boy." She tried to calm him.

"Here," Sand held out his hand, "allow me."

She handed the lead to him and Scout seemed to settle just a little. They said their goodbyes to her mom, dodging questions all the while, and headed for the park. They walked for a few minutes in silence. Scout sniffed everything between bouts of bounces. He'd bounce and then sniff and then bounce some more. "He's a great dog. No wonder you couldn't stop talking about him."

"What are you doing here?" she asked, getting to the point. "We shouldn't see one another anymore. In fact, we should probably add that to the list of rules."

"Screw the rules." He stopped walking, or maybe she did. Macy couldn't be sure. They were also already in the park. When had that happened?

"You can't say that," Macy said. Scout seemed to sense that something was brewing because he sat down and was quiet for a change.

"I can, Mace. I hate those rules. I hate that you left—"

"Stop right there. I'm not entering into some casual thing with you. I can't be your fuck buddy anymore. In fact, I wish that whole thing had never happened." She shook her head.

"I'm glad it happened because I met you, Mace." He stepped forward. "Because I found out that I want things I never knew I wanted. They're important things. They're things that matter."

"What things?" she asked.

"I want love and a committed relationship. I want to be a father and I want those things with *you*." His eyes pierced right into her.

Oh shit! She pushed out a breath, feeling overwhelmed right then. "Where did this come from?" She frowned.

"I was lying to myself. I lied while we were together. I lied when we got out. I lied when you left. I managed to hold onto the lie for a day or two, but then…" He shrugged. "I just couldn't do it anymore. I love you, Macy. I love everything about you. Your smile, how sweet you are, I love the way you snore… yeah, you heard right," he chuckled. "Not just when you're on your heat. I love it all the damn time. It's as cute as hell. I love you… all of you. I'm not sure how it happened, or when it happened, only that it did. I would be the biggest idiot on earth if I let you slip away. If I let what we have go."

Part of her felt such joy. Such happiness… but the other part, that logical part, had to suppress those emotions. "It was those damned rules." She tried to smile but her lip wobbled. "I told you we should have followed them more closely. This would never have happened if we had."

"They're a bunch of bullshit and you know it." He took a step towards her, taking her hand, but she pulled away.

"I might never be able to have kids." Her eyes filled with tears. "I went to see a doctor yesterday. Louise was right. I have endometriosis. My MRI is booked for next week. It's bad though, Sand." A tear rolled down her cheek. Hot and wet. "If you want kids then I'm not the right person for you. I might not be able to have any."

"I want you, Macy. I love you." He put his arms around her. "You need to understand that. I want kids… but only with *you*. If it doesn't happen…" He shrugged.

She sobbed and put a hand over her face. Tears coursed down her cheeks. She hadn't told anyone about her prognosis.

"We'll figure it out." He hugged her tight. "We'll tackle it as a team." He kissed the top of her head. "Fuck, Mace… I'll do anything. What do you want me to do? Just say it."

"Hold me," she sobbed into his chest. His arms felt good, reassuring. He felt right. *They* felt right. She finally lifted her head. "Do you really love me?"

"Yes." He was smiling.

"And you're sure my fertility issues won't get in the way of…?"

"No," his voice was choked up. "I know you want whelps and I'll do anything to make that happen, but if it doesn't, we'll be okay. We'll have each other. We can see the best doctors and we can try really, really hard."

She laughed. "You like the thought of all that trying."

"I do! I'm not going to lie." He shook his head, a gorgeous smile on his lips.

She laughed some more.

"Can I kiss you yet?" He cupped her face. "On the mouth, that is. I never want to kiss your cheek ever again. Unless we're talking butt cheek… then I'm okay with it."

She laughed. "I love you too, by the way."

"I know." He pressed a kiss to her lips. "I've known for a while. I'm sorry I acted like such a dick. I don't know why it took me so long to figure things out. I won't fuck up like that again, I swear."

"Sand…"

"Yes?"

"Kiss me already." He leaned in and covered her lips with his. Soft, gentle… so… wet? Scout had decided to join in on the action.

They broke away, laughing. Sand sobered up. "I want to mate you soon, Mace. I hope you're game. We've waited long enough."

She rolled her eyes. "Is that your idea of a proposal?"

He got a shocked look. "Oh, shit." Sand dropped to one knee. "What I meant to say was…" Scout bounced around him. "I love you so damned much and will you mate me? Fuck!" His expression morphed into panic. "I don't have a ring. I'm winging it here!"

"Get up," she laughed. "I was joking. Yes! My answer is yes! That was as from the heart as it gets."

"Good." His eyes lit up. "Let's go to Vegas. What do you say, boy?" Scout bounced up and down, trying to nip at Sand's arm. "Do you want to go to Vegas?" There was more jumping, this time there was whining as well. "He agrees." Sand grinned.

Macy laughed. "I'm afraid that my mom would kill me. It's going to have to be a white wedding with all of the family."

"Anything for you!" He turned serious. "And I mean that." He planted a kiss on her mouth.

CHAPTER 28

Stone felt uncomfortable as he looked around the table. The female across from him glared. Her eyes were hard and cold. They were a bright yellow color. Strange as hell and yet… interesting. Pity she wanted to kill him. Or to tear off his balls. Or both. Hopefully, she'd kill him first. Save him some unnecessary pain.

Thing was, she was a Feral female. She was strong enough to be able to do whatever the hell she wanted to him. He was a sick fuck because other things instantly came to mind. His eyes moved down to her chest. The Feral wore a tight tank top. She had nice-looking, perky tits with the plumpest nipples Stone had ever seen. He lifted his gaze back to hers, not lingering.

"Um…" He turned his body slightly, and even though he spoke to Topaz, he didn't take his eyes off the Feral while he did so. She continued to stare daggers at him. Eyes narrowed. Jaw tight. Frown evident. "I thought the brief said a male and a female from each species. Why am I the only male in attendance?"

The female across from him snorted. "The brief recommended that a male and a female attend." She scrunched up her face, looking both irritated and confused. "The word 'recommended' is key here. Who would send a male? What would a male know about issues concerning females? You should not be here." Her eyes sliced into him. Or, at least it felt that way.

Stone had to fight not to squirm in his seat, or to run the fuck away. This female didn't want him here.

"Our king was the one who made the call," Topaz put forward. "Stone was ordered to attend, as was I. The male is eager to contribute to our discussions surrounding—"

"Then your king is a fool," she spat, eyes glowing like amber in a flame.

"Do not—" Topaz began, clearly angered at the Feral's harsh words against their Blaze.

Stone touched her arm, it wouldn't do them any favors to start an argument before this conference even started. "I am already here," Stone was sure to keep his voice even, "so, I would appreciate it if we could make the most of it. I assure you I will take my role very seriously."

The Feral snorted. "We are here to discuss the predicament of infertile, non-human females. You are neither of those. In fact, why aren't you with a human right now? Making young? You have absolutely no idea what it is like to—"

"Come now, Cordia. The dragon sounds like he has genuine concern for our plight. He has been tasked with attending, as have we. Let's not—"

"I don't like it." Cordia pushed her dark hair back off

her shoulder, her mouth set. "Maybe we should take a vote. Your king can send a female in your place when everyone votes for you to leave. Someone sympathetic to what we are going through. That person is not you." She widened her eyes.

"Stop right there! You have no idea—" Topaz began.

"Leave it," Stone urged the dragon next to him. "It's not worth it," he added.

"You said we should vote," a female from down the other end of the table piped up. "I vote that the dragon stays." She smiled at Stone, giving him a wink. By her scent, he could tell that she was a vampire.

"I agree," the wolf shifter sitting next to the Ferals said, licking her lips. "Let him stay. The rest of us are all are infertile females. One male will help us see things from another angle."

The Feral rolled her eyes so hard that Stone wasn't sure that they would even come back from the other side of her skull. "You are only saying that because the male is attractive. He has pretty eyes and a decent-sized prick. You're hoping for a rut and want to get on his good side. I saw the way all of you looked at him when he came into the room. This is serious."

"You looked at my dick?" Stone had to hold back a laugh.

The Feral made a face. "Not on purpose. Your midsection is at exactly eye level. I was already sitting here when you came in. You are wearing those thin cotton pants." She shrugged. "It was hard to miss. I assure you, I wasn't looking." She snorted.

Topaz giggled.

Just then, another vampire female walked in. She wore

a navy dress suit with a white blouse. She was holding a glass bowl with folded pieces of paper inside. "Morning!" She smiled warmly. "I am Gazelle. I have been tasked with coordinating our conference over the next few days. We have a couple of interesting topics up for discussion. I thought it would be a good idea if the species were split up. I want each of us out of our comfort zones and learning about one another, while we figure out a way forward for all females," she cleared her throat, "like ourselves." Sand noticed she avoided looking at him as she spoke. He glanced at the Feral, who was glaring at him like he had been the one to personally rip out her womb and stomp on it.

He looked back at the vampire.

"Here," Gazelle put the glass bowl on the table, "I want each of you on this side of the table to take one piece of folded up paper. Do not open it yet!" The bowl began making its way down to him. Each one of them removed a slip. Stone did too, placing the empty bowl on the table in front of him.

He held onto the paper, a bad feeling slowly making its way into his bones.

"On three, you can open up and see who your partner will be for the duration of the conference. You will work closely with this person. I am sure that together, we can find a way forward. You may open your papers now and then we will take a one-hour recess so that you can get to know your partner better." She smiled broadly, sucking in a deep breath before counting down. "Three. You may open the paper now."

Sand held onto the paper for a few more seconds before finally opening it.

Cordia. Feral Species.

How had he known that this was coming? His heart fucking sank. This was going to be a long-ass couple of days. He was about to be partnered with a female who not only hated his guts but could use them for garters if she felt like it.

"Go and enjoy some light refreshments," the vampire added. "Make sure you go somewhere private with your partner. I want you to fully understand one another, as a species, by the time this conference is over."

"Why the need for the whole team-building thing?" he had to ask.

"We all share a common problem," Gazelle said. "However, it is far more complex than that and aspects may differ between the species. Who knows? Maybe one species can help another. Knowledge is always power. We will never know unless we share. Our kings would also like for this to be an opportunity where we improve our interspecies relationships. Take it as a chance to learn and to grow. You hour has started." She looked at the watch on her wrist.

There was loud chatter and chairs scraped as new pairs began to leave. Everyone left, including Gazelle. Eventually, it was only the two of them remaining. Still sitting there across from one another. "I do not wish to improve interspecies relationships." Cordia shook her head. "I don't like you."

"How do you even know that? You don't know me."

"You're a non-human and a male. Both reasons enough."

"Bullshit," Stone threw back.

Cordia raised her brows. "Dragon, vampire, Feral,

shifter or elf. You are all the same."

"What?" he snorted. "I've never heard such shit in all my life."

"You looked at my breasts… sized me up when you first arrived. You pictured rutting me at least once in the short time we have been in the same room. In short, you reduced me to an object before you knew anything about me. If I offered to rut you right now, you would jump at the opportunity."

"Are you offering?" He folded his hands on the table.

She rolled her eyes, before narrowing them on him. "You wouldn't last even one round." One side of her full mouth lifted in what may have been the start of a smile. "I would hurt you."

Stone snorted. "Like hell you would."

"Then again," she raised her brows, "if you were hurt, you would need to return to your lair, tail between your legs and I wouldn't have to look at you anymore. I quite like that idea."

He laughed, feeling a touch nervous. *Did he really want to go down this road?*

Cordia stood up, those golden-yellow eyes on him. She leaned forward, placing her hands on the table. "You're afraid." She smiled. "I can tell… and so you should be. Walk away now before you are injured… or worse."

END

AUTHOR'S NOTE

Charlene Hartnady is a USA Today Bestselling author. She loves to write about all things paranormal including vampires, elves and shifters of all kinds. Charlene lives on an acre in the country with her husband and three sons. They have an array of pets including a couple of horses.

She is lucky enough to be able to write full time, so most days you can find her at her computer writing up a storm. Charlene believes that it is the small things that truly matter like that feeling you get when you start a new book, or when you look at a particularly beautiful sunset.

BOOKS BY THIS AUTHOR

The Chosen Series:
Book 1 ~ Chosen by the Vampire Kings
Book 2 ~ Stolen by the Alpha Wolf
Book 3 ~ Unlikely Mates
Book 4 ~ Awakened by the Vampire Prince
Book 5 ~ Mated to the Vampire Kings (Short Novel)
Book 6 ~ Wolf Whisperer (Novella)
Book 7 ~ Wanted by the Elven King

Shifter Night Series:
Book 1 ~ Untethered
Book 2 ~ Unbound
Book 3 ~ Unchained
Shifter Night Box Set Books 1 - 3

The Program Series (Vampire Novels)
Book 1 ~ A Mate for York
Book 2 ~ A Mate for Gideon
Book 3 ~ A Mate for Lazarus
Book 4 ~ A Mate for Griffin
Book 5 ~ A Mate for Lance
Book 6 ~ A Mate for Kai
Book 7 ~ A Mate for Titan

The Feral Series
Book 1 ~ Hunger Awakened
Book 2 ~ Power Awakened

Demon Chaser Series (No cliffhangers)
Book 1 ~ Omega
Book 2 ~ Alpha
Book 3 ~ Hybrid
Book 4 ~ Skin
Demon Chaser Boxed Set Book 1–3

The Bride Hunt Series (Dragon Shifter Novels)
Book 1 ~ Royal Dragon
Book 2 ~ Water Dragon
Book 3 ~ Dragon King
Book 4 ~ Lightning Dragon
Book 5 ~ Forbidden Dragon
Book 6 ~ Dragon Prince

The Water Dragon Series
Book 1 ~ Dragon Hunt
Book 2 ~ Captured Dragons
Book 3 ~ Blood Dragon
Book 4 ~ Dragon Betrayal

The Earth Dragon Series
Book 1 ~ Dragon Guard
Book 2 ~ Savage Dragon
Book 3 ~ Dragon Whelps
Book 4 ~ Slave Dragon

Excerpt

Dragon HUNT

WATER DRAGONS BOOK 1

CHARLENE HARTNADY

CHAPTER 1

She should be happy.

What was she thinking? She *was* happy.

Happy, excited and nervous all rolled into one. Nervous? Hah! She was quaking in her heels. This was a huge risk. Especially now. Her stomach clenched and for a second she wanted to turn around and head back into her boss's office. Tell him she'd changed her mind.

No.

She would regret it if she didn't take this opportunity. Why now though? Why had this fallen into her lap now? What if it didn't work out? She squeezed her eyes closed as her stomach lurched again.

"You okay?" Rob's PA asked, eyebrows raised.

Jolene realized she was standing outside her boss's office, practically mid-step. Hovering.

"Fine." She pushed out the word together with a pent-up breath. She *was* fine, she realized. More than fine, and she had this. The decision was already made. Her leave approved. She was doing this, dammit. Jolene smiled. "I'm great."

"Good." Amy smiled back. "Just so you know," she said under her breath, looking around them to check that no-one was in hearing distance, "I'm rooting for you." She winked.

"Thank you. I appreciate that," Jolene said as she headed back to her office, trying not to think about it. Not right now. It would make her doubt her decision all over again. She'd made the right one. The only thing holding her back was fear of failure. It was justifiable and yet stupid. She wasn't going to live with regrets because fear held her back. She was going to embrace this. Give it her all and then some. Her step suddenly felt lighter as she walked into her office. *Do not look left.* Whoever designed this building had been a fruitcake. This floor was large and open-plan. Fifty-three cubicles. There were only two offices. One was hers, and one was—*Not looking or thinking about her right now.* Both offices had glass instead of walls. Why bother? Why even give her an office in the first place if everyone could see into it?

It had something to do with bringing management closer to their staff, or the other way round – she couldn't remember. The Execs were on the next floor. *Not going there and definitely not looking left.* She could feel a prickling sensation on that side of her body. Like she was being watched. Jolene sat down at her desk and opened her laptop. Her accepted leave form was already in her inbox. She had to work hard not to smile. It was better to stay impassive. Especially when anyone could look in on her. This was going to work out. It would. All of it.

No more blind dates.

No more Tinder.

No more friends setting her up.

She was done! Not only was she done with trying to find a partner, she was done with human men in general. Jolene bit down on her bottom lip, thinking of the letter inside her purse. She'd been accepted.

Yes!

Whooo hooo!

It was all sinking in. She couldn't quite comprehend that this was actually happening.

The sound of her door opening snapped her attention back to the present. She lifted her head from her computer screen in time to see Carla saunter in. No knock. No apologies for interrupting. Not that Jolene had been doing anything much right then, but still. She could have been.

A smug smile greeted her. "I believe I'm filling in for you starting Friday for three weeks." Her colleague and biggest adversary sat down without waiting for an invitation. "Rob just called to fill me in."

"Yes," she cleared her throat, "that's right." Jolene nodded. *Don't let her get to you.* "I have too many leave days outstanding and decided to take them."

Carla folded her arms and leaned back. She seemed to be scrutinizing Jolene. It made her uncomfortable. "Yeah, but right now? You're either really sure of yourself or…"

She let the sentence drop. "I believe you're going on a singles' cruise?" The smirk was back. Carla's beady eyes—not really, they were wide and blue and beautiful—were glinting with humor and very much at Jolene's expense.

It was her own fault. She should never have told Rob about why she was taking this trip. Why the hell had he told Carla? It was none of her damned business. *Stay cool!* She smiled, folding her arms. "I thought it would be fun."

"You do know that I'm about to close the Steiner deal, right? Work on the Worth's Candy campaign is coming along nicely as well."

"Why are you telling me this?" Her voice had a definite edge which couldn't be helped. Carla irritated the crap out of her.

The other woman shrugged. "It might not be the best time for you to go on vacation. Not that I'm complaining. It works for me." Another shrug, one-shouldered this time.

Jolene pulled in a breath. "I need a break. That's the long and short of it."

"Yeah, but right now and on a singles' cruise… do you really think you'll meet someone?" She scrunched up her nose.

"Why not? It's perfectly plausible that I would meet someone. Someone really great!" she blurted, wanting to kick herself for the emotional outburst.

"It's not like you have the greatest track record." Carla widened her eyes. Unfortunately, working in such close proximity for years meant that Carla knew a lot about her. In the early days, they had even been friends.

"But you should definitely go," Carla went on. "You shouldn't let that stop you," she quickly added. Her comments biting.

"I'm not going to let anything stop me. Not in any aspect of my life," Jolene replied, thrilled to hear her voice remained steady.

Carla stood up, smoothing her pencil skirt. "I'll take care of things back here. The reason I popped in was to request a handover meeting, although I'm very much up to speed with everything that goes on around here." She gestured behind her. "I'll email a formal request anyway." She winked at Jolene.

Jolene had to stop herself from rolling her eyes. "Perfect." She refolded her arms, looking up at Carla who was still smiling angelically.

"I need you to know that I plan on taking full advantage of your absence."

"I know." Jolene smiled back. "I'm not worried."

The smile faltered for a half a second before coming back in full force. "You enjoy your trip. Good luck meeting someone." She laughed as she left. It was soft and sweet and yet grating all at once. Like the idea of Jolene actually meeting someone was absurd.

That woman.

That bitch!

Stay impassive. Do not show weakness. Do not show any kind of emotion. She forced herself to look down at her screen, to scroll through her emails.

Two minutes later, there a knock at her door. Jolene looked up, releasing a breath when she saw who it was. Ruth smiled holding up two cups of steaming coffee.

Jolene smiled back and gestured for her to come in.

"I was in here Xeroxing—our printer is down yet again

– and thought you could use a cup of joe." Ruth ran the admin department on the lower level. Her friend moved her eyeballs to the office next door to hers. The one where Carla sat, separated by just a glass panel.

"You were right," Jolene exclaimed.

Ruth sat down. "Are you okay? That whole exchange looked a little rough."

"I thought I kept my cool. Are you saying you could see how badly she got to me?" Carla was all about pushing buttons. She only won if Jolene retaliated and she'd learned a long time ago it wasn't worth doing so.

"You looked fine. What gave it away and – only because I know you so well – was the way you tapped your fingers against the side of your arm every so often. I take it when 'you know who' said something mean." Ruth handed her the coffee and took a seat.

"Mean doesn't begin to cut it. Thanks for this." She held up the mug before taking a sip.

"What's going on?"

"Things have happened so quickly, I didn't get a chance to tell you. I'm going on vacation." Jolene briefly told her friend all about her real upcoming plans, as well as about what had transpired between Carla and her.

Ruth smiled. "I can't believe you're this excited." She looked at her like she had lost all her faculties. "It's not that big of a deal. Quite frankly, I'm inclined to partly agree with Carla, for once." She made a face. "Maybe you shouldn't be going on a trip right now."

"It's a huge deal, and you're right, I'm excited," Jolene gushed. "One in five hundred applicants are accepted, and I'm one of them. The shifter program is just the place for a woman like me. I'm ready to settle down, to get married and to have kids. Lots of kids. Four or five… okay, maybe five's too many, but four has a ring to it. Two boys and two girls."

"Two of each." Ruth chuckled under her breath.

She smiled as well and shook her head. "Actually, I'm not too fazed about that. I just can't believe they actually selected me."

"You're nuts!" Ruth laughed some more. "Why's it so hard to believe? Just because you've had a bad run doesn't mean you're not… worthy."

"I'm thirty-four. I turn thirty-five in two months' time."

"And that's a big deal why?"

"Because thirty-five is the cut-off for taking part in the program." She had to undergo a whole lot of testing – including ones of the medical variety – and she'd been selected anyway. "I'm so done with guys running away as soon as they realize I'm serious."

"How is being a part of this program going to change anything? I love you long freaking time, but you do tend to scare men away. You're a little… pushy."

"I'm not pushy! I know what I want and I go after it. After everything I've been through, I'm not interested in anything less, and shifters actually want to settle down. They want kids. They want what I want. For once, I'm going to meet someone who doesn't run scared at the prospect of commitment and family." She sucked in a deep breath.

"Human guys also want commitment." Ruth raised her brows, taking another sip of her coffee. "They want kids."

"Just not with me they don't. None of them wanted anything other than sex or casual dating. Sure, they're more than willing to take the plunge as soon as they move on to the next one, but not with me."

"Have you ever stopped to consider that you're maybe coming on just a little too strong? You can't start out a relationship talking about marriage. Guys can't handle that."

"I'm not coming on too strong. I'm done wasting my time… that's all." Jolene took a sip of her own coffee, feeling the warm liquid slide down her throat. "I know what I want. Casual sex, endless dating…" She shook her head. "That's not it. Even living together. Have you ever heard the saying, 'why buy the cow if you can get the milk for free'? No… not for me. Never again!"

"You seem to think it's going to be different with a shifter. Can't say I know too much about shifters." Ruth shrugged. "Except that they're ultimately guys too."

"For starters they're hot. Muscular, tall and really, really good-looking."

"Okay, that's a good start." Ruth leaned forward, eyes on Jolene.

"They have a shortage of their own women, just like with the vampires. It's actually the vampires who are helping them set up this whole dating program."

"Oh!" Ruth looked really interested at this point. "No women of their own you say, now that's interesting."

"I didn't say no women, just not many women. Their kind stopped having female children, so there's a shortage. They have a natural drive to mate and procreate, which is exactly what I'm looking for." Jolene put her coffee down and rubbed her hands together. "I can't wait to get my hands on one."

"You might just be onto something here. Where do I sign up?" her friend whisper-yelled while smiling broadly.

"I can't believe you told Rob you're going on a cruise. Where did you come up with that?"

"I shouldn't have said anything at all." She shook her head. "I don't know why I disclosed as much as I did."

"Yeah!" Ruth raised her brows. "I can't believe he told," she looked to the side while keeping her head facing forwards, "her."

"I know. Thing is, I've made up my mind. I'm going."

"That cow is going to move in while you're gone. She might just get the edge in your absence and take the promotion out from under you."

"I realize that, and yet I can't miss out on this opportunity. I'm willing to risk my career over this. It's a no-brainer for me." She sighed. "Don't get me wrong, I'm freaking out about it, but as much as I love my job, having a family would trump everything. I have a good feeling about this."

"Those shifters sound so amazing." Ruth bobbed her brows.

"I'll show you the website online. They only take three groups a year and then only six women are chosen each time. Just a handful from thousands of applications." Jolene's heartbeat all the faster for getting accepted. She was so lucky! Things had to work out for her. They just had to.

"You say these shifters are hot and pretty desperate?" Ruth smiled, her eyes glinting. "Why didn't you tell me about this sooner? We should have entered together."

"Not exactly desperate, but certainly looking for love. Ninety-six percent of the women who sign up end up mated... that's what the shifters call it, mated. It's not actually the same as marriage, it's more binding. Ninety-six percent," she shook her head, "I rate those odds big time."

"I can't believe you didn't tell me sooner." Even though she was still smiling, Ruth narrowed her eyes. "I thought we were friends."

Jolene made a face. "I didn't tell you anything because I didn't want to jinx it."

Ruth rolled her eyes. "I wouldn't get too excited until you get there. Until you actually meet them." Ruth snickered. "With your luck, you'll get one of the bad apples."

"You shut your mouth. Don't be putting such things out in the universe."

Ruth looked at her with concern. "I don't want you getting your hopes up, that's all."

"Well too late, my hopes are already up." Jolene was going to win herself a shifter. Someone sweet and kind and loving. A man she could spend forever with. "I just wish it wasn't right now. This isn't a good time to be leaving."

"Not with that big promotion on the horizon." Ruth shook her head. "Not when *she* could take it."

"We're both on the same level. We both started at the same time. I hate how evenly matched we are."

"You're the better candidate though. I've never known anyone to work as hard as you."

"Carla works hard too. She's also brought in several big clients in the last couple of months, and she's not going on vacation. She'll be here day in and day out, whispering sweet nothings into Rob's ear."

Ruth made a face. "It's not like that, is it?"

"No, no." She waved a hand. "Sweet nothings of the

business kind. It's still a threat just the same to me, and honestly, that's the only downside to this. I stand a good chance of losing to Carla if I go."

"But you are still going anyway." Ruth took a sip of her coffee, frown lines appearing on her forehead.

"I have to." She pushed out a breath. Hopefully, Ruth was wrong about the whole 'bad apple' thing.

Out now!

Printed in Great Britain
by Amazon

27771291R00158